Christina Brett is a retired Chartered Surveyor and an avid fan of Jane Austen since first reading *Pride and Prejudice* at the age of twelve. The entail that so often features in Austen's books has fascinated her in the way it alters the destiny of her heroines. *The Norland Inheritance* seeks to redress this.

Dedicated to Jane Austen, who has brought me so much joy.

Christina Brett

THE NORLAND INHERITANCE

AUSTIN MACAULEY PUBLISHERS™
LONDON * CAMBRIDGE * NEW YORK * SHARJAH

Copyright © Christina Brett 2024

The right of Christina Brett to be identified as author of this work has been asserted by the author in accordance with sections 77 and 78 of the Copyright, Designs and Patents Act 1988.

All rights reserved. No part of this publication may be reproduced, stored in a retrieval system, or transmitted in any form or by any means, electronic, mechanical, photocopying, recording, or otherwise, without the prior permission of the publishers.

Any person who commits any unauthorised act in relation to this publication may be liable to criminal prosecution and civil claims for damages.

This is a work of fiction. Names, characters, businesses, places, events, locales, and incidents are either the products of the author's imagination or used in a fictitious manner. Any resemblance to actual persons, living or dead, or actual events is purely coincidental.

A CIP catalogue record for this title is available from the British Library.

ISBN 9781035855308 (Paperback)
ISBN 9781035855315 (ePub e-book)

www.austinmacauley.com

First Published 2024
Austin Macauley Publishers Ltd®
1 Canada Square
Canary Wharf
London
E14 5AA

Chapter 1
An Unexpected Invitation

Barton Cottage basked in glorious June sunshine, a chocolate box house surrounded by a blaze of summer blooms. Its sheltered position at the foot of the downs created a suntrap, while a faint smell of the sea wafted in on a southerly breeze from the creek beyond. This was the time of year Margaret Dashwood loved best when the great outdoors beckoned and she was safe from the impracticalities of the cold stone building and the smoky parlour fire. On such a summer's day, Margaret forgot to regret the past, almost believing herself to be settled at Barton. Today, she toiled in the shade of the kitchen gardens behind the house, her pride and joy since the family's removal from Norland, her beloved childhood home. Growing the vegetables her impoverished family needed to save them money at the market and, more latterly, herbs for culinary and medicinal purposes, provided her with a sense of purpose and helped to compensate for her devastating loss. Despite her satisfaction with the work, she kept a sharp ear out for the carriage expected from Delaford, carrying her two elder sisters to Barton. Her mother had been in a state of high dudgeon since yesterday but would only tell her that she had some important news. Despite Margaret's pleading, her mother was adamant she would reveal nothing until she could tell all three of her daughters together. At the sound of carriage wheels, her face lit up with pleasure and instantly drew her attention from the garden. She jumped up eagerly and ran to the front gate to welcome her dear sisters as they sprang from the carriage and enveloped Margaret in affectionate embraces. With difficulty, Margaret disentangled herself, impressing upon them the urgency of their summons, and all three hastened to the parlour, where her mother was pacing up and down impatiently.

"My dear girls, at last!" cried Mrs Dashwood, embracing her two eldest daughters. "I summoned you here this morning because I received a very unexpected letter yesterday." Mrs Dashwood paused to examine the upturned faces of her three daughters. Margaret was amused to note her mother had donned her Sunday best for this important announcement. Never one to waste an opportunity for drama, Mrs Dashwood's hands gesticulated wildly, and her face was flushed with the enthusiasm of the moment. Her two eldest gazed at her with mystified expressions, knowing nothing more than Margaret and unable to guess what could possibly have occurred to so animate their mother.

"Do go on, Mama," pleaded Marianne with her usual impetuosity. "We are all agog." Elinor merely waited calmly for her mother to continue, sensing she was enjoying the moment and would spin it out for as long as she could. Margaret, of late more used to her mother's dramatic tendencies, was starting to become bored, now certain that the announcement could not possibly relate to her. In her experience, it never did, being the youngest and least important. Fidgeting impatiently, she found the long suspense had caused her initial curiosity to dwindle, and the protracted wait for enlightenment had considerably lessened her desire for the secret to be revealed. Gazing longingly out of the window, she was now desperate to return to the garden and could not subdue a loud sigh. What had begun as a daily chore was now a real pleasure. It had been very dry of late, and there had not been time to water her most tender plants before her sisters' arrival. She was concerned they might be wilting in the heat, and some of her carefully nurtured herbs needed harvesting before they went to seed. Her mother noticed this indifference with annoyance and hurriedly proceeded with her announcement.

"Very well, I shall allay your suspense directly," she resumed, aware that her pause had not quite delivered the suspense she'd hoped for. Margaret was clearly already beginning to lose interest and very little disturbed Elinor's serenity. Only Marianne had risen to her mother's bait. Nothing much happened in Devonshire, so when something this interesting occurred, Mrs Dashwood felt obliged to make the most of it. Clasping her hands together in excitement, she proceeded to enlighten her daughters.

"Well, girls, yesterday morning, I received a letter from your half-brother, John. It appears that he has had a change of heart and, at last, decided to honour the promise he made to your father on his deathbed." She paused again to allow her audience time to take in the magnitude of these tidings and was rewarded with incredulous gasps from all three daughters. John and his wife, Fanny, were not known for impulsive generosity, and six years had elapsed since their father's death. Thus, all hope of any financial help from that quarter had long since evaporated. Mrs Dashwood held up her hand to quell the multitude of questions that followed, quite content now she had finally succeeded in gaining their undivided attention. She waited for the excited babble to die down a little before interrupting them stridently.

"Please hear me out, and you shall learn all in good time. Since the death of young Harry, in that dreadful riding accident last year, it would appear there has been a great deal of soul searching, on John's part, at least. I will now read you his letter, which will make their intentions clear."

My dear Mrs Dashwood,

I hope this letter finds you and my sisters well.

I sincerely apologise for my negligence in not writing to you for many months, but I am sure your kindly nature will appreciate how the untimely death of our only son has overwhelmed our lives and forgive me.

I will do you the honour of coming straight to the point. You will understand that although Fanny is not yet beyond the years of childbearing, we are quite without hope in that direction. It does seem extremely unlikely that she will ever conceive again as nine years have elapsed since our son was born. I am sure you can imagine what a grievous disappointment this has been. When I inherited Norland from my father, we envisaged a long family tree stretching far into the future. Sadly, that is now very unlikely to be the case, and my uncle's son, Charles Dashwood, will inherit the estate upon my death. I am, however, a relatively young man, and we hope and pray that will not be for many years yet.

The shock of the death of our son has caused me to do some soul-searching, and I find that my conscience has been troubling me greatly about the promise I made to my father, your husband, upon his deathbed. It is almost as though divine judgement has been visited upon me for my neglect of his wishes. I freely own that I have done nothing for your daughters, my half-sisters, as my father asked, and I hope to make amends for this negligence on my behalf. As Elinor and Marianne are happily settled in life and do not require my assistance, my thoughts have naturally turned to Margaret. In short, my dear Mrs Dashwood, we would be delighted to launch her into society at our expense for this London season. We owe this debt to you and my father, but, I confess, you would also be doing us a great favour by adding youth and vitality to our household and giving Fanny something to turn her attention to. The death of our son and heir has hit us both very hard.

Please take time to consider this proposal, but I hope you will come to see that it would be to the advantage of all concerned.

Yours affectionately,
John Dashwood.

Mrs Dashwood looked up to gauge her daughters' reactions but was dismayed to observe that Margaret, to whom this news chiefly was related, remained ominously silent. She waited patiently for her elder daughters' exclamations to subside before turning to her youngest daughter.

"Well, Margaret, is this not a marvellous turn of events?" Mrs Dashwood began enthusiastically, trying to elicit a reaction, although she strongly suspected her youngest daughter was not exactly ecstatic to be invited to London. Having made up her mind already that Margaret should accept the invitation, she was disappointed and steeled herself to battle with her youngest child, knowing she could be strong willed and obstinate at times.

"I am not a ship, Mama, to be thus launched," was all Margaret could think of to retort while she wrestled with a multitude of emotions, most of them negative. Mrs Dashwood laughed at her youngest daughter's ironic reference to a ship, thinking how it had been her greatest ambition as a child to be a sea captain. Quite out of the question for a girl, of course, as was any form of employment, beyond that of a governess, and Mrs Dashwood was determined Margaret would never be that. She endeavoured to speak kindly despite her increasing irritation with Margaret's negativity. She recognised Margaret was the most unconventional of her daughters, and it was going to be more difficult for her to accept the narrow lot of a female. Elinor's common sense has always come to her rescue, and Marianne's romantic nature had decided her fate.

"No indeed, my dear, but you are about to set sail on the most important voyage of your life. I should tell you that I have given John's request a great deal of consideration, and I am of his opinion, that this proposal will be to the advantage of all concerned. Naturally, Fanny and John will be delighted if you accept their invitation, but consider, Margaret, London and all its attractions. What an adventure for a girl on the brink of womanhood."

"Yes, indeed, Margaret!" cried Marianne, barely able to contain her excitement at this unexpected turn of events. "I intended to try and persuade the colonel to take a house in London for part of the season this year, and if you were there, it would help to convince him."

She turned to her elder sister. "Elinor, you must persuade Edward to join us. We shall be such a merry party." Elinor frowned, being far less enthusiastic than her middle sister for a sojourn in London, remembering just how ill-natured Fanny, John's wife and Edward's sister, could be, and there was also Edward's general dislike of town to consider. The rift between her husband and his mother, Mrs Ferrars, had barely healed, so it would not help that she also resided there, but she turned to Margaret sympathetically.

"You are still silent, Margaret. Can it be that you really dislike the idea?" Margaret hesitated, tossing her unruly curls as she paced the room, clearly very agitated.

"As a matter of fact, I do dislike the idea. How could I not? Fanny has been no friend to us, and although I have never been to town, I am sure London would not suit me. I have grown up a country girl and have developed a passion for nature. Besides, I am convinced that this scheme is merely a way of John salving his conscience and a desire to fill the void left by the loss of Harry. I wonder that Fanny has agreed to it, bearing in mind her usual indifference to our welfare. I am very sure she has been coerced by John. Fanny has never shown the remotest interest in me personally, and I'm sure it will be as disagreeable to her as it will be to me. Frankly, I think Fanny would regard the idea of divine judgement as ridiculous. I know it is ill natured of me, but I distrust their motives." Margaret's heart was thumping after her long speech, and, turning to her mama in distress, she was surprised to see a deep frown directed at her from that quarter. Mrs Dashwood decided to be frank with her youngest child. It was high time she faced facts.

"Margaret, I will not hear this. It is most generous of John and Fanny, and, after all, what are your options?" Margaret could see her mother was incensed by her ingratitude.

"How else are you to meet eligible young men? I do not see them lining up here in Devon," Mrs Dashwood observed bluntly to her daughter, but secretly, she was very concerned that Margaret was becoming isolated at Barton Cottage now that her sisters were married. In her view, it was unhealthy for a young girl to be so obsessed with gardening and studying. Margaret must marry as her sisters had done, and it was about time she recognised that fact.

"Elinor, what is your opinion?" Mrs Dashwood called on her eldest and most sensible daughter for support, but Elinor was interrupted by Marianne, also irritated by Margaret's ungrateful outburst, seeing her hopes of a London season disappearing rapidly.

"Mama is right, Margaret; you are of an age now when you must look to your future. Just think of it, a whole season in London at no expense. You will be treated to an entire new wardrobe. It is what every young woman dreams of, and what other options do you have?" Marianne added weight to her mother's argument, but Margaret raised her eyebrows at Marianne's attempt to persuade her with finery in which she had no real interest, remembering a time when Marianne would also have scorned such shallow attractions.

"Elinor, you still haven't given your opinion," Margaret prompted, turning to her eldest sister for support. She valued Elinor's advice above all others, and Elinor, knowing this, considered carefully before replying. Ever the peacemaker, she saw that emotions were running high and felt the immediate necessity for calming matters down. The practical side of her nature agreed with her mama that Margaret's options were few, but she sympathised strongly with her sister's reluctance to stay with John and Fanny. She also agreed with Margaret that Fanny had absolutely no conscience to trouble her about divine retribution. Their mother's pecuniary embarrassment, however, was a fact, and it was out of the question that she could provide Margaret with such a chance in life. Elinor was also well aware that Margaret was in danger of becoming hermitized by her life in Devon, where they had so few young people around them. She had also strongly suspected for some time that Marianne, much as she loved and respected her husband, was a little bored and longed for the variety her youth craved. With Margaret in London for the entire season, Marianne would have every excuse to be there herself and thus be able to persuade the colonel, who had a soft spot for his wife's younger sister. Elinor resolved to play the role of diplomat.

"Well, I dare say I can persuade Edward to be one of the party," she conceded, knowing her husband would also distrust his sister's motives. Edward was also very fond of her little sister, and Margaret adored Edward, so the prospect of his presence in London would certainly be another inducement for her to accept. She was immediately rewarded with grateful looks from her mother and Marianne. Elinor was also relieved to see that Margaret was beginning to calm down after her initial negative reaction. It was not in Margaret's nature to be obstructive for the sake of it, and Elinor had been a little surprised by the vehemence with which she had rejected the proposal. She also recognised that Margaret was becoming a little ashamed of her uncharitable outburst and knew this would be the right time for gentle persuasion, so she added weight to her previous arguments.

"I understand your reservations, Margaret, but it is only for one season, and you have the rest of your life ahead of you. Why not think of it as an adventure, as Mama suggested? Where is the brave Captain Margaret I once knew?" Elinor cajoled her younger sister and was rewarded with a rueful smile.

"Despite what you all think, I am not a child any longer, and I know it's my duty to find a husband. It's just that I thought I'd have longer. This invitation has brought matters to a head and much sooner than I would have wished. I do not like to be disobliging, and, of course, it's very generous of John and Fanny." She sighed in submission. "I suppose if you are all in London at the same time, it would be more agreeable to me. Will you come too, Mama?" Although Mrs Dashwood had no intention of going to London and was certain Fanny would not brook her interference, she had no wish to discourage Margaret, just as she was coming around to the proposal.

"Perhaps just for a week or two, my dearest," she promised vaguely, and Margaret had to be content with that.

"Very well, I will give John's proposal my consideration and let you know in an hour or so. In the meantime, let me go out into the garden. It will help me to think clearly." Margaret hurriedly left the room before they could refuse, leaving them all to stare after her departing back. There was no doubt that Margaret was growing up and had surprised them all by taking a stand. Nevertheless, she returned well within the hour, poking her head around the door jamb mischievously. She laughed at their expectant faces, still somewhat surprised at being the centre of attention.

"Well, if it's what you all wish, then I suppose it is settled. I shall accept John and Fanny's offer and allow her to turn me into a lady fit for the marriage mart." Margaret laughed again at her family's enthusiastic response, knowing there was really no other option open to her. It had not taken her long to recognise that further argument would be fruitless, but she took some comfort in that it was months away and she had the rest of the summer to get used to the idea. As Elinor had pointed out, it would be an adventure and would broaden her mind, if nothing else.

Two months later, Fanny Dashwood was seated in her private morning room, at the pretty escritoire given to her in happier times by her husband as a wedding present. She was about to write her weekly letter to her mother, Mrs Ferrars, which occurred even though her mother lived but a mile distant from the Dashwood house and they saw each other regularly. This was a time Fanny enjoyed when she could bare her soul, safe in the knowledge the recipient would be sympathetic to her cause. This time, however, the subject was a difficult one, and she chewed the end of her pen thoughtfully, wondering just how much she could take her mother into her confidence. After all, her mother was now a frail old lady, although Mrs Ferrars would never have admitted this to anyone. Fanny was under no illusions about her relationship with her mother, knowing her brother Robert to be the favourite child. Nevertheless, she and her mother had formed an alliance, two women that stood together in a man's world, first against the tyrant husband and father and then against the male sex in general. Edward, the eldest, had been different from birth and did not count.

Dearest Mama,

I hope this letter finds you in excellent health, as always. (It was generally helpful to add a little flattery where her mother was concerned.)

I have some news. I have just found out that John has invited his sister Margaret to come and stay with us, and I am sure you will understand when I admit to you that I am greatly annoyed at the prospect. The imposition of having to entertain one of the Dashwood girls as our guest! Particularly so, because I have come to understand that the invitation was made and accepted two months ago without my knowledge. I am sure you will remember that you did not admire the two elder sisters when they came to London some five years ago. I remember well how appalled you were that Elinor Dashwood had designs on becoming your daughter-in-law. Sadly, that has now come to pass, and Edward is lost to us forever, but I do not wish to dig up the past. It is the future that has me concerned. I confess, I do not understand John's motives for this visit as he keeps his plans hidden from me. In truth, I could even believe he means to make Margaret his heir if I did not know the impossibility of such a notion. The entail would not allow it, so it's not in his power to bequeath the Norland Estate to Margaret. Nevertheless, he still has his mother's money. I daily praise your foresight in having the lawyers draw up my dowry so that he cannot touch it without my consent. At least, that will be safe from the grasping Dashwood girls.

Fanny's face flushed in anger, and she banged her fist on the desk, suddenly very angry with her husband and his youngest sister. How dare he impose on her so. Of late, he seemed to shut her out entirely, almost as if he blamed her for their son's death. Fanny did not deny, insisting on their son taking riding lessons because she'd wanted Harry to grow into a young man of fashion, like her brother Robert. It was sad, but Fanny had to admit she had never really taken to her only son. Unfortunately, Harry was a sensitive boy, reminding her of her eldest brother, Edward, and Edward had always been a severe disappointment to the Ferrars family. Especially so, now that he had married the penniless Elinor Dashwood instead of the rich Miss Moreton they had all hoped for. Elinor Dashwood was a scheming hussy, if ever there was one. The terrible accident that killed their son had hardly been his mother's fault; however, for who could have foreseen the fallen tree? John had not spoken to her of his grief. In fact, he had ceased to confide in her at all. Their relationship had deteriorated into a polite routine on his side but silent and seething resentment on Fanny's part. Following the accident, John Dashwood had withdrawn into himself and barely noticed his wife at all.

That Margaret Dashwood was to be their guest at Grosvenor Street without any prior consultation with her and, just this morning, presented to her as a fait accompli, was unbearable to Fanny. She recalled that morning's conversation with anger.

"My dear," John had addressed her over breakfast, "I have long been thinking that I have never honoured the promise I made to my father on his death bed…" He hesitated.

"Go on," Fanny urged suspiciously, looking him straight in the eye, finding he was unable to look at her directly.

"Well, I have invited Margaret Dashwood to stay with us for the London season. She is the only sister unmarried, and it's the least I can do." At last, he met her eyes with a challenging stare, and Fanny bit back a cry of dismay, remaining silent.

"I expect you to launch her into society and equip her with everything a girl needs. Do I make myself clear, Fanny?" His voice held a menacing note, and Fanny thought better of a flat refusal.

"Who will pay, John?" she asked bluntly.

"I will, out of my mother's money." Fanny was only a trifle mollified by this, but she could see he was adamant and there would be no point in arguing. Nevertheless, she was most put out.

"Very well, John, if that is what you wish," she agreed submissively, swearing retribution under her breath.

Fanny had never had much time for Margaret, nor indeed any of John's half-sisters. She couldn't quite put her finger on it, but despite their lack of fortune and distinct lack of fashion, the Dashwood girls managed to make her feel inferior. Elinor was pretty, sensible and clever, which Fanny found infuriating but also slightly intimidating, although she would never admit it. Marianne was a renowned beauty and a talented musician with an unfortunate propensity to look down her nose, mostly at Fanny. Bitterly resenting this haughty behaviour, Fanny had barely spoken two words to Marianne since her father's death. As for Margaret, Fanny remembered only a spoilt tomboy with an eccentric desire to be a sea captain. Her mother had clearly overindulged her youngest in Fanny's opinion. The latter Fanny was now expected to turn into a polished young lady and launch her into the London season. If John thought it would give her a pastime to compensate for the loss of Harry, he was very much mistaken. Harry may have been a disappointment to her, but he did have one great advantage, that of being the heir to Norland. What would have been compensation for the loss of their son and heir was denied her, the fact that she had not conceived again. This too she felt was entirely John's fault. After the birth of their son, he had lost interest in that side of the relationship, and although Fanny was no more interested than he, if truth were known, she would have liked an heir and spare. They had lost their only child and, with him, the Norland inheritance in perpetuity. It didn't help that the prospect of being the future mistress of Norland was the only reason Fanny had allowed herself to be persuaded to marry John. Now, at the age of thirty, married to a man ten years her senior, Fanny felt life had passed her by and there was little chance of another child. Nevertheless, she was not going to take the loss of the Norland inheritance to a distant cousin lightly. Something must be done to either prevent it altogether or somehow make it more palatable to her than it was at present.

Fanny resumed her letter to her mother, hurriedly summarising the situation, not troubling to hide the parts that might show her in an uncharitable light, trusting that mother and daughter were always of the same mind. Ringing the bell for it to be delivered, she got up and paced the room, trying to calm her temper. Fanny caught the curious look of the maid as she collected the letter and tried to suppress her anger, knowing she must remain calm if she were to succeed. She was shrewd enough to realise that angry people achieved little, and Fanny was nothing if not enterprising. It was mostly because of her ingenuity that John had inherited Norland in the first place, thus disinheriting the second wife of his father and his half-sisters. Fanny had gone to work on John's great uncle with immediate effect, completely charming him with her baby son, until he made his will, leaving his estate to John's father for life only. Then entailed to the male line, away from Mrs Dashwood and her daughters, making John his heir. Fanny had absolutely no scruples about making herself agreeable for gain, which gave her a material advantage over the Dashwood ladies, who would never have dreamed of such scurrilous behaviour. Fanny was clever enough to recognise this and took every opportunity of ingratiating herself with the old man, merely despising the Dashwood ladies for their lack of foresight. It was unacceptable to Fanny, to be beaten now by this change in circumstances. She told herself firmly any setback she was suffering at the moment was temporary only, but for the time being, she must make the best of things, appearing to comply meekly with John's wishes and taking Margaret Dashwood under her wing. Fanny resolved to keep her eyes and ears wide open until a solution turned up, as it always did, in her experience. She, therefore, made all proper preparations for the arrival of Margaret, sending to Devon for her measurements, preparing an appropriate bed chamber and training up a kitchen maid to serve her. John witnessed all this with surprise and pleasure, greatly relieved to see his wife so compliant, especially as he'd expected strong opposition from that quarter. In fact, it was for this reason he'd delayed telling Fanny of his invitation to Margaret, waiting until the last moment, unable to face the scene he thought she'd create. It was simpler to present her with a fait accompli than endure two months of argument. John was not a perceptive man in general, and despite their many years of marriage, Fanny's true character was as much a mystery to him now as it had been in the beginning. It was his misfortune; therefore, he remained in complete ignorance of his wife's true feelings.

Chapter 2
The Journey Begins

One month later, as the trees were losing their leaves, Margaret found herself travelling to London in the company of Colonel Brandon, who had business in town. The summer had flown by, and the intervening months had not reconciled her to the visit. Nevertheless, she was resigned to it, heartened by the knowledge she was doing her duty. Elinor had reassured her of that before her departure, saying she was proud of her courage. Margaret looked up as the colonel addressed her, profoundly grateful for the supportive company of her old friend at this challenging time.

"Well, well, I did not think to see the fearless Captain Margaret capitulate to such a scheme so easily." Colonel Brandon twinkled at her, and Margaret laughed self-consciously, remembering the unruly child she had been.

"No, Colonel, you are quite right, but Captain Margaret no longer exists. In her place, there is a young lady who must take a different course." Margaret sighed, thinking how unfair life was for a girl.

"Do not be so quick to judge, Miss Margaret; you may yet enjoy your adventure, and London is most diverting," the colonel sought to encourage his young friend.

"I know you are trying to cheer me, Colonel, but you are well aware my tastes are simpler now. Give me a garden of herbs with space to make my tinctures and salves, and I am happy. Such a scheme as this is not at all to my liking, but as my mother has set her heart on it, I felt obliged to accept." She paused to look out of the window before turning back to the colonel again. "Although, you must acknowledge, Colonel, it is a very generous offer, and it's not as though I am overwhelmed with alternatives, matters situated as they are," she finished with a sigh, and the colonel admired her the more for her stoicism. Colonel Brandon was concerned for his young friend, having never been impressed with John and Fanny Dashwood, particularly Fanny, whom he thought shallow, vain and greedy. He chose not to share this opinion with Margaret, knowing it would hardly be helpful in the current circumstances as she continued to justify her acceptance.

"Anyway, Elinor thought it would be an adventure, and I didn't want to appear faint-hearted." Margaret finished with a mischievous smile worthy of her previous persona. The colonel laughed heartily, reminded of the impish child who had first charmed him, and he sympathised with her predicament. At thirteen, Margaret's eccentricity had been tolerated with some amusement, but at eighteen, she must comply with the restrictions that society imposed upon her. Her options were few: to marry, to become a governess or to remain an old maid, and none seemed ideal for his spirited friend. He sighed, thinking of Marianne's pleading face as she begged him to take her to London for the season.

"No, I suppose not," he agreed, "but it was not just your mother and Elinor, was it? I understood that Marianne was quite an advocate of you accepting the invitation." He looked at her so quizzically that Margaret turned away in embarrassment, unable to meet his eyes, acutely aware that her sister was restless in her marriage to the colonel.

"Yes, Colonel, they all wanted me to accept," Margaret agreed uncomfortably, and the colonel saw her discomfort and let the subject drop much to Margaret's relief. She could not help remembering the hapless love affair between her sister and a feckless young man called Willoughby, by whom they had all been taken in. She and Marianne had been very close at that time, and Margaret followed her middle sister's lead slavishly, seeing her through childish eyes as a romantic heroine. Of late, she had been forced to admit that such excessive sensibility, as displayed by Marianne at that time, had only led her sister to blind impartiality. With hindsight, it was clear to Margaret that Marianne had almost died of a broken heart because of her inability to control her feelings. Margaret now recognised that Colonel Brandon had been the hero of the hour, stepping in to escort her sister's home and fetching her mother from Devon in Marianne's hour of utmost need. That kind of devotion was hard to find, and Margaret considered Marianne had made a very good bargain.

Margaret stole a look at the colonel from beneath her hat and was pleased to see his features had returned to their normal sanguine expression. He was still a fine figure of a man, belying his forty years and commanding the respect of everyone he met. Despite the disparity in their ages, he and her beautiful sister were very really very well suited, even lucky enough to share the same tastes in literature and music.

They didn't travel far on the first day as the colonel had to meet a horse dealer in Exeter, and Margaret was charmed by the bustling town on market day. Feeling her spirits lifting, she felt a sense of wellbeing and a growing optimism for the future. Her mama was right, she did need to broaden her horizons. They so rarely visited Exeter from Barton Cottage, it being just too far to make the return journey in one day, and Margaret was beginning to recognise her circle of acquaintance was narrow, indeed. They stayed at the busy coaching inn overnight, and, emboldened by a couple of glasses of wine, Margaret felt able to question the colonel about the past. Embarking on this journey to London, there were a few outstanding matters, little discussed in her presence, on which she needed clarification. She and the colonel were rarely alone together, so Margaret took full advantage of the convivial moment over dinner.

"Colonel, could I ask you about that time in London when my sisters visited Mrs Jennings?" He looked up in surprise.

"Why, of course, my dear. What is it you want to know?" he answered evenly, suppressing his astonishment.

"As I will be meeting most of the main protagonists in London, I wish to be clear about the facts," Margaret explained reasonably, and the colonel nodded in understanding as she continued. "Of course, it is impossible for Marianne to dissemble, so I know all about Willoughby and his desertion of her for the rich Mrs Grey. I have no wish to revisit the dreadful consequences emanating from that, but Colonel, could you tell me more about Elinor's experience? Elinor is not like Marianne. She keeps her council, and I was a child at the time. Therefore, much was spoken about behind closed doors, and I am still not in possession of the facts," Margaret pleaded gently.

"It is true, Miss Margaret, your sisters are very different in character. Elinor is the practical one of the two, and Marianne wears her heart on her sleeve, it being impossible to conceal her feelings. I see your predicament clearly. Of course, you want to know more of the characters you will be mixing with in London. How can I help?"

"If you could fill in the gaps in my knowledge, it would be of great assistance to me, Colonel. I know that Lucy Steele, now Mrs Robert Ferrars, was first secretly engaged to dear Edward, and she confided all this to Elinor, who was sworn to secrecy." Margaret looked at the colonel for verification.

"Yes, that is entirely correct; no one knew of the engagement until Lucy, emboldened by Fanny's patronage, was encouraged to confess all to her." Margaret gasped in surprise, knowing Fanny to be very protective of the Ferrars family.

"Oh dear, I'm sure her confidence in Fanny's sympathy was quite misplaced."

"You could say that, my dear. Fanny threw her out into the street without her belongings. She was obliged to seek the protection of Mrs Jennings, and Edward was immediately called into his mother's illustrious presence. She ordered him to break off the engagement, on pain of disinheritance." Margaret nodded, recalling a conversation overheard between her mother and Elinor on the subject.

"I guessed as much, but no one has actually confirmed that to me. What happened then, Colonel?"

"Edward refused, nobly standing by his promise to Lucy, even though his affection for her was long over and it was Elinor he loved. Of course, his mother was entirely without pity and settled his inheritance irrevocably on his younger brother, Robert. I was much impressed by Edward's honourable behaviour and sorry his mother had been so unjust, causing me to offer him the living at Delaford. The rest, I believe you know," he finished.

"Yes, Colonel. Lucy Steele instantly transferred her affections to Robert, freeing Edward to marry Elinor."

Margaret was impressed by Elinor's behaviour and her dignified approach to an impossible situation. She had kept her composure, no matter how difficult it was, going about her business as normal. Being sworn to secrecy by Lucy Steele, Elinor could not speak of the matter to anyone and was forced to bear this burden for many months alone. Fortunately, it had all turned out well in the end. Lucy was now married to Robert Ferrars and Elinor to Edward, but Elinor had no way of knowing that at the time. Margaret was sketchily aware of these events but was pleased the colonel had now confirmed the full facts. She counted herself fortunate to have received an early lesson on how to conduct herself from watching the different ways her two sisters reacted to being crossed in love. She saw that Elinor's behaviour had been superior; even Marianne acknowledged that now. Margaret tried not to judge her sisters, but, inadvertently, her role model switched from Marianne to Elinor, and her respect for both sisters' husbands was profound. Honourable to the core, Edward had been prepared to stand by Lucy despite foolishly contracting himself to her at an immature age. It didn't matter that he had made a mistake, now loving Elinor and Lucy no longer.

He was prepared to honour his engagement until his mother rescued him by settling all the money irrevocably on his brother, Robert. Lucy instantly switched her affections from one brother to the other, thus releasing Edward to marry Elinor, revealing the true nature of her grasping character. It had been a very happy outcome for everyone, except perhaps Robert Ferrars, Margaret mused. It appeared to Margaret that marriage was very much a matter of luck, and both her sisters had been lucky in the end. She allowed herself to hope that such luck might run in threes.

On the following day, their journey was a long one as the colonel wished to make Salisbury by nightfall. The soporific motion of the carriage caused her thoughts to wander back to her own childhood, and she now recognised, as the baby of the family, she had been utterly spoiled, given to hiding herself away to avoid lessons and unwelcome chores. The young Margaret had created a daydream world as a refuge from the harshness of reality. The loss of her father and Norland within a couple of months of each other had been too much to bear.

"I hope that I was able to clarify matters a little for you yesterday, my dear," the colonel interrupted her thoughts.

"Yes, Colonel, thank you for your honesty," she answered him gratefully. "It was more or less as I'd thought, but your confirmation was welcome. One is never quite sure how much the facts may have become muddied over time."

"I'm afraid the truth doesn't show the characters of Fanny or Lucy Ferrars in a very good light, but it's best to be aware of the pitfalls before you begin your visit to Fanny. It is inevitable you will also meet Lucy and Robert Ferrars, so forewarned is forearmed."

"Yes, Colonel, you are quite right. I will tread warily. Fanny's character is already known to me from my own experience but not that of Lucy Ferrars. Edward made a lucky escape." Margaret remembered, with a shudder, as if yesterday, one occasion when she happened to be hiding under the table in the library, perusing her beloved Atlas. The door opened as John and Fanny entered, and she'd heard herself the subject of discussion between them. At first, Fanny made general complaints of all the Dashwood women and their lack of respect for her as the new mistress of Norland. Bored by her monotonous complaining, Margaret was just dozing off when she heard her name mentioned specifically.

"What do you make of Miss Margaret?" asked Fanny of her husband.

"She seems a good-humoured sort of girl," he answered indifferently, and Margaret suspected he was unwilling to admit to his wife that he hadn't really noticed her at all. Fanny sniffed in contempt.

"Well, in my opinion, she has a head stuffed so full of romantic nonsense and such little formal education that I cannot see how she can possibly turn out well. She spends most of her time up trees or hiding in cupboards."

"I bow to your greater knowledge, my dear Fanny, but do not upset yourself on her account. She and her mother and sisters will have very little to do with us when they have all moved out of Norland. They can hardly move in the same circles in such straightened circumstances," John soothed his wife's ruffled feathers as they left the room, and Fanny smiled to herself. At least she had succeeded in putting all thoughts of financial assistance out of John's mind.

At first, Margaret could only think of Fanny as unjust, to judge a child so harshly. A thirteen-year-old, so recently bereaved of a beloved father, but the more Margaret pondered Fanny's words, the more she recognised truth in them. Sometimes an insignificant event can change the course of a life, and thus it was with Margaret. She became determined to prove Fanny wrong, and from thence forward, she devoted a great deal more time to her books. Her new interest in serious study, coupled with Elinor's sensible example, meant that Fanny's prediction had been avoided. At eighteen, Margaret was both educated and clever, with a great deal of common sense. She didn't see herself as being particularly pretty, having stronger features than those normally attributed to beauty, but a tall, elegant figure, fine blue eyes and a mop of strawberry blonde curls caused most people to pronounce her a very handsome girl.

The colonel, noting her silence, was curious, interrupting her long reverie. "A penny for them, Miss Margaret," he enquired with a smile.

"I was just thinking of Norland and wishing I was invited there and not London."

"Perhaps you may be yet; Norland is not a great distance from London," he reminded her, noting Margaret's eyes sparkled in anticipation.

"Miss Margaret, it is my turn to ask a favour from you. May we go back to the beginning of our conversation yesterday? I'm not such an old fool that I can't see Marianne longs for a wider society. She is a young woman, and I am nearly an old man. It is only to be expected. Perhaps if there was a child," he added wistfully. "What is your opinion, as her sister? Should I take her to London as she wishes and risk her health? She has never been strong after that illness five years ago." Margaret was saddened to see her dear friend so pensive but did not attempt to deny his statements, offering consolation where she could be truthful.

"Colonel, you are nowhere near being an old man, so please don't make yourself uneasy. I am sure matters between you and Marianne will resolve themselves in time. As you say, Marianne is very young, and she has always been excessively romantic. She does not view the world as the rest of us do. It is not in her nature to be happy in the normal contented way that suits most of us. Her life swings between great joy and brooding heroine. For what it's worth, I don't believe Marianne's health to be in danger, rather that she is a little melancholic from the monotony of daily life in the country. She is stronger than she seems, and she will have you by her side to care for her. I think a change of scene will do her good, and she will see for herself that the grass is not greener in London. If you deny her, Colonel, she may harbour resentment." The colonel was surprised to witness such mature reflection in one so young, but he saw the wisdom of Margaret's advice. He made up his mind in that instant and nodded in agreement.

"So be it; we shall go then. How shall you like residing with our dear Fanny?" he enquired, changing the subject with a sardonic smile, and Margaret sighed.

"I do not know, Colonel, but I am resolved to give her the benefit of the doubt and try to make the best of the situation." Margaret spoke with such grim determination that the colonel laughed.

"Well done, indeed. Spoken like a true adventurer. What cannot be cured must be endured."

They travelled on in companionable silence, the colonel occupied with his papers and Margaret with the scenery along the way. It would be wonderful if an excursion to Norland was included in her visit. As the colonel confirmed, it was not far from London, and she let herself hope that such an invitation may occur, visualising the park wearing her autumn colours, a blaze of glory in the wintry sunshine. Her love of plants had begun there in the kitchen gardens with the head gardener. He'd befriended the solitary child and was glad to impart his knowledge about horticulture. She felt almost sick with longing for those happy, carefree days when her future had stretched out before her, so safe and secure. It would be almost possible to bear Fanny at Norland. She longed to wander in that dear place and visit all her old haunts again, especially the treehouse, constructed lovingly by her father. There was nothing he did not do to ensure the happiness of his family. Dear Papa, she sighed. Elinor and Marianne had not been much interested in the treehouse beyond an initial curiosity, so Margaret had made it her special place, a place of childhood secrets and magic. Now Elinor and Marianne had found new homes at Delaford and moved on from the cramped cottage and memories of Norland. Only Margaret hankered after the past and her old home, which Barton Cottage had never really replaced in her heart. This time of year was particularly poignant, as it was in the autumn they'd all departed from Norland. She remembered the copious tears shed by her mother and Marianne whist Elinor stared stoically out of the coach window, dry-eyed. Margaret also did not cry at the time, but a lump formed in her throat as sadness overwhelmed her, the dying year reflecting her shattered hopes.

The journey to London passed much more quickly than Margaret anticipated. It seemed like no time at all before they arrived at Grosvenor Street. Margaret stepped out of the coach in some trepidation to greet her hosts, awaiting their arrival at the entrance of their London residence. John was kindness itself as he shook her hand enthusiastically, beaming all over his face.

"My dear Margaret, we are delighted to welcome you to Grosvenor Street. You must make our house your home over the forthcoming months." He turned to his wife for support, but to Margaret's dismay, Fanny merely sniffed and looked down her nose. Margaret had never warmed to John, not able to forget the conversation overheard in the library, but tonight she felt sincerely he could have been an amiable person had he not married Fanny. Fanny, true to Margaret's expectations, appeared unable to find an agreeable word to say to her young guest, satisfying herself with barely concealed criticism.

"My dear Margaret, it is very fortunate that you have arrived in plenty of time, for there is much to do," observed Fanny, with another sniff of disapproval, eyeing Margaret's country attire and wild curls with obvious dismay. Margaret felt shabby indeed, confronted by her hostess dressed in the height of fashion, the very picture of elegance. Her haughty composure, belying the role of a grieving mother, swiftly dispensed with any sympathy Margaret might have felt for her. Despite Margaret's intention of giving Fanny the benefit of the doubt, in her heart she knew her invitation came from John alone. Fanny did not approve, but coerced by her husband, she was forced to accept the situation. Of that, Margaret was now absolutely sure. All she had to look forward to from Fanny was a long round of dressmakers, deportment and dancing masters and whatever else Fanny thought necessary to make her presentable for the London season and the marriage mart. It was more than she could bear after the loss of her family and the long coach journey to London. She swayed visibly on her feet and would have fallen to the ground if the colonel hadn't caught her in time. Watching from the sidelines, the colonel had witnessed Fanny's dubious welcome with increasing dismay.

"Dashwood, help me. We must get her upstairs."

His sharp tone roused John, and together they supported Margaret upstairs to bed, with John calling for a maid to follow them directly. Fanny was left to stare after them resentfully, aware that she had fallen short of her husband's expectations, once again. She shrugged her shoulders as she went back into the house alone.

"No matter," she voiced aloud, defiantly.

Chapter 3
A Lady Is Born

With the resilience of youth, Margaret felt decidedly more cheerful the following morning, completely revived after a restful night's sleep. Her irrepressible sense of humour enabled her to view Fanny's reception of her with some amusement, sympathy even. The long journey could hardly have enhanced her appearance in Fanny's fastidious eyes, with her shabby attire crumpled and travel stained. With a smile, she turned her attention to her new surroundings, noting her allotted bed chamber was so capacious, it was hard to believe it was for her alone. Staring around in awe as daylight flooded the room, she was delighted with its elegant simplicity, seeing that every detail had been designed with comfort in mind. Even the chosen colour of pale rose added significantly to the ambience and feeling of warmth. Margaret felt bound to acknowledge that whatever else Fanny was guilty of, she had exquisite taste and a real eye for design. Revelling in the luxury of remaining in bed, a new feeling for her and one that was difficult to resist after the long journey, a sharp knock at the door made her start guiltily. Before she could reply, the door opened to produce a smart young maid carrying a tray, which she set down on the bedside table. To Margaret's surprise, she dropped a curtsey.

"I've brought your chocolate, ma'am," the maid informed her, unable to conceal her curiosity, staring at Margaret with round eyes. Margaret eyed her in dismay, ashamed to be caught in such deshabille by this pert young person and very uncomfortable to be scrutinised so blatantly.

"And you are?" Margaret's discomfiture made her unintentionally brusque.

"Lily, miss, Lily Parks. Your new maid. You should call me Parks," the girl answered, quite unperturbed by her new mistress's curt manner, whilst pouring the chocolate into a delicate cup. Another unimaginable luxury for Margaret. In Barton Cottage, there were only two servants employed, so no one could afford the indulgence of remaining in bed. Margaret would have been up hours ago to help with the household chores and cut the garden produce needed for the day, let alone reclining in bed with a cup of chocolate. Such a luxurious commodity had not been seen since the Norland days.

"My first duty is to help you to dress," explained the maid, handing Margaret the steaming cup, and she sniffed appreciatively, watching as Lily Parks picked up the battered valise discarded unopened on the floor. Mindful of its shabby contents, Margaret tried to stop her when another knock on the door produced a timely intervention. Lily opened it to reveal a footman, completely overladen with parcels, which she received in obvious excitement. To Margaret's amazement, they contained a rich assortment of finery. First came the morning dress, followed by all the underclothes and accessories needed to complete the ensemble. Then came new half boots and the sweetest bonnet Margaret had ever seen. Lily was clearly delighted.

"I think this will do very well, miss, for your first appearance," the young maid approved enthusiastically, fingering the fine fabric. "See the quality, miss." Margaret stroked the beautiful material lovingly, entirely agreeing with Lily Parks, somewhat ashamed to realise her lack of enthusiasm for finery was probably born out of never having had any of her own. Any dress she now possessed had formerly been one of her sisters', let down or altered to allow for her height.

"Is this all for me? How is it possible?" Margaret asked in astonishment, hardly able to believe her eyes as her new maid shook out the elegant gown.

"I believe Mrs John Dashwood had your measurements sent up from Devon, miss, and this was all made up in advance of your arrival." Margaret, for all her inexperience, could see that the dress was fashioned in the latest style and the fabric picked with taste, its simplicity chosen to suit the youth of the recipient exactly. The delicate green stripe fitted Margaret's colouring perfectly, bringing out the highlights in her strawberry blonde curls. The bonnet was trimmed in the same shade of silk, complimented by a matching reticule. For the second time that day, Margaret was obliged to acknowledge Fanny's exemplary taste.

"I'll say one thing for the mistress: she does have the eye," praised Lily, unwittingly voicing Margaret's thoughts aloud.

"I think we should get you dressed, miss." After helping Margaret to wash, she insistently held out the gown for her to step into. Margaret grinned, suddenly as excited as any young girl could be at the prospect of such elegant new clothes.

"Oh, Lily, is it wrong to be overwhelmed by such frippery?"

"No, miss, definitely not." Lily grinned back in collusion.

Margaret decided to call her maid Lily, to which she was much better suited than plain Parks. Young Lily, however, was eyeing Margaret's unruly hair with some consternation.

She had been taught by a skilled hand, but that hair was going to take some doing. Margaret caught her look of concern.

"Forgive me, we have not yet been formally introduced. I'm Margaret Dashwood." She smiled at the girl, holding out her hand in a friendly gesture, but Lily knew her station and did not take it, merely bobbing another curtsey.

"Miss Margaret, I think we should make a start on your toilette if you are not to be late for breakfast." Lily's tone was firm, and Margaret nodded in agreement, giving herself over entirely to the maid's ministrations.

Lily had been right, Margaret mused as she descended the stairs to the breakfast room, somewhat astounded by her elegant appearance. The green striped gown and new hairstyle, tortured into something resembling elegance by Lily's skills, made a new woman of her. In general, Margaret was not a vain girl, but today she felt quite unusually satisfied with her appearance. John and Fanny were already at breakfast, and Margaret was gratified by John's blatant astonishment at the contrast in her appearance, from the bedraggled waif that landed on his doorstep the night before. Fanny also looked up and nodded unsmilingly. "I see young Lily Parks has risen admirably to the occasion," Fanny remarked to her husband without addressing Margaret, merely gesticulating that she should serve herself and join them.

"Yes, my dear, do sit down," encouraged John kindly, embarrassed by his wife's rudeness. He turned to Fanny in disapproval.

"Lily Parks? I thought she was from the orphanage and employed as a kitchen maid." He frowned at his wife.

"No longer, my dear, she has been under the tutelage of Crane. I have sacrificed the time of my own maid to train her, and I think she will do very well for Miss Margaret and at such little expense. She was so keen to take the post that I was able to agree on a fraction of Crane's wages." Fanny congratulated herself on the thrifty way she had dealt with the provision of Margaret's personal maid. On no account would she have shared hers, as John had first suggested. John was not satisfied and said so.

"I do not think expense is the main consideration here, Fanny. I am correct, am I not, that Miss Parks came from the orphanage originally? How could she possibly have suitable qualifications for preparing a young lady for her first London season?" His disapproval of the arrangement was evident to Margaret, but Fanny chose not to answer, applying herself to her breakfast. John was a fool, surely the evidence of young Lily's suitability was before his eyes. Margaret was acutely embarrassed to find herself the topic of a disagreement between husband and wife. She was further dismayed to see John's face had turned puce with anger at being so ignored.

"Fanny?" he barked, but his wife smiled disarmingly at him.

"Oh, John, such a to do. Surely you can see for yourself that Miss Margaret's appearance is all you could wish for. Crane has trained Lily Parks meticulously, and we are lucky that the girl proved quick to learn. Besides, it is charitable to give a helping hand up the ladder to an orphan," she added smugly, although charity had been far from her mind. John couldn't very well dispute this fact, so he remained silent. *Yes*, thought Fanny, *Lily Parks had done very well, certainly well enough for Margaret Dashwood*, she muttered under her breath.

After breakfast, John politely excused himself to Margaret, pleading an early engagement, giving his wife a compelling stare.

"Fanny, I would like a word with you before I leave," he said forcefully, so Fanny had no choice but to follow him out of the room. She returned after a few minutes to finish her coffee, wearing a mutinous expression. An awkward silence ensued, neither party knowing what to say to the other now that they were entirely alone. Margaret searched frantically for a suitable topic to begin the conversation, without success, but when it became clear that Fanny was content to remain in frosty silence, Margaret could bear it no longer and blurted out in desperation.

"I wish to thank you for this gown, Fanny. It is a perfect fit and shows exquisite taste." Although feeling extremely awkward, Margaret remembered her manners and the thanks due to her hostess. Fanny scrutinised the ensemble in question with a practiced eye and nodded.

"It is true that I know all the best warehouses and dressmakers in town," acknowledged Fanny, unbending a little at the compliment. Margaret then recalled that Fanny always responded to flattery, but it was not something she was prepared to stoop to on a regular basis in order to ingratiate herself with her hostess.

"My friends all say that I definitely have the eye," Fanny continued to boast, and Margaret inclined her head, not knowing how to answer. She was pleased to have broken the silence and induced a favourable reaction from Fanny, at last. Fashion, it seemed, was Fanny's passion, but it was a subject Margaret knew nothing about, and she was relieved when Fanny rose from the breakfast table, putting an end to their enforced tête-à-tête.

"Well, no time to waste if we are to be prepared in time. Today, we shall sally forth in search of your wardrobe for the season. I have ordered the carriage for ten o'clock, so please do not keep me waiting, Miss Margaret," she said sternly, implying Margaret had already been late for breakfast. With that, she left the room like a ship in full sail, leaving Margaret to finish her solitary coffee and ponder gloomily about the prospect of a whole day with Fanny. She had to admit she was not looking forward to it, but her curiosity to see more of London somewhat outweighed her reluctance.

At ten o'clock precisely, a very smart carriage stood at the front door of the Grosvenor Street House. Margaret, mindful of her hostess's warning, had been waiting at the door for five minutes, spending the time examining her surroundings, impressed by the elegance of the Dashwood town residence and the convenience of its situation. It was built over four storeys, and the front windows looked out on the best part of town. By the time Fanny appeared, four matching horses were straining at the bit in readiness, and Fanny and Margaret were carried swiftly away. Conversation between them remained stilted, but even that was better than the awkward silence of the breakfast parlour. At least Fanny remembered her manners enough to enquire about Margaret's family.

"Pray, Miss Margaret, how does your mother?" Fanny asked in her society voice, furious that John had so far forgotten himself that morning as to criticise her manners to his sister. Margaret answered her as positively as she could, perfectly sure that Fanny had no real interest in her answer.

"Thank you for enquiring, Fanny; my mother is very well and hopes to join us for a few weeks as the season progresses." Fanny frowned but deemed it wiser to say nothing at this point, although she had absolutely no intention of sanctioning such a visit to Grosvenor Street.

"Mrs Brandon is also well, I trust, and Edward and Mrs Edward Ferrars?"

"Perfectly so, I am pleased to say. The Brandons are discussing whether to take a house in London for at least part of the season this year." Fanny's ears pricked up in satisfaction at this unexpected good news. If the Brandons were in London, then they could bear the brunt of a visit from the odious mother, and their presence would remove some of the responsibility for Margaret from her shoulders. They fell into silence again, broken only by Margaret's occasional futile attempts to draw her hostess out.

Despite their reluctant companionship, Fanny came alive at the cloth warehouses, which were an eye-opener to Margaret, just up from the country. If Fanny was not an enthusiastic communicator, Margaret soon saw she was quite at home in such places. There was no doubt she knew her business, and nothing but the best would do for Mrs Fanny Dashwood. Margaret was quite astonished to find her an astute negotiator, waving away inferior materials without so much as a second glance and driving a very hard bargain for those she approved of. It appeared no amount of haggling was beneath her hostess, and despite her misgivings, Margaret found herself feeling very grateful to have such guidance on matters that were quite beyond her experience. She felt bound to acknowledge a reluctant admiration for the efficient way Fanny conducted herself. That Margaret found herself the centre of attention, surrounded by fawning assistants, was not quite so satisfactory. These ladies were extravagant in their praise of Fanny Dashwood's young charge, and Margaret was dismayed to be the recipient of such obvious flattery.

"Mrs Dashwood, your ward will be the talk of the town. I have rarely seen such an elegant figure. It is a great privilege to be able to dress such a beauty," the chief assistant simpered to Fanny, who was clearly a regular customer and obviously needed to be pandered to excessively. Margaret was overcome with embarrassment, utterly dismayed at being prodded and poked, her tall figure exclaimed upon as though she were a doll without feelings at all. It was some compensation, however, that the cloth was of the most exquisite kind, and if she had difficulty choosing between them, Fanny did not. Thus, the bales of muslins, cottons and silks were soon on their way to the dressmakers, where Fanny had already placed her orders in advance of Margaret's arrival, knowing exactly what a young girl would need to impress society for a London season. It all happened in such a whirl that Margaret felt quite giddy, not at all used to the London pace of life.

"Although I have given them your precise measurements, we will need to attend the dressmakers at a later date for fittings, of course," Fanny explained as they left the warehouse for an appointment with the milliner and then onwards for gloves, boots, undergarments and the purchase of two very smart velvet pelisses. Not surprisingly, Margaret was quite exhausted when they arrived back at Grosvenor Street, laden with a great assortment of parcels and somewhat astounded at the expense laid out on her behalf. Margaret felt that Fanny's company was better taken in very small doses, so she hurriedly excused herself and retired to her chamber. Fanny did not protest, and Margaret saw that Fanny was as eager to be rid of her, as she was of Fanny. After closing the floor firmly behind her, she thought over the events of the morning in peace. Fanny might stint on a lady's maid, but she knew what was needed to satisfy all outward appearances. Margaret was not fooled, knowing Fanny's chief motivation was the good opinion of London's fashionable society. It certainly would not do for her charge to let the side down.

"Miss Margaret." Margaret woke on hearing her name called as Lily entered her chamber.

"I'm sorry to disturb, Miss Margaret," said Lily, noting with sympathy that Margaret had been asleep, "but it's time to dress for dinner, and the mistress will have my guts for garters if you are late again." Lily was still smarting from the dressing down she'd received from Fanny about punctuality at mealtimes, delivered sharply after the scant praise for Margaret's appearance. She busied herself tidying away Margaret's outer garments, randomly discarded and scattering the chamber. Margaret sat up, rubbing her eyes guiltily.

"What time is it?" Then, seeing that Lily had just opened the closet, she jumped out of bed in alarm. Unfortunately, not quickly enough to prevent Lily from examining the contents hanging there with a deepening frown. Clearly, to Margaret's extreme embarrassment, someone had unpacked the valise in her absence. Finally, after much deliberation, Lily pulled out a pink silk dress, which had been Margaret's best in Devon but now looked excessively dowdy after the business of the day. Margaret eyed the gown with some consternation, seeing it through Fanny's eyes, but Lily was busy smoothing out the creases with a little smile of satisfaction.

"I think we can make something of this, Miss Margaret, until the dressmakers are finished. They will be quick about their business as Mrs Dashwood is a most valued customer, and if I'm not much mistaken, the first of the gowns will be delivered tomorrow," Lily encouraged, seeing Margaret's doubts.

"If you say so, Lily." Margaret remained unconvinced on both scores. Whilst Lily worked diligently, the two girls discussed the day's shopping with much enthusiasm. Lily was filled with curiosity about their purchases, wanting exact particulars of all the cloths chosen and the number of gowns on order from the dressmakers. Margaret was happy to regale her with all the details and noticed

Lily's comments on the choices made, which revealed her to be very well trained. Margaret began to see that she would be a very useful asset.

"If I know anything about the mistress, she will have demanded the first of the morning dresses be delivered before breakfast tomorrow," Lily repeated.

"But Lily, how is it possible that a gown could be made up so expediently? The sempstresses would have to work all night." Margaret was appalled when Lily nodded sagely.

Her growing respect for young Lily increased tenfold when Margaret examined the results of her labours in the mirror. Her much-worn pink silk had been transformed by a few clever additions, drawing the eye from its dowdiness. An exquisitely embroidered satin sash disguised the seams where the dress had been let out more than once, and a necklace of rosy pearls drew the eye upwards to Margaret's slender neck. Matching pink satin ribbons wound into her hair added the finishing touch to what passed for a fashionable appearance. Shockingly, Lily also applied a dab of rouge on each cheek, and when Margaret saw how it instantly wiped out the pallor of a fatiguing day, she resisted the strong urge to rub it off. It was a good thing her mother wasn't present as her disapproval would be certain. Full of curiosity, she picked up the little pot that had so dramatic an effect.

"What gives this little pot its red colour?" she inquired with genuine interest.

"Cochineal, Miss Margaret. It is a kind of beetle."

"How fascinating. Who would have thought that an insect could have such an effect on feminine beauty? In my limited experience, it is wonderful indeed what can be found in nature. You really are a treasure, Lily," Margaret praised, and Lily flushed pink with pleasure, drawing Margaret to the conclusion the young maid was not used to receiving appreciation in a household run by Fanny. Lily silently reflected that you couldn't make a silk purse out of a sow's ear, so the fact that Miss Margaret was tall and graceful helped her task considerably. Besides, it was a pleasure to work with so kind and appreciative young mistress. Even the cook, her special friend and mentor, was known for her sharp tongue.

When Margaret entered the drawing room that evening, she was astonished to find Colonel Brandon already there, deep in conversation with John, and she greeted him in genuine delight.

"Good evening, John and Colonel Brandon, what a charming surprise! I had no idea that you were expected!" Margaret exclaimed, giving him her hand, and the colonel bowed over it ceremoniously.

"Miss Margaret. I came upon Dashwood this morning, and he extended the invitation, which I accepted, as you see. I was worried by your near faint last night so could not pass up the opportunity to see for myself how you are settling in. Although I am completely reassured now that I have. How very well you look this evening, Miss Margaret." He smiled his approval of her fashionable appearance, thinking how grown up she appeared in the short time since leaving Devon. Before Margaret could answer him, they were interrupted by Fanny making a stately entrance, dressed in a cerise silk gown, obviously expensive and the very height of fashion. Margaret could not help but admire her. Although Fanny was no great beauty, her stylish dress sense and poise always made one forget that. She greeted their guest most graciously, and John and Fanny led the way into dinner, followed by Margaret on Colonel Brandon's arm.

"I have some news." He twinkled importantly at Margaret when John and Fanny were occupied at the other end of the table. Margaret looked up at him expectantly, her eyes sparkling in anticipation as he gave her an expressive look.

"I am pleased to confirm I have taken your sage advice, Miss Margaret, and given into extreme duress, you can guess from which quarter. I am happy to inform you that I have seen a house that I intend to rent for the entire London season this year. In fact, I will sign the lease tomorrow, and then I will repair to Devon to fetch Marianne immediately. I also understand from my wife, Mr and Mrs Edward Ferrars have been persuaded to join us for the first month." Margaret's face lit up in delight. Although she had been half expecting this news, it was gratifying to have it confirmed.

"Oh, Colonel, I am sure you won't regret your decision. Marianne will be so pleased, and have you really persuaded Elinor and Edward to come too? I did think Elinor would have some difficulty convincing Edward, matters situated as they are between him and his family. What about Mama? Will she accompany you also?" Her questions were so many that the colonel didn't know which to answer first. He decided on the latter.

"I'm afraid not, Miss Margaret; Elinor could only be persuaded to come if Mrs Dashwood undertook to take care of little Kitty. Perhaps Mrs Dashwood can be prevailed upon later in the season when Elinor returns to her child." Margaret nodded in understanding.

"Of course, that is quite proper. We cannot leave my little niece absolutely alone. So, nearly everyone is to be here, as we discussed. This means I shall not be alone with John and Fanny," she finished in a whisper. "I cannot tell you what a relief that is, as I find Fanny completely unchanged. How kind of you, Colonel." He looked a little embarrassed by her fulsome thanks.

"Please don't thank me, Miss Margaret. You know it was not done on your behalf. My wife can be very persuasive when she has the bit between her teeth, but it was your advice that made me see sense. I am such a doting old fool that I am in danger of wrapping my wife in cotton wool, forgetting she has a life to lead. Although I am glad you will have other company in London, as I saw for myself, Fanny's behaviour with you last night," he whispered back before turning his attention to Fanny, who, now bored with her husband, had been struggling to hear their conversation for the past few minutes and was trying to catch his eye. Margaret observed, not for the first time that day, that all was not well between Fanny and John. Currently, Fanny's face was pink with suppressed fury at something that had passed between husband and wife. Fortunately, the colonel was in very good spirits and soon managed to soothe the ruffled feathers of his hostess until she became all smiles and social affability again. Thus, Margaret's first dinner at Grosvenor Street passed off without any awkwardness, mainly thanks to the presence of the colonel.

Chapter 4
An Exchange of Letters

A week had passed since Margaret's arrival, and Lily was regaling the cook with a full description of her new young mistress. Dinner was over, and the guests assembled in the drawing room, meaning they could spend a precious hour together. As Mrs Jenkins spent most of her life below stairs, she had not yet seen the new house guest and was extremely curious. Lily had also been much occupied with her new post, and this was the first opportunity they'd had for a tête-à-tête. It was clear to the cook that Lily was full of enthusiasm for her new mistress.

"Oh, Mrs Jenkins, I can't believe my luck. Miss Margaret is beautiful, tall and slender but, more importantly, kind," praised Lily, who was delighted with her change of fortune. This first appointment, as a lady's maid, was very important to her, and she'd awaited the arrival of her first young lady with some trepidation. Having been informed by Fanny she should not expect too much, she was extremely surprised when Margaret exceeded all expectations, and Lily counted herself blessed. This gladdened the heart of the cook, who'd taken Lily under her wing from the start.

"Moreover, she has a sense of humour and doesn't talk down to me, as all other employers have done. Miss Margaret is completely unaffected, and I wish her every good fortune for the season ahead. It will not be my fault if she's not a success. She puts me in mind of a wild flower," Lily enthused, and the cook nodded sagely.

"If what you say is true, Lily Parks, there is little doubt she will be a great success. I'd say, it's a refreshing change from all those hothouse roses. It was a lucky day for you, Lily, when Miss Crane picked you out for training amongst the other maids."

"I think I've you to thank for that, Mrs Jenkins. It was you who gave me a character." Lily threw her friend a grateful smile.

"Rue the day, as I'm left to fend in the kitchen without any intelligent help," Mrs Jenkins complained.

"Go on with you; Sarah's not that bad," Lily chided, knowing the cook liked a good grumble.

Lily had found Crane intimidating and an exacting teacher, but she was quick to learn, and the older woman had no hesitation in recommending her for the post of Miss Margaret's maid. Fanny, knowing a bargain when she saw one, was delighted to award her the job. Fanny kept a close eye on household expenditures and was very reluctant to employ a new lady's maid for their lowly guest. She was still smarting with indignation at her husband's solution that she should share her own maid with his sister, but Lily Parks was a good compromise. Of course, Lily knew she was underpaid for such a post but accepted it philosophically. One had to gain experience somehow. Besides, now that she had her own young lady to wait on, it promised to be an interesting season. Much as she respected Mrs Jenkins, she had no ambition to make a career in the kitchens. Even the mistress herself had grudgingly congratulated Lily on the results after seeing Margaret dressed by her for the first time, and that was almost unheard of in Lily's book. She had been employed in the Dashwood household for two years, since the mistress had plucked her from the orphanage and not had a kind word from Fanny since. Miss Crane had a keen eye for fashion, much needed to be Fanny Dashwood's maid, and was skilled in all the latest hairstyles. The older woman had taken great pains to pass this knowledge onto Lily, making her work very hard to master the art, and she was very grateful for her diligent instruction. The young maid knew she would need to be at the top of her game if Miss Margaret's season was to be a success.

The following morning, Margaret was overjoyed to receive a line from Marianne confirming the colonel's words.

Dearest Margaret,

It is official. We are to join you in London for the entire season. I could not be more pleased, especially so because you will not now be entirely at Fanny's mercy. I dared not hope her character has improved, and the colonel informed me she is the same as ever. Enough of Fanny. My dear husband has found us a delightful residence in Bath Square but a stone's throw from Grosvenor Street, so, in addition to every other happiness, we will be near neighbours. We will arrive next week, and Elinor and Edward are to accompany us.

Naturally, they will be our guests in Bath Square, and I believe they plan to remain for about a month, depending on how Kitty fares with Mama. Mama is mollified at losing all her company by the fact she is to have the care of her only grandchild, and the Middletons have promised to invite her to dinner, probably more frequently than she would wish. So it is finally all settled, and we look forward to meeting you in London, my dearest Margaret.

I am writing to John and Fanny to inform them of our plans and issue an invitation to dine at Bath Square on Friday next. You will appreciate that this is a tedious duty but one I cannot neglect, so I may as well get it over with quickly. I apologise for the brevity of this letter, but there is much to be done in preparation for our journey, and I will soon have the pleasure of seeing you in person.

Bear up with Fanny. Remember, it is all in a good cause.

Your affectionate sister,
Marianne Brandon

Margaret's happiness at the news pricked her conscience, reminding her she had only sent a line to her mother to inform her of their safe arrival, resolving to rectify that directly.

Dearest Mama,

Please forgive me for keeping you waiting for my first proper letter. I'm sure you will have no trouble imagining how occupied I've been. Fanny has insisted on escorting me on shopping excursions every day, but I do believe I'm now in possession of everything a young lady needs for a London season. Three more of the dresses arrived yesterday, and we expect the rest early next week. There are nine in all. Three cotton day dresses, three muslins and three silks. I would describe them all to you now, but I cannot do them justice in the time allotted before dinner. Suffice it to say, they are much finer than I deserve, and I am afraid the cost has been great. I did try to remonstrate with Fanny, but she would brook no refusal. I repeat her exact words to you:

"If John wishes to make amends, then make amends we will, whatsoever that takes, and we cannot have you looking like the poor relation. Whatever would people say?" Then she added, rather strangely:

"Although let it be known that the expense is taken from the Dashwood inheritance and my own fortune remains as intact as ever." What is your opinion of that, Mama? Her manner to me is as cold as it's always been, although John makes every effort to be kind when we meet, but he is very often from home, which means that I am left alone here with Fanny. Not that she ever takes the trouble herself to entertain me, quite the contrary, in fact. Once the business of shopping is done, she orders the carriage for herself, almost daily, without troubling to invite me on these afternoon excursions. This brings me to another point. Since being in London, I have noticed there seems to be an estrangement between John and Fanny. Of course, I haven't been in their company since Marianne and the colonel's wedding, but I can clearly see relations between them are not as they were then. They are quite distant in their treatment of each other and spend very little time together. There are also times when Fanny lets her guard down, that I catch her looking at John with positive dislike when his back is turned.

Enough of Fanny and John. I hear you are not to come to London, which is a great disappointment for me, but I do understand that you must take care of your first grandchild in the absence of Elinor and Edward. I am delighted, however, to hear that Marianne and the colonel are to host Elinor and Edward in Bath Square. You must know what a great comfort their presence will be to me at my debut. I am now looking forward to the rest of my visit to London as I have not done before. I hope the Middletons do not plague you constantly to dine at Barton Park as I know how bored Sir John becomes when he is deprived of company. It is fortunate that you have little Kitty as a ready excuse.

On to other news. I am sure you will be most interested to hear that I made the acquaintance of the new heir to Norland yesterday. Fanny and John gave a small soiree to include Charles Dashwood, the son of John's uncle, the odious cousin (according to Fanny), who is to inherit Norland and his mother, Marguerite Dashwood. I have to inform you that they are both exceedingly handsome, which was a pleasant surprise, although I like the mother better than her son. Lucy and Robert Ferrars were also present, and she and Fanny are such kindred spirits now, you would never suspect their grand falling out. I am sure Fanny is still of the opinion that both her brothers made a very bad bargain, but she could hardly say as much before me, and to Lucy, she is everything that is amiable. It appears Lucy has also forgiven Fanny for the beating she gave her when Fanny found out she was engaged to Edward, and they treat each other now as fond sisters, at least to all outward appearances. Mr Robert Ferrars remains much as I remember him, but I was greatly relieved to hear their mother, Mrs Ferrars, was unable to attend as she was suffering from a cold. It appears the excellent health she always boasted of has deteriorated, so she rarely leaves her home these days. I cannot pretend this will be a source of regret, as it means I will be spared her severe company and critical contempt. I see your frown, and I'm sorry, Mama, that was thoughtless and unkind of me. Charlotte and Mr Palmer were also part of the company, which turned out to be a blessing. Of course, you will recall that Mrs Palmer does not draw breath from one sentence to another, so between her and Mrs Marguerite Dashwood, who is as charming as she is beautiful, any awkward silence went entirely unnoticed.

I know you will be eager to hear my opinion of the heir to our darling Norland, especially as I've already hinted that I was not impressed. I've already told you that he is handsome; how could he not be as the son of such a mother? But as to his character, I cannot say. I only know that he is a physician by profession, and I believe he has a very lucrative practice. This fact was impressed upon me by John before the event, but during the evening, Doctor Charles Dashwood remained largely silent and grave. Fortunately, I was seated between Mr Palmer and Mr Ferrars, so it did not fall to my lot to engage him in conversation. He, likewise, showed absolutely no interest in me, beyond the initial introduction. He did not trouble himself to speak to me at all, although I flatter myself, I was looking my best in a new blue silk gown. Oh dear, am I growing vain, Mama?

His mother, however, was completely the opposite and utterly entertaining. Imagine, Mama, her mother was French, and they managed to escape the reign of terror in the revolution, fleeing to the safety of England. I longed to ask her more about it but did not have the opportunity. She reminds me of an exotic plant, the waxy kind that retains its beauty long after our English roses have bloomed and faded. She must be over forty to be Charles Dashwood's mother, yet she doesn't look older than mid-thirties. Her hair is dark and lustrous, with no sign of grey, and her skin is as unlined as my own. Perhaps it is her French heritage. I have heard much of their style and elegance. I would like to know more of her,

Mama, and wish you could meet her in person. Although, come to think of it, perhaps you did meet her long ago, as your husbands were brothers.

On reading through my letter to you so far, I think perhaps I have been unfair to Charles Dashwood. It is wrong to dismiss someone you hardly know in so peremptory a fashion, even if he was not attentive to me personally. Unfortunately, he was seated between Fanny and Lucy Ferrars, so it is likely he found no subject in common with them. Bearing in mind how mistaken we all were in Willoughby, I will try not to judge him on first acquaintance, as Elinor always advises me. You cannot judge a book by its cover, and still waters run deep. I hear her voice reminding me of the veracity of these cliches.

I am sorry to have to report that Lucy Ferrars is not improved by her advantageous marriage to Robert Ferrars. I think perhaps she now regrets exchanging one brother for the other, albeit that brother has all the money for himself. Our dear Edward is by far the more amiable character, in my opinion. Mr Robert Ferrars is a gentleman of fashion and quite the man about town, but I still find him shallow and vain. His conversation is not well informed and is largely confined to carriages and horses. That Robert is clearly bored with his choice of bride and doesn't trouble to hide it from Lucy might also explain her uncertain temper. It is to be hoped that this longed-for child will eventually be the means of bringing them together. Sorry, Mama, I haven't yet told you that Lucy is expecting their first child in January, so perhaps she will also grow softer with motherhood.

Charlotte Palmer is just the same as ever and sweetly asked to be remembered by you. Even Mr Palmer was pleased to see me and very kindly invited us all to visit in Somerset. Did you know that Mrs Palmer and Lady Middleton have inherited the house in London from their mother, and Mrs Palmer informed me they intend to make good use of it? In fact, we are also invited there whenever we wish. Dear Mrs Jennings, how I miss her sense of humour now that she is no longer with us. I must confess, Mama, I do not enjoy staying with Fanny and John and would much rather stay with Marianne and the colonel, but I must not be ungrateful and will endeavour to try and make the best of things. I know John would be deeply hurt if I voiced as much, although I doubt Fanny would lose any sleep over the loss of my company.

I have to finish now, Mama, but you may depend upon me writing again soon. My maid, Lily, (how grand that sounds!) has come to dress me for dinner. She is proving a dear girl and a considerable asset, with such excellent skills at *presenting me respectably, just as you would wish. I cannot tell you what a great consolation it is to me to have an ally in this household of malcontent.*

Your affectionate daughter,
Margaret.

The following Thursday produced two letters for the attention of Miss Margaret Dashwood.

The first, from Elinor, was short and to the point.

Dearest Margaret,

Forgive me for so short a note.

We have arrived at last! Considering the time of year, we had a tolerable journey on remarkably dry roads. Although the house is everything we could wish for, there is still much to do to make it our home. I am assisting Marianne in preparing it in readiness for our soiree tomorrow evening, when I very much look forward to seeing you and John and Fanny, of course. Although the prospect of Fanny's critical eye makes my current tasks more of a burden than is normal in the circumstances. I hear you say that I shouldn't mind what Fanny thinks, and I know you are right. Nevertheless, I do mind, for Edward's sake, if nothing else. Until tomorrow, then.

I enclose a letter from Mama, which is more worthy of your attention.

Your affectionate sister,
Elinor.

Margaret was not at all surprised at receiving so short a note. She knew that Elinor was likely to be bustling around, overseeing all the housekeeping whilst Marianne wafted around, arranging flowers and playing on the pianoforte. Her sister and this instrument were inseparable, so the colonel was under strict instructions to make sure the London house contained one and to have it tuned in time for her arrival. Not that Marianne was lazy, thought Margaret fondly, just a little unworldly and unpractical. She turned eagerly to the letter from her mother.

Dearest Margaret,

I was delighted to hear all your news and did not blame you in the slightest for making me wait. I can, of course, imagine how occupied your life has now become. I am well aware that the pace of life in London is vastly different to Devon, although I have not visited town for some time.

I am disappointed, however, to hear of Fanny's cold treatment of you. I hoped so much that the death of her son would have softened the rough edges of her character and rendered her a little more agreeable. I see now that you were right in your suspicions and it was John who wished to make amends and she was forced to agree. No matter, you now have the consolation of your own sisters with you at this time, so Fanny's companionship is not so important and you have family to turn to if needed. I am pleased, however, to hear Fanny is at least willing to do what is right and introduce you in the proper manner. I never had any fault to find with her taste, only her manners, which are rendered agreeable enough in company when it is necessary to make a show. As to what you say of Fanny and John, I cannot say I am much surprised. These fashionable marriages are often without strong attachment, and the death of a child must be a test for even the strongest match. I always suspected it was the prospect of being Mistress of Norland that attracted Fanny to John, so it must be particularly galling for her to see it inherited by an outsider. Although, I daresay she and John will rub along tolerably well for the rest of their lives by finding their separate pastimes. Many a society marriage is managed in this way, so it is not unusual, and I am very sure Fanny will find other consolations. I know that my dear Henry and his brother were estranged, so for John, it will also be extremely difficult to have to welcome his uncle's son into the family fold as the heir. I do not recall that I ever met Marguerite Dashwood, and from what you say of her, I'm sure I would remember if I had. I do recall, however, Henry speaking of Marguerite Dashwood, his brother's wife. Although I can't recall the particulars, I believe that she may have been part of the cause of the rift between them, possibly something to do with her lack of fortune and connections. That is the usual way of such matters. With regard to Fanny's comments about the Dashwood inheritance, I can well believe that Mrs Ferrars had her lawyers tie up her daughter's fortune in such a way that John could not touch it. He would have to obtain his wife's signature first, which, I am sure, would not be given for your benefit. Therefore, it does not come as a surprise to me that John will be footing the bill for all your expenses as I am positive Fanny still remains in tight control of her fortune. I doubt if they have even touched the capital and probably draw only on the interest.

As to what you say of Charles Dashwood, I have been doing a little digging myself. The Middletons are acquainted with his professional reputation, and it appears he is a physician of some renown with a very profitable practice. Apparently, he is the toast of every fashionable young wife in town when she expects an addition. Nevertheless, it seems unfair, my dear Margaret, that Norland is destined to be inherited by those who have no need of it. I still cannot believe it is justifiable to entail an estate away from the female line. Enough! If I start on that subject, I will never leave it alone.

I am very glad to hear you are properly equipped to make the best of impressions on society and that you will have the opportunity to move in such a wide circle. Margaret, I cannot entreat you enough to make the very most of this opportunity as it will not come again. I know I can rely on you to do your best. I must be patient and wait for Elinor's homecoming to describe the exact shade and style of your new gowns and all your personal triumphs. Be assured, I will exact from her all of the details.

With regard to Lucy and Robert Ferrars, we cannot suppose that there was any strong attachment on her side, so Robert must now feel rather foolish for being so taken in by her flattery. I have often observed in life that the old adage is correct: we reap what we sow. Let us all hope you are right and that children will be the saving grace in that unfortunate match. I do not believe Edward and Elinor regret the money, so happy as they are with each other and little Kitty. They have just enough money to be comfortable, and Elinor is skilled at making economies, as we well know. Edward was all that Elinor ever wished for, and of course we all agree that Edward is the most amiable of the Ferrars family. He alone has the principles that none of the others possess.

I wish I could be with you at such an important time in your life, but in my absence, you may rely on your sisters' guidance. Take care of yourself, my dearest child.

Your loving mama.

If Margaret had been in any doubt before, she now recognised it was incumbent upon her to end the season as an engaged woman, for what other options did she have? This thought did not fill her with enthusiasm, valuing her independence as she did. Nevertheless, she vowed she would do her best, and if she didn't end the season engaged, it would not be her fault. Tomorrow, they were to dine with her sisters, and Saturday night saw the first of the balls. She couldn't help but feel a little excited at the prospect.

Fanny, at last, found time for a belated letter to her mother, having neglected her for longer than usual. She had missed these moments of cathartic revelations and picked up her quill with relish.

Dearest Mama,

Please accept my sincere apologies for having neglected you for so long, but I have been much taken up with arrangements for our guest. I am sure your generous nature will make allowances and forgive me for this omission. (Mrs Ferrars was far from generous in nature and had probably complained, most bitterly, to anyone who would listen of her daughter's neglect, but Fanny knew it wouldn't do to point this out.)

I am pained to have to admit, Mama, Miss Margaret hasn't turned out to be as hopeless as I originally predicted. I am sure you will understand how provoking this has been, to be unable to say to John, I told you so.

Here, Fanny paused to consider how to continue. It was true, the tomboy had been replaced by a tall, elegant girl with a strong air of independence and an unfortunate liking for books. Although John would not have agreed, Fanny found this incomprehensible and wrote many sentences deploring this habit to her mama. In Fanny's opinion, this trait would not enhance her task of finding Margaret a suitable husband. At which point, she was sure her mama would agree entirely. Mother and daughter thought alike about the only qualities that were important to make a good match, and these were money and connections. Fanny did not openly admit to Mrs Ferrars the real grounds for her rejection of Margaret. The grown-up Margaret, like her sisters, also made Fanny Dashwood feel inferior again for reasons she couldn't quite fathom. It was also true that Margaret made absolutely no attempt to ingratiate herself with her hostess and had no talent for the flattery Fanny thrived on, so the thought of having Margaret as a guest for six months filled her with dismay. Fanny and Margaret had absolutely nothing in common. There was nothing for it; she must do her best to get Margaret married off, as soon as she possibly could, to the first presentable suitor. Thus, Fanny would have absolved herself of all responsibility and could turn her full attention to the problem of the Norland inheritance. This decision was vindicated by the pleasure that John appeared to take in his sister's company and his determination that she should receive every attention and courtesy. Fanny found this incomprehensible, considering his cold treatment of her, his wife and his constant criticism of her manners towards Margaret. In truth, Fanny was beginning to boil with suppressed anger towards her husband and his guest.

On the night of the soiree, Fanny had been forced to give in Margaret's honour; she walked into the drawing room to find her husband and Charles Dashwood in the middle of what seemed to be a confidential discussion. Head-to-head, their voices lowered, at first, they failed to notice her entrance as evidenced by the fact they sprang guiltily apart as she walked towards them. By then, Fanny's sharp ears had heard enough to know that the subject of their conversation had been Margaret Dashwood, and a strong suspicion began to form in her mind about John's intentions for their young guest. Now that John had lost the Dashwood inheritance for his immediate family line, perhaps he intended to try and ensure it passed to one of his sisters. Of course, this could not be done directly as John was powerless to break the entail, but if he could persuade the new heir to marry Margaret, then she would become Mistress of Norland. Fanny was appalled. It was not to be borne after all Fanny's hard work to see them disinherited. She was not going to allow herself to be pushed out of Norland when the time came by Margaret Dashwood of all people.

Hence another reason why Fanny was so delighted to hear that Margaret's sisters were soon expected in town. Not that she was very eager to meet them again but it meant Margaret would have company other than her own and John's to rely on. If John was trying to match make between his cousin and Margaret, it was better he had as little time for this purpose as possible. At first, she'd tried to suggest to her husband that Mrs Brandon would be a more appropriate person to launch Miss Margaret, but John wouldn't hear of it. When Fanny had persisted, pointing out that they had already borne the expense of Margaret's wardrobe and the Brandons could easily afford the rest, John became quite angry with her. To add insult to injury, he also informed her that he had every intention of inviting all the Dashwoods to Norland for Christmas. On top of everything else she was obliged to endure at the hands of her husband, Fanny would soon have the whole family as her guests for the prolonged Christmas season. With grim determination, she decided that something must be done before that event took place.

Chapter 5
The Season Begins

Although it was only an informal family affair, the dinner in Bath Square was Margaret's first engagement away from Grosvenor Street, and Lily took extra care in dressing her young mistress. Knowing Margaret was keen to demonstrate to her sisters her transformation from schoolgirl to young lady, Lily chose an ensemble that would reflect this newfound sophistication. Margaret was keen to be taken seriously, but being the youngest by five years, everyone was still inclined to think of her as the baby. This attitude would no longer do if her season was to be a success, so it was high time this changed. As they would be attending the same events, it was important she was treated as a serious debutante by everyone, including her elder sisters. Lily carefully laid out a white muslin gown, simple but entirely appropriate, enhanced by the delicate quality of the material and the perfect cut of the garment. It showed Margaret's slender figure to enormous advantage, and the coral accessories, supplying just a touch of colour, gave the whole outfit a distinct air of fashion. Such an ensemble was not to be found in Devonshire, and Margaret felt very smart indeed. She was imbued with a new feeling of self-confidence as she descended the stairs to find Fanny and John already waiting for her. By now, they were used to her elegant appearances, but tonight, even Fanny gave her a slight nod of approval. She saw, with grudging respect, Margaret was gaining poise in her new role and starting to enjoy the power it gave her. They set off for Bath Square in the carriage; despite it being near enough to walk, Fanny wished to arrive in style.

"How fashionable you look, Margaret; I hardly recognised you!" cried Marianne a little enviously when they were shown into the drawing room. Marianne was not used to feeling dowdy beside her little sister and privately resolved to make some additions to her own wardrobe whilst she was in London. Elinor nodded in agreement, smiling her approval without a trace of jealousy.

"Our little duckling has become a swan," she corroborated. "Not that she was ever an ugly duckling. Edward, what do you think of your charming younger sister? Where is our Captain Margaret now?" Edward bowed formally over Margaret's hand, but his eyes twinkled up at her conspiratorially.

"Oh, I think she's still hiding in there somewhere," he replied, winking at Margaret. "I expect to be ordered to swab the decks at any moment." Margaret laughed, pleased she had so easily accomplished her aim and not minding his teasing as it made her feel at home, but Fanny was quick to intervene with a sharp retort.

"Goodness, Edward, I sincerely hope not. Such childish nonsense should have been left behind long ago," Fanny chided him crossly with a frown. "My efforts would have all been in vain, indeed. You had best keep quiet about Captain Margaret if we are to have any chance of her making a good match for her in London." Edward sighed, thinking Fanny could never see the humour in anything.

"I do not think there is any hurry, Fanny. Margaret is very young." Edward was quick to defend himself and Margaret from his sister's ire, winking at Margaret when Fanny wasn't looking. Fanny sniffed, rolling her eyes heavenward at her brother's naivety.

"She is eighteen, Edward, and quite old enough. A match must be accomplished before the bloom goes off the rose." Edward sighed in resignation, feeling very sorry for Margaret. There was no arguing with Fanny. She always knew best.

"I am so very happy to see you all," said Margaret, ignoring Fanny and beaming at the small family party. Her brothers-in-law were the best of men and wore the mark of true gentlemen. Not that she had made the acquaintance of many gentlemen in her short life, but compared to the dashing Willoughby, who had deceived them all, they were exemplary. She also thought of Edward's brother, Mr Robert Ferrars, who seemed shallow and vain by comparison. She wondered where Willoughby was now and whether he was as unhappy in his marriage of convenience to the rich Mrs Grey as Robert was to Lucy Ferrars. It seemed to Margaret that both men richly deserved their fate of loveless marriages.

"I am very pleased to welcome you to Bath Square, Mr and Mrs Dashwood," interrupted the colonel pacifically, demonstrating his excellent manners and taking Fanny's arm placatingly. "Shall we go in for dinner?" Marianne followed his example, linking her arm with John's, and the small party followed them through to the dining room.

It was a merry family reunion, so unlike the formal diners at Grosvenor Square, and everyone was in high spirits. Even Fanny was so unbent as to be heard laughing on several occasions, but she was seated next to the colonel, who was exerting himself to entertain her. Glancing over to where they were seated, it was clear Fanny was enjoying herself, unused to such attention and being largely ignored by her husband.

"Tell me all the news from Devon." Margaret turned to her sisters eagerly, keen to put Fanny and John out of her mind for the evening. Marianne shook her head.

"Better that you tell us all the news from London, for there is no change to tell of in Devon. Everything is just as you left it," she replied a little sourly, stifling a yawn.

"Well, that is certainly not true, Marianne," Elinor chided her sister. "Devon has shaken off its autumn colours and tipped firmly into the winter season, so whilst I admit it's the perfect time for a little diversion, Devon could never be dull. Although even I have to acknowledge the countryside is never at its best in winter, with the evenings so long and dark. Sir John is already becoming bored with the lack of sport and is thinking of joining us in town. That is, if he can possibly persuade Lady Middleton to leave the children." Elinor loved the countryside and considered Marianne unfair in her condemnation of their home, but even she has to acknowledge the advantage of being in London in winter.

"That would leave Mama all alone!" cried Margaret, dismayed at the thought of her mother alone at Barton Cottage, but Elinor was reassuring.

"I do not think Mama minds it. In fact, she may even enjoy a rest from Barton Park. Don't forget, Margaret, she does have Kitty to keep her occupied." Margaret couldn't help laughing, thinking of the relentless invitations that arrived from Barton Park when Sir John was bored and housebound by the weather.

"Tell us about the ball tomorrow," interrupted Marianne eagerly, bored with the talk of Devon. "I am sure it will be a great crush, but will we have any special acquaintance there? Do you know, Margaret?" Marianne was greatly looking forward to this first ball, especially as her previous visit to London had not been a success. She regretted there was not enough time to have a new gown made up but was relieved she'd had the forethought to buy a gown in Exeter on her last visit. It was not quite the latest fashion, but it would have to do. Margaret's considered answer interrupted her thoughts.

"Well, all the present company will be there, of course," Margaret pondered. "Mr and Mrs Robert Ferrars are also likely to attend if Lucy is well enough." At this, she glanced at Elinor to see her reaction, mindful of past differences, but Elinor wore her usual sanguine expression, and Margaret felt safe to continue.

"Mr and Mrs Palmer may be there if they are not too occupied with taking possession of Mrs Jennings' town house," Margaret added.

"Oh, yes, a delightful house. Elinor and I will never forget our stay there. Such a pity it couldn't have been in happier circumstances. I shall be happy to see them again. They were so very kind to me," interjected Marianne.

"Yes, indeed," said Elinor with feeling, remembering the dreadful time when Marianne had nearly died in the Palmers' residence in Somerset. She recalled with eternal gratitude Mr Palmer's speedy summons of the apothecary to Marianne's sick bed.

"Perhaps also Mrs Marguerite Dashwood and her son Charles, who is to inherit Norland, much to Fanny's annoyance," Margaret added in a whisper, audible only to her sisters. Her sisters' eyes widened with excitement at the thought of meeting the next heir.

"Oh, yes, we are all very eager to meet him. We read the report in your letter to Mama, but it was not very forthcoming. All we can deduce is that he is not ill-looking and he is a physician by profession. For shame, Margaret, you must have known how curious we would be," Marianne teased mercilessly.

"Forgive me, Marianne, but that is really all I know. When I met him, he was silent for most of the evening. I thought I'd made that clear, so you must form your own opinions. In any case, I think you will approve of his mother, especially you, Marianne, as she cuts a very romantic figure. I don't think I've ever seen such a beautiful woman." Margaret was unable to elaborate further as Marianne was just then called on by her husband, who gave her the nod to withdraw with the ladies and leave the gentlemen to their port. At this point, Fanny turned to her husband, who was preparing to leave with the others.

"I think we may not stay long this evening, John, as tomorrow is Miss Margaret's debut and she must be in her very best looks. I am sure you will all agree." She eyed him sternly, putting an end to his hopes of an enjoyable discussion with the colonel and his brother-in-law.

The next morning, Margaret woke with a strong sense of anticipation. Tonight would be her very first ball, and it was impossible not to feel excited at the prospect. Everything was in readiness, and yesterday she had received strict instructions from Fanny to rest and be sure she was looking her best for the evening. Easier said than done, she thought, but how was she going to endure the waiting with a stomach full of knots and butterflies? She forced herself to stretch luxuriously in bed, gently sipping the hot chocolate Lily had supplied her with. She had to admit it was pleasant to be without morning shopping engagements for a change. Margaret was thankful she'd arrived in London early as the shopping expeditions had been relentless and exhausting, right up to the last moment. Only yesterday she had been obliged to accompany Fanny in search of matching ribbons of every description, but she had to admit these excursions had given her time to familiarise herself with London's ways. She was no longer the country mouse who'd first arrived at Grosvenor Street. In addition, the arrival of her dear sisters buoyed up her confidence as much as her new clothes and her newfound polish. She had reluctantly come to accept it was the right decision to accept John's offer. London was filling up for the season, and she was starting to enjoy the hustle and bustle. In frustration at being unable to relax, she rang the bell for Lily to keep her company during the long wait, and they spent the time experimenting with hairstyles and giggling over the outrageous results.

That afternoon, Margaret was bathed and perfumed until she felt like Cleopatra, the queen of Egypt, who had so fascinated her in her youth. Then Lily, with a serious expression, began the business of preparing her first young lady for her very first ball. It was a momentous occasion for them both, but not one that could be taken seriously for too many minutes. Before long, they were both giggling and laughing, predicting all the fine conquests Margaret would make that evening. Lily bowed ceremoniously before her young mistress, in exact imitation of a pompous old man soliciting a dance, and Margaret laughed out loud. "I shall want a full account tomorrow morning, Miss Margaret; you can be sure of that." Lily laughed.

"And you shall have it, Lily," Margaret promised. "That is, if there is anything much to tell," she added doubtfully, and Lily smiled to herself. It pleased her that Margaret was not vain. At last, Margaret was ready. Used as she was to Lily's skills, tonight she had surpassed herself, and Margaret thought she looked well enough to be presented to royalty. On this first formal occasion, Fanny felt obliged to oversee the process, choosing a cream silk gown, which,

Margaret had to admit, was perfect in every way, despite thinking it a little plain at the time of purchase. She had much preferred a showy blue satin, but now she saw Fanny was right, and the cream enhanced her complexion and colouring far more than the blue would have done. Lily entwined pearls in her hair to match the pearl necklace, and the whole effect was nothing short of miraculous.

"There, Miss Margaret," she said, stepping back to review her handiwork. "If all the unattached young men don't end the evening in love with you, then it won't be my fault."

"No, Lily, indeed, it won't," agreed Margaret earnestly, hardly able to believe it was herself she was looking at as she twirled before the mirror.

At Fanny's insistence, they arrived at the ball fashionably late to find a great crush within. Margaret had never seen so many people in one place, and they had to fight their way through the rooms to find the rest of the party, having all agreed to meet up the night before. Margaret found it all very daunting, even with her newfound experience of London. In Devon, the largest parties she'd attended were groups of around twenty, and they never visited Exeter for the assemblies as it was too far. At last, Margaret spotted her sisters on the other side of the ballroom with Mr and Mrs Robert Ferrars. Pushing through the crowd, they finally reached the party, and Robert Ferrars, who had been eyeing Margaret's approach appreciatively, was quick to monopolise her attention. Before she could greet any of the others, he stepped forward and ogled her rudely with his monocle.

"Charming, delighted to see you again, Miss Margaret, and welcome to your first London assembly." Robert smirked with the only certainty of a man quite sure of his attractions. "May I take the opportunity of engaging you for the next dance?" He bowed smugly, clearly sure of her acceptance, and Margaret was taken by surprise. She was not fond of Robert, nor did she want to dance with him, but she couldn't think of how to refuse him on the spur of the moment.

"I…I thank you, sir," she mumbled in reluctant acceptance, turning quickly away from him to talk to Lucy. She was just in time to catch a look of pure dislike directed at her, quickly hidden by an ingratiating smile.

"I do not intend to dance tonight for the reasons that are clear." Lucy indicated her thickening waist, quick to offer an explanation as to why her husband preferred to dance with Margaret and not herself. Margaret had just time to acknowledge the rest of the party before she was whisked away by Robert to join the rows of couples lined up for the dance. Mr Robert Ferrars, who was dressed in the height of fashion and clearly had a very high opinion of his manly attractions, was enjoying the questioning looks of his cronies as he led Margaret in the dance. A beautiful new face, as well he knew, was always sure of attracting attention, and he meant to make the most of his connection with the lady. Meanwhile, Margaret gave very short answers to his probing questions and used the time to look around the ballroom. It was with some shock she suddenly saw Willoughby watching her from the sidelines. An older Willoughby, without any of the sparkle she remembered so well, with greying hair and lines around his eyes and mouth, giving him a discontented look. He didn't recognise her, of that she was certain because he looked puzzled, as if trying to place where he had seen her before. He was just then joined by a tall, young lady wearing fashionable attire and a sour expression, clearly out of humour with her husband and the rest of the world. Margaret assumed this to be the shrewish Mrs Willoughby, nee Miss Grey, who had been preferred over Marianne for her fifty thousand pounds. She was surprised to feel nothing but pity at seeing him again, and it was a great relief when the dance was over and Robert led her back to her seat. As soon as it could be discreetly accomplished, she would let Marianne know she had seen Willoughby. It was a long time ago, but Marianne had been deeply in love, and Margaret was still concerned about her reaction. If she encountered him unexpectedly, there was no telling what might happen. The intervening years had not cured Marianne of sensibility, and she still wore her heart on her sleeve. To dissemble was simply not in her nature.

Margaret found her sisters engaged with Mrs Marguerite Dashwood and Colonel Brandon. Margaret was also curious to see Edward engaged in an intense conversation with Mr Charles Dashwood, and she wondered what they could possibly have in common.

Marguerite seemed very pleased to see her again and immediately beckoned her son over to join her. Margaret was dismayed to note that though he obeyed his mother at once, it was with obvious reluctance.

"What can I do for you, Mama?" he asked with a frown, completely ignored by his mama.

"Charles, I must have you dance. See, here is Miss Margaret, who will make a charming partner." Her tone brooked no refusal, but Margaret had the strong impression he disliked the idea. His hesitation before complying with his mother's request confirmed her suspicions.

"If you are not engaged, may I have the next Miss Dashwood?" he asked dutifully, and she also hesitated, wondering if she could possibly refuse such a reluctant invitation, but Marguerite was eyeing her expectantly.

"I am not engaged, sir," Margaret was forced to reply, unable to think of an excuse as she was obviously not engaged, nevertheless mortified by the thought he was only doing it to oblige his mother.

He led her out for the allemande, and the first part of the dance was conducted without a word. He completely dispensed with the usual polite exchanges and remained resolutely silent, and, to her intense annoyance, Margaret also found herself utterly tongue-tied in his presence. Fortunately, he was an accomplished dancer, and she had to be content with that until, at last, she plucked up the courage to break the silence.

"Do you usually attend these assemblies, sir?" she finally enquired, unable to endure the strained atmosphere any longer.

"I do not, Miss Margaret. I am here to accompany my mother tonight," he answered briefly.

"I hear you are a physician by profession, so that must leave you with little time for social interaction," Margaret tried again.

"Indeed, ma'am," he replied, and Margaret was thoroughly discouraged from any further attempt at discourse. They ended the dance with Margaret being none the wiser about the character of Mr Charles Dashwood, and she was profoundly affronted by his treatment of her. He had been abrupt to the point of rudeness, clearly resentful of being forced into her company by his mother. What had she possibly done to deserve his contempt, for contempt it appeared to be? Angrily, she decided he was not worth the trouble and resolved to think no more of him. Fortunately, this was not difficult as the evening offered many other diversions. Fanny had been busy on her behalf and speedily introduced her to two naval officers, who proved more than happy to dance with a pretty new face. Margaret was pleased to have their enthusiastic attention, especially after the bruising indifference of her last partner. It was balm to her wounded vanity. Especially as the elder and more senior of the two officers was exceedingly handsome. She danced two dances with the younger before being claimed by the dashing Captain Dunning for the last two. Thus, Margaret ended her first ball having danced every dance, excited by the curiosity of many of the onlookers and being taken into supper by a handsome naval officer. Captain Dunning was the man every lady had her eye on, and Miss Margaret Dashwood was the fortunate girl he chose to favour with his attentions. She left the ball with her head in a whirl, astounded by the speed with which the evening had flown by.

"I think that can be counted as a success," crowed Fanny triumphantly on the way back to Grosvenor Street.

"What young lady could wish for more on her first introduction into society?" She turned to John with a smile, expecting his praise and naturally taking all the credit for herself. John did not smile back as he was more inclined than his wife to give credit where credit was due.

Chapter 6
A Private Party

Fanny wrote to her mother the next day, unable to resist boasting of her triumph at the season's first ball. In any case, her mother liked to be kept abreast of all the details, despite her recent decision to retire from society. Fanny was also smarting from John's reluctance to give her any credit for Margaret's successful performance and yearned for her mother's congratulations.

Naturally, Fanny attributed Margaret's beauty and elegance to herself and the talents of young Lily Parks, failing to recognise that it was Margaret herself who had captured the interest of the ton. Fanny was also extremely conscious of her standing in society, so it was of the utmost importance to her that Margaret should be well received by London's most fashionable inhabitants. She could not deny it was also very gratifying that Margaret had attracted the eye of one of London's most notorious bachelors, for where he led, others would surely follow. It would certainly do Miss Margaret Dashwood no harm in society to have captured the handsome Captain Dunning's notice, so Fanny decided it would be wise to encourage him as much as possible. The dashing captain was fatally attractive to females and certainly capable of winning the heart of a simple chit just up from the country. In fact, Fanny had to acknowledge even her own hardened heart had skipped a beat when he'd bowed over her hand in greeting. It was true, there were whispered rumours circulating about his gaming habits, which did not bode well for his financial standing, but Margaret's future happiness was not her business. All that was required of Fanny was to find a match for the girl, then her duty was done. Fanny was certain her mother would be sympathetic to this course of action and sat down to pour out her heart to a known ally.

Unused to such late hours, Margaret was quite worn out the following day, but Lily insisted she rose as normal to be properly attired for any morning calls. Such calls of congratulations were a tradition on the morning after a ball, and from what Margaret had told her, Lily expected her to receive many such visitors. Thus, duly attired in the green-striped morning gown, Margaret was seated in the parlour in expectation. True to Lily's prediction, there was an early knock at the door to admit Mr and Mrs Palmer and Sir John and Lady Middleton. Although they had not been present last night, Margaret's success had already reached their ears through the contacts of Lady Middleton, who loved to gossip.

"Sir John, Lady Middleton, Mr and Mrs Palmer. We were so sorry not to see you last night. What a delightful surprise!" cried Margaret, rising enthusiastically to greet them as they were shown in, and Charlotte crossed the room to take her hands affectionately as Sir John's voice boomed above the others.

"Good morning, Miss Margaret. Delighted to see you, m'dear. We were very sorry to miss the ball last night, but we opened up the house in Hanover Square only yesterday and will be in town until Christmas. Lady Middleton could not be persuaded to be separated from the children any longer," Sir John explained, and Lady Middleton nodded solemnly, corroborating this statement.

"Yes, the little darlings. I shall be quite bereft without them. But I hear congratulations are in order, Miss Margaret. A little bird told us you were very well received in society last night. You are the talk of the town, and your first outing has been counted as quite a success." Margaret was at a loss as to how Lady Middleton had received this information as she had not been present at the ball.

"Thank you, Lady Middleton," replied Margaret, thinking this was the most notice she had ever had from her. Lady Middleton did not normally notice any children but her own, and Margaret was only just out of the school room. Last night's triumph changed everything, and Lady Middleton's respect for the young girl had increased tenfold. It appeared Mr Palmer felt the same as he shook Margaret's hand vigorously.

"How do you do, Miss Margaret? I hope not too fatigued after last night's exertions," he enquired, with unusual solicitude in the longest speech he had ever made to her.

"No, sir, I am quite well, thank you." Another indication she was considered firmly out of the schoolroom and he viewed her as a young lady worthy of his notice, but, as usual, his wife took over the conversation.

"Miss Margaret, how charming you look. Quite the young lady. We are all overcome to be at the townhouse, having not set foot there since Mama died last year," cried Charlotte in anguish, dabbing her eyes with a handkerchief, and Margaret took her hand in sympathy.

"Dear Mrs Jennings. How well we remember her lively sense of humour. She would have been so delighted to be here in London with us all together," responded Margaret warmly, remembering Mrs Jennings' love of company, even though her wit had sometimes been too direct for her sisters, whom she had teased relentlessly about their beaux. Margaret, being too young to be the butt of her matchmaking, had found the old lady genuinely amusing. She hadn't minded her direct sense of humour, appreciating her blunt honesty and kind heart. Mrs Palmer smiled through her tears at Margaret, grateful for her kindness.

"She would indeed, Miss Margaret, and, to that end, we have come to issue an invitation in her honour. It is just what she would have wished. There is nothing she so much enjoyed as a party. We are at home on Tuesday next and would be delighted if you and Mr and Mrs John Dashwood could join us."

"Yes, indeed," seconded Lady Middleton with unusual enthusiasm. "Please tell Mrs John Dashwood that I shall quite depend upon her. One does not often meet with such a woman of sense." Margaret was forced to hide a smile at such a description of Fanny.

"I am not engaged," Margaret responded, "although I cannot speak for Fanny and John as they are from home at the moment, but I'm sure they will be delighted to accept if they are free." Mrs Palmer nodded.

"Well then, my dear, I will leave our card and hope for the best. Now, we must take our leave as we are in the process of giving invitations to all our acquaintance personally. Mr Palmer will not rest until this is done. He is so eager to meet with your dear sisters again, I can hardly contain him. Good day, Miss Margaret, until Tuesday," Charlotte gushed, as usual speaking for everyone as they all took their leave. Margaret was amused to note Mr Palmer meekly followed his wife with an expression of silent resignation.

It transpired that Fanny and John were not otherwise engaged, so on Tuesday next, they accompanied Margaret to Hanover Square. Margaret felt a strong curiosity to see the place where Marianne and Elinor were invited on that first fateful visit to London. There, Marianne had arrived in such hope and learned of Willoughby's defection within days. It must have been a terrible shock to meet him in the company of another woman at a ball. Margaret looked around her, taking in every detail of the charmingly appointed residence, as Fanny evinced surprise at finding such a large gathering. Margaret, knowing Charlotte Palmer's and Sir John Middleton's love of company, had prepared herself for a proper party, and she was not at all surprised to find upward of twenty people present at the soiree. She waved to Marianne and Elinor from across the room, currently occupied with Marguerite and Charles Dashwood but was prevented from joining them by the arrival of Captain Dunning and First Lieutenant Carter. They claimed her attention immediately, and for a while she had neither leisure nor desire to speak to anyone else. The officers were so effusive in their praise that she did not know where to look, being unused to such compliments from young men.

"Miss Margaret, how charming you look this evening," admired the captain, smiling boldly at her.

"Allow me to compliment you on being the belle of the ball last night. All London is talking of the beautiful Miss Margaret Dashwood," First Lieutenant Carter interjected, not to be outdone by his superior officer. Margaret stared at him in disbelief, but extravagant compliments aside, she was glad to take the arm the captain proffered and allow him to lead her towards the refreshments, with the lieutenant following closely behind them. Their laughter could be heard all over the room as they talked of the ball, while the officers proved themselves to be witty as well as handsome. That Margaret was enjoying their attentions immensely was evident to the rest of the company. The captain cut a particularly dashing figure, being tall and well-built with a commanding military deportment. He reminded Margaret of a younger version of her brother-in-law, the colonel. She could not help but be flattered at his particular notice, although she was at a loss as to why he had singled her out. He must be at least thirty, and she was just eighteen. She was particularly gratified to notice Mr Charles Dashwood frequently glanced over to where they were standing and was quite disappointed when Charlotte Palmer approached purposefully, interrupting their easy camaraderie.

"Captain, Lieutenant." Charlotte pretended to be annoyed, cutting across their merry banter and rapping the captain playfully on the knuckles with her fan.

"I simply cannot allow you to keep Miss Margaret to yourselves all evening. I wish to introduce her to the other young people present, and there are other young ladies requiring your attention." Reluctantly, Margaret was forced to allow Charlotte to lead her towards a small group of ladies, who curtseyed eagerly as she approached.

"Miss Margaret, may I introduce an old friend of Mama's, Mrs Louisa Parker and her two daughters, Miss Caroline and Miss Catherine Parker. They are visiting town from Yorkshire and have taken a house nearby, so we are to be neighbours. I do hope you will be friends." Margaret curtsied, observing that Miss Caroline was perhaps a little older than herself, while Miss Catherine appeared almost too young to be out in society, possibly because her deep blush revealed she was unused to company. Mrs Parker was exceedingly fat and rather young to be a friend of Mrs Jennings, although Margaret was able to discern she had once been a beauty. Before either of the others could speak, Miss Parker interjected determinedly, monopolising the conversation at once.

"I've so long been wanting to meet you, Miss Margaret," she gushed. "Mrs Palmer's letters to Mama have been so full of the Miss Dashwoods, I've barely heard anything else; isn't that so, Mama?" Without waiting for her mama to answer, Miss Parker took Margaret's arm rather forcefully and proceeded to walk her away without so much as a backward glance at her mother and sister, leaving them to stare after her in askance. Margaret was extremely surprised and very disconcerted by this forward behaviour and decided to discourage Miss Parker immediately.

"You will soon find others in London more worthy of your attention, Miss Parker. I suspect there is not much else to talk of in the small circle of acquaintance we have in Devon." Margaret was now quite discomforted to find herself parading around the room on the arm of this brazen stranger. They continued on for a few minutes in silence, whilst Margaret desperately tried to think of an excuse to extricate herself from this awkward situation and such an impertinent girl.

Miss Parker was remarkably pretty with black curls and a very neat figure, so there was no doubt in Margaret's mind this was the reason for the display. She was sure Miss Parker was well aware of how much she appeared to the advantage and very much enjoying the attention they were attracting from the gentlemen present. She turned to Margaret, pressing her arm in an affectionate gesture.

"Oh, no, I've been led to believe the Miss Dashwoods are all very superior beings. Will you do me the honour of introducing me to your sisters?" Miss Parker begged, looking eagerly over to where her sisters were talking to Charles Dashwood, who was now thoroughly engrossed in the conversation and appeared not to notice Margaret and her new acquaintance.

"Of course," said Margaret, leading the way, relieved to have a course of action that would put an end to their intimate discussion. She had been conscious of her sisters' puzzled stares, which confirmed her own opinion: they were making a bit of a spectacle of themselves. Margaret quickly made the necessary introductions, and Elinor politely began the conversation with Miss Parker.

"And do you stay long in town, Miss Parker?" Elinor asked while Marianne looked down her nose, rather bored, and Margaret detected she had taken a dislike to Miss Parker on first sight. Marianne thoroughly deplored any kind of pert behaviour for the sake of occupying the limelight. Undaunted by Marianne's silent disapproval, Miss Parker answered Elinor with enthusiasm, but her eyes sought those of Charles Dashwood as she looked at him from under her lashes.

"Papa has taken the house for the whole season, so I hope we will often meet," she simpered, still looking at Charles.

"I pray you will all excuse me," Marianne bluntly interrupted her, quite disgusted by her obvious flirting with a complete stranger. "I have been prevailed upon by Charlotte to play some country dances as some of the guests wish to dance." Marianne walked away, and Caroline Parker called after her departing back.

"How kind of you, Mrs Brandon! I long to dance." Miss Parker again looked pointedly at Mr Charles Dashwood, at whom this hint was chiefly aimed, but he looked away, embarrassed. As Marianne began a lively tune, a line of dancers began to assemble, and Elinor took pity on Miss Parker. Being less censorious than her sister, she was always the first to give anyone the benefit of the doubt. She turned to Charles Dashwood with an encouraging smile.

"Mr Dashwood, I am sure you will be kind enough to oblige Miss Parker," Elinor urged, eager to see him dancing anyway. To her mind, this young man was far too serious for his own good. His horrified expression revealed this was the last thing on his mind, but good manners prevailed. He had no choice but to lead a triumphant Miss Parker to the dance floor, quickly followed by Margaret and Captain Dunning. First Lieutenant Carter was left to Miss Catherine Parker, to whom her mama had quickly affected an introduction. Margaret was pleased to see him encouraging his shy partner, whilst she responded to his boyish charm with timid smiles. Margaret saw then that Miss Catherine Parker was also very pretty, only lacking confidence. Most probably eclipsed by an elder sister who was constantly putting herself forward, Margaret decided. She resolved to put as much distance between her and Miss Parker as was humanly possible and concentrate on enjoying the dance.

After the first two dances, Marianne was relieved at the pianoforte by Mrs Marguerite Dashwood and persuaded to join the dance by Captain Dunning, recently released by Margaret. Edward proudly led out his wife, meaning Margaret was able to catch her breath and watch from the sidelines. It was a lively affair, and Margaret was pleased to see Marianne enjoying herself as she had been a little depressed in spirits of late. Clearly, London was doing her good, and she looked radiant as Captain Dunning flirted with her outrageously. Charlotte and Mr Palmer were standing next to her, also watching the dance.

"Five couples, Mr Palmer!" Charlotte cried, shaking his arm vigorously, to his obvious dismay. "Our little party is a great success. How delightful! Mama would have so enjoyed it." Charlotte was ecstatic, while Lady Middleton looked on in askance at such an uncivilised way of spending an evening.

At supper, Margaret was dismayed to find herself sitting in a party that included the Miss Parkers, the captain, Lieutenant Carter and Charles Dashwood. Obviously, Charlotte had been very busy in her endeavours to keep the young people amused. Margaret couldn't help thinking they were an ill-assorted group and was relieved when the captain began the conversation.

"I hear you are a physician, Dashwood. What is your specialism?" inquired the captain politely, mainly to break the awkward silence. Charles looked surprised by such a question from a military man but answered him confidently enough.

"Obstetrics," he confirmed bluntly, "but I am interested in all forms of medicine."

"How fascinating, Mr Dashwood." On hearing him speak, Miss Parker's ears pricked up, and she interrupted, favouring him with a charming smile, hanging on his every word. It was then that Margaret began to suspect the reason her company had been so eagerly sought by Miss Parker. Of course, she had been the means by which Miss Parker effected a speedy introduction to Charles Dashwood. Charlotte Palmer would, no doubt, have informed her of his excellent prospects, and it was becoming obvious that Miss Parker had been brought to London with one aim in view: to catch herself a husband. But who am I to judge? Margaret inwardly reproved herself, as it had been made very clear to her that she was on the same mission. Charles Dashwood interrupted her thoughts by answering Miss Parker with enthusiasm, and Margaret was surprised to see him so animated.

"Exactly so, Miss Parker. It is extremely interesting. I studied under the famous Alexander Gordon. Obstetrics has come a long way in the past twenty years, and the childbed has become a much safer place. That fact I am very happy to be able to confirm to the ladies present," he said, warming even further to his subject. Miss Catherine blushed an even deeper shade and didn't know where to look, but Margaret's interest was piqued, and she said so, unafraid to break into such a conversation.

"How so, sir?" she asked, keen to learn more as she had recently embarked on a private study of the efficacy of herbs with medicinal properties. He looked surprised by her direct question but answered without hesitation.

"Well, infection for one, Miss Margaret. That is much less likely as we now have new methods of preventing the transference." Captain Dunning looked horrified at the turn the conversation had taken as a result of his polite question and swiftly tried to change the subject. Miss Parker persisted, however, and would not let it drop, seeing it as a sure way of keeping the doctor's attention focussed on her.

"We ladies are all very relieved to hear that, Mr Dashwood," Miss Parker interjected, succeeding in her object of regaining his attention immediately. "We are very glad to learn we will be in such safe hands when the need arises." She gazed at him seductively with her large, dark eyes.

"Perhaps not a suitable subject for the supper table, though," said the captain dryly, now very keen to put an end to a discussion in which he could play no part and divert the attention of the ladies away from Mr Dashwood. Margaret was disappointed to lose the opportunity of questioning him further as her studies had excited her curiosity. All forms of medicine fascinated her, and she had ideas of her own she would have enjoyed discussing with him.

Margaret joined her sisters after supper, eager to hear their opinion of the new heir to Norland.

"Well, now that you have made his acquaintance, what do you make of Charles Dashwood?" she enquired.

"He seems like a serious young man, but that is no bad thing," said Elinor with feeling, remembering Willoughby's high-spirited but ingenuous charms.

"No, indeed," agreed Marianne thoughtfully. "I found him very willing to talk, albeit on serious topics, but he was not without taste on the subject of literature when I introduced it into our conversation, and it cannot be denied, he is rather handsome." She smiled teasingly at Margaret. "If I remember correctly, I think it was you that first pointed that out." Margaret was dismayed to find herself blushing under Marianne's intense scrutiny.

"Don't look at me in that way, Marianne. I have had not heard more than two words from him since we were introduced. I'm sure that he has taken a dislike to me. In fact, he was most impolite at the ball. When we were forced to dance together by his mother, he made it very clear to me he would rather not."

"Surely not, Margaret. You must have mistaken the matter. Why ever would he object to dancing with you?" cried Elinor incredulously.

"I hardly know," said Margaret, glancing over to where Charles Dashwood was being monopolised by the two Miss Parkers. At that moment, he looked up and caught her eye, and to her extreme annoyance, she found herself blushing, for the second time in as many minutes. To cover her embarrassment, she told Marianne of her sighting of Willoughby at the ball and was sad to see her sister pale at the mention of his name.

"Thank you for preparing me that he is in town, Margaret, although I do not see how meeting him can possibly distress me after all this time." Despite her protests to the contrary, Margaret noticed her face quickly turn from white to red as she denied any lingering feelings. Fortunately, they were distracted from further conversation by Fanny and John, who joined them at that moment.

"My dear Elinor, Marianne and Margaret, I am very glad to have found you all together. Fanny and I have decided to take a rest from London at Christmas and would like to invite you all to join us at Norland. It will just be family, of course, but we would be delighted to receive you. The colonel and Edward have already agreed to my proposal, subject to your approval, naturally. You would be doing us a favour as the house seems so empty without…" John trailed off miserably, while Fanny stood expressionless by his side.

"I should be delighted to join you, John," said Marianne with feeling, having long desired to see Norland again, but Elinor was doubtful.

"I think we may be needed back in Devon to relieve Mama of the sole responsibility for our daughter, Kitty."

"If that is your only objection, my dear Elinor, then let me put an end to your doubts. The colonel has undertaken to send his carriage for your mother and daughter, if they can be persuaded to join us, and to that end, I have already written to Mrs Dashwood in anticipation of your acceptance." John was happy to be able to reassure Elinor that all details for her happiness had been considered.

"In that case, John and Fanny, I should be delighted to accept," said Elinor, satisfied that everything had been properly done and secretly very curious to see the home of her youth again. John was so pleased by their unanimous acceptance that he failed to notice the stony silence of his wife.

At the earnest pleas of her hostess, Marguerite Dashwood sat down at the pianoforte, and couples lined up for the dance again. The two officers were quick to claim the hands of Marianne and Margaret, who was surprised to see Charles Dashwood had so overcome his initial reluctance to dance as to invite Miss Parker to stand up with him for the second time. She watched in amazement as he engaged her in lively conversation, reflecting how different his behaviour was with other young ladies. It just proved her assumption was correct; it must be her that set his teeth on edge. Could it be that they were forming an attachment then, after so short an acquaintance? Well, what if they were? He is handsome, and she is pretty, and it was nothing to her who he danced with. She turned her attention back to the captain, who looked as though he had something to say to her.

"Miss Margaret, would you do me the honour of taking a drive with me in the park tomorrow?" She was surprised beyond belief and couldn't think of how to refuse such a forward invitation from a man of the captain's sophistication.

"I…that is why, I thank you, if Fanny has no objection, Captain. You must know I cannot do anything without her approval." Margaret was not quite sure of the propriety of accepting his invitation but couldn't think of a suitable reason for refusal, and she was afraid he would think her missish. Seeing her hesitation, he was at pains to reassure her.

"Of course, there can be no objection. I assure you, Miss Margaret, there is nothing improper in my invitation, and I shall ask Mrs Dashwood's permission directly after the dance." Captain Dunning then proceeded to kiss her hand rather forwardly, in Margaret's opinion. She was very uncomfortable that his attentions seemed to be taking on a more serious note so soon after their introduction. She was not at all sure whether she felt pleasure or dismay at this change of tempo after such a short acquaintance. She found it difficult to believe he had formed a violent attraction for a girl barely out of the schoolroom, so what could be his motive? The fact that she had only known him for a few days only added to her disquiet about being so singled out. It was one thing to accept his attentions with pleasure in company, but to drive out with him alone was quite another matter. She felt, instinctively, it was wrong and had been very reluctant to accept, no matter that conventions in London were very different from those in Devon. He left her after the dance, and she saw him approach Fanny purposefully, rather surprised to note that he remained by her side for some time. Fanny, it seemed, was enjoying his company immensely, and Margaret thought she looked remarkably well. Later, she learned from Fanny that the captain had asked her permission for the drive, and Fanny had freely given it. This surprised Margaret enormously as she'd expected Fanny to repudiate his advances and refuse her permission for such an intimate drive, but Fanny merely informed Margaret, with a significant look, that he would be calling for her at Grosvenor Street at ten o'clock in his curricle.

"Quite a conquest, my dear," Fanny congratulated with a rare smile. "Although he is only the second son, word has it that he made his own fortune in the Navy. You have done very well, child." Margaret was considerably alarmed. Fanny was talking as if it were already a settled thing, even before her wishes were consulted. She liked the captain and was flattered by the attentions of such a dashing soldier, but no more than that. Was she expected to accept the first man with prospects who proposed to her, then? She made a last attempt to save herself from the ordeal by voicing her doubts aloud.

"Fanny, are you sure it is quite proper for me to drive out with him alone? Such behaviour would not be approved of in Devon. It would be deemed quite fast," Margaret demanded, earnestly looking at Fanny, but she only laughed derisively.

"My dear, Miss Margaret, you are not in Devon now and must allow me to be the judge of what's best for you." Margaret gave up, knowing herself to be beaten and refrained from further argument.

"Very well, I will go for the drive, but no more than that." Margaret was adamant, and Fanny shook her head in amazement.

"Do you meant to tell me, Miss Margaret, if the gallant captain makes you an offer, you would refuse him? I cannot believe it. Why, half the debutantes in London have set their caps at him this season alone." She was incredulous as Margaret shook her head and replied with determination.

"I've no reason to expect him to make me an offer, Fanny. Why, I hardly know him." She was incensed, but Fanny had already turned away to talk to an acquaintance, and Margaret felt caught in a tide she couldn't control. Elinor and

Marianne had married for love, even though there had been immense difficulties to overcome at first. She had always hoped of doing the same, but it appeared that Fanny had other ideas.

Much to her astonishment, Fanny had enjoyed the soiree at Hanover Square immensely. She was always pleased to meet Lady Middleton, with whom she had so very much in common. It was a shame they could no longer discuss their children on an equal footing, but Lady Middleton had expressed her deepest sympathy in such sincere terms, Fanny quite forgave her fecundity. Nevertheless, they still found plenty to talk over, gossiping at length about the ton and people of fashion that formed the very stuff of their lives. It had been a long time since Fanny had enjoyed anyone's company more, but another introduction had also given Fanny very great pleasure. Caroline Parker was a charming girl, and Fanny liked her immensely, being remarkably pretty without giving herself airs, unlike the Dashwood sisters. She also possessed a great talent for the kind of flattery that was balm to Fanny's wounded vanity. As such, she was a great success, so much so that Fanny was keen to see more of her. She had already resolved to invite Miss Parker to Norland for Christmas, thinking she was the perfect person to distract Charles Dashwood from Margaret. Fanny, always a keen observer, saw Caroline's overtures to him, and she was in a position to make sure they had every encouragement. If she must lose Norland to another woman, then better it be a strong ally of hers, one who has every reason to be eternally grateful. It was Fanny who had put pressure to bear on Charles Dashwood to ask Caroline to dance a second time, which she knew would give rise to speculation. Of course, she must also include the sister, Catherine Parker, in the invitation to Norland, but she was a meek little thing and easily dictated to. It would kill two birds with one stone. Fanny congratulated herself in delight. She would have the means of preventing John's plot to marry Margaret to Charles, and she would gain much-needed allies against the Dashwood camp.

Charles Dashwood and Caroline Parker was not the only match Fanny was planning; she had also succeeded in planting a seed of expectation in Captain Dunning's head. Margaret was his latest flirt, but Fanny knew of his reputation; it would go no further than that without a little help, but it had been such a simple matter for Fanny to give the captain the merest of hints, implying Margaret was likely to be made heir to the Norland Estate, and he had taken the bait. His eyes had lit up with speculation, and if Fanny was any judge, he could even propose in the park. Perhaps by the time he came to realise his mistake, he would already be in too deep to extricate himself. The speed with which he had asked her permission to take her young charge for a drive seemed to indicate his ardour or his desperate need for money. Of course, Margaret's doubts were not without foundation; it was not entirely proper for a single girl to go on such an outing unchaperoned, but if Margaret was a little compromised, then there would be even more reason for her to speedily marry the captain. There was no doubt about it; he was an absolute rogue, but a very attractive one, she had to admit. Fanny's cheeks grew warm, remembering their conversation from the previous evening. Clearly, his intentions to Margaret had not prevented him from dancing attendance on herself for the best part of half an hour, and this flattering interlude had made her feel young and desirable again. Yes, indeed, Fanny thought to herself, it was very satisfying to be a woman of influence and standing in society. It was so much easier to manipulate people into doing her will. Yes, all in all, it had been a very successful evening.

Chapter 7
A Drive in the Park and a Surprise Meeting

The following morning, Margaret was surprised to find Fanny in remarkably good spirits. Over breakfast, her conversation overflowed with enthusiasm for the previous evening's gathering, so much so that John was also puzzled.

"Why, Fanny, I thought the evening was pleasant enough but nothing remarkable in terms of people of fashion." Fanny favoured her husband with a rare smile.

"My dear, I disagree with you; the Middletons and the Palmers are people of standing, and I greatly enjoy the company of Lady Middleton, as you well know, but I am also quite delighted with the elder Miss Parker. Did you not think her a charming girl?" Fanny felt obliged to explain away her jubilant mood, not wishing to arouse his suspicions on the other matter that pleased her. John did not deign to answer his wife, merely shrugged his shoulders indifferently, making it obvious to Margaret that he had not been at all impressed by Caroline Parker. Margaret silently agreed with Fanny that Lady Middleton and she had a great deal in common, both having limited sense and valuing the importance of fashionable connections above everything else. She had also been nearby when Fanny and Miss Parker had been introduced by Charles Dashwood, thus overhearing much of their conversation.

Hence, she was not surprised that Fanny had a new protégé. Their conversation had mostly taken the form of outrageous flattery on Miss Parker's part, in a shameless effort to ingratiate herself with Mrs Fanny Dashwood. She had succeeded, it appeared, for Fanny informed Margaret that she had invited Miss Parker to call that morning. Margaret was almost pleased she had an engagement. Although she was not particularly looking forward to the drive with Captain Dunning, it was better than having to endure Fanny and Miss Parker. It was now her firm opinion that the latter, though pretty enough, was a shameless social climber who would stop at nothing to achieve her aims.

If Margaret had hoped the captain would think better of his invitation in the cold light of day, she was destined to be disappointed. As good as his word, he was waiting for her in a very smart curricle at precisely ten o'clock. Margaret was looking anxiously out of the window, dreading his arrival, fashionably dressed in her warmest pelisse and a smart new hat.

"My dear Miss Margaret, how charming you look this morning." He bowed gallantly as she descended the steps of Grosvenor Street. "We are very fortunate in having such unseasonably fine weather to make our outing possible at this time of year."

"Indeed, Captain," she agreed, unable to meet his eye as he helped her into the seat beside him, and they set off at a sedate pace for the park. Although she couldn't look at her escort, she had already observed his dashing appearance and the very smart carriage he was expertly handling.

"You have a very fine equipage," Margaret observed, breaking the awkward silence in an attempt to overcome her embarrassment at being in such close proximity to a gentleman she hardly knew. He appeared gratified at her praise.

"I am pleased it meets with your approval, Miss Margaret." There was another long pause before he turned to look at her and observed in an intimate tone.

"You are very fortunate in your family connections, Miss Margaret. Mr and Mrs Dashwood seem very well situated in life. I understand that you are John Dashwood's youngest and favourite sister?" He continued to probe impertinently, and Margaret answered him with stiff reservation.

"John is only my half-brother, and as to me being his favourite, it is not true at all. He invited me because I am the only one of his sisters not yet settled and married," she explained coldly, hoping her answer would dampen his curiosity. Nevertheless, he persisted with his questions.

"I understand that Norland is a very great estate," he observed, changing the subject.

"Yes, indeed, it is very well situated, being just fifty miles from London in the beautiful countryside surrounding Midhurst," Margaret corroborated enthusiastically, always pleased to speak warmly of her erstwhile home. His attention was called to his driving, and Margaret could not help admiring the expert handling of the horses as they took a corner. He returned immediately to their former topic of conversation.

"Yes, I have heard much of its beauty, and it cannot be denied that being just fifty miles from London is most convenient. But you are too modest, Miss Margaret; it is very clear to me that Fanny and John both think very highly of you. Did I hear that they lost their only child last year in an unfortunate accident?"

"Yes, it was very sad," agreed Margaret, unwilling to be drawn further on that subject to a relative stranger. "Poor little Harry." She looked away, brushing away an involuntary tear, which the captain ignored.

"I understand they have now taken you into their personal protection, almost as their own child," he continued insensitively, but Margaret interrupted him indignantly.

"I do not believe I am their guest as a substitute for Harry. That is not how Fanny and John think of me, Captain Dunning." She was irritated by his interrogatory tone, as if he were in possession of a secret he was trying to winkle out of her through these incessant enquiries.

"I would lay a wager that they do." He laughed, and the penny dropped. So that's it, she thought with a blinding flash of insight. He mistakenly believed she would be made heiress to the Norland Estate. Where had he got that idea? Surely, he couldn't have leapt to that conclusion merely because she was staying with Fanny and John. Margaret decided it was time to disabuse him of his mistake without further delay.

"Please, Captain Dunning, I think you may have misinterpreted the nature of my relationship with John and Fanny. Let me disabuse you at once. They are introducing me into society in payment of an old debt, so to speak. Their intentions go no further than that; indeed, they cannot, for Mr Charles Dashwood is to inherit the Norland Estate following the untimely death of little Harry. The Norland Estate has been entailed to the male line since the death of my father's uncle, so it would be impossible for me to inherit, no matter how much John and Fanny may wish it. Indeed, this is the reason that Charles Dashwood is so often in their company of late." Margaret delivered this speech in such a manner, no one could doubt it was the truth. The captain's face darkened immediately, and she saw her assumption was correct, although he remained silent and pensive. Margaret could tell that her revelation had greatly disconcerted him, and they drove on in awkward silence. But how had he leapt to such a conclusion? Certainly, she had never given him any reason to believe herself to be the heir to Norland. Nevertheless, it was the perfect explanation for his unaccountable, whirlwind courtship. The dashing captain was nothing but a fortune hunter. Her embarrassment was now so acute that she longed for a means of escape.

After what seemed like an age, they reached the park, which was almost empty of people at such an early hour, just as the captain had hoped, but now that his planned seduction was out of the question, he decided to have some fun and derive some enjoyment from the unfortunate situation. Even though this mistaken entanglement had been of his own making, he was exceedingly angry at being so misled and resolved to have it out with Mrs Fanny Dashwood at the earliest opportunity. Besides, she had a roguish twinkle in her eye, and he wouldn't object to seeing her again for other reasons. A most attractive lady and married. In his experience, the married ones were always grateful for any attention they no longer received from their husbands, so they were always the most compliant. He had been very impressed by last night's gathering. There had been some real beauties present: Mrs Brandon and Mrs Marguerite Dashwood, to name but two. He doubted the former could be persuaded into a dalliance, but it had been a great pleasure to lure her onto the dance floor. Mrs Marguerite Dashwood was quite another matter entirely, however, and a woman of the world, if he were any judge. Fanny Dashwood was no beauty by comparison, but there was something about her that intrigued him greatly. He was fascinated by her complete self-absorption, which was something they had in common. As a strategist, he saw she would make a considerable ally but a very dangerous foe, and that husband of hers was a fool if he couldn't see his neglect was turning her into the enemy. It was true that Fanny was not in his usual style of dalliance; nevertheless, there was something he couldn't put his finger on. Smiling wickedly at the thought of Fanny's encouragement of his advances, he turned to Margaret, and she was alarmed by the look in his eyes.

"I think perhaps we can now have some sport if you do not object, Miss Margaret." He made a pretence of deferential consultation without any intention of adhering to her wishes. She had made a fool of him, and he was equally angry with her but with far less justification.

"Well, perhaps some very gentle sport, Captain," agreed Margaret nervously, not wanting to appear missish and disobliging, aware that he was grossly disappointed in her prospects and wanting to avoid any further tête-à-tête. He laughed fiendishly, whipping the horse into a fast trot, forcing Margaret to hold tight to her hat and the seat as the curricle swept down the central avenue. At that moment, a spirited black stallion galloped into view, carrying a lady rider attired in a striking crimson riding habit. Her horse reared as it approached them and took the captain completely by surprise, startling his horses so they veered off course onto the grass, tipping the curricle slightly as one wheel made an impact with the soft ground. Unfortunately, it was enough to throw Margaret from the carriage, having momentarily loosened her hold. She lay stunned for a few seconds as the captain brought the horses to a halt, and the rider leapt from her horse to kneel by her side.

"Good God, Miss Margaret, are you injured?" a familiar voice cried, and Margaret opened her eyes to see the perfect face of Marguerite Dashwood leaning over her in great concern.

"I do not think so," she replied and tried to stand. "Oh, my ankle." She fell back down as her ankle gave way. Do not panic, she told herself firmly, it is probably a sprain, remembering the time when Marianne had suffered a similar incident. Although Margaret was convinced there was no real cause for alarm, for the moment, she was completely helpless. The captain and Marguerite Dashwood were clearly not so certain, and both looked extremely worried.

"Is the leg broken, Mrs Dashwood?" the captain asked in a frightened voice, happy to let Marguerite take charge with quiet efficiency, and she looked up at him in concern.

"I cannot tell you, Captain, but it is badly twisted, and I dare not move her. I beg of you, take my horse and fetch my son." She took charge, seeing the gallant military man was helpless in this situation. "He is not five minutes from here," she urged. "I will stay with Miss Dashwood and look to your horses. See, they are beginning to graze and look not at all upset by the accident. Here is my son's direction. Please go quickly and impress on him the urgency." Her imploring tone girded him into action, and without another word, the captain mounted her horse, taking only a few moments to gain control of the spirited beast before galloping off at breakneck speed. Marguerite watched him leave the park, with reluctant admiration, before turning her attention to Margaret and beginning to examine her carefully for any other injuries. At last, she smiled with relief.

"Well, child, I think you've been extremely fortunate as there is no head injury or indeed any other that I can see, but I do not think you will be dancing for a while. It was lucky you fell on grass, which also slowed the carriage. Nevertheless, Captain Dunning was driving at quite a pace considering he had a passenger. Although perhaps it was also my fault for breaking into a gallop, but in my defence, I had only my own safety to consider." Margaret also thought the captain had been rather reckless, but unlike Marguerite, she was aware of the reasons for his frustration. It was his own fault he had been deceived, but a man like that would not enjoy being proved wrong.

"Does Fanny know of this adventure?" Marguerite asked with a frown, changing the subject. "I cannot believe that she would approve of such an outing." Margaret was ashamed that Marguerite Dashwood could believe she would do anything behind Fanny's back and hastened to reassure her.

"Yes, Mrs Dashwood," she replied emphatically. "Fanny and the captain arranged it between them last night, and she encouraged me to accept, even though I questioned the propriety. I would not do anything without her approval." Marguerite looked surprised at her vehemence.

"No, of course not. Do not upset yourself, Miss Margaret. I did not mean to imply that you would, but I am surprised that Fanny sanctioned such an outing." She looked questioningly at Margaret, who didn't know how to answer her as she was thinking the same thing. For some reason, Margaret couldn't quite fathom; she then confided the whole sorry tale to Marguerite Dashwood, who listened in increasing astonishment.

"Do you meant to tell me that the reason for the captain's pursuit of you was because he thought you were the heiress to Norland? What or who made him think that, and why?" Marguerite mused, almost to herself.

"I cannot give you the answer to those questions, perhaps Fanny herself." They looked at each other in some alarm, both wondering what possible motive Fanny could have for such deception.

"You are a most proficient rider, Mrs Dashwood," said Margaret admiringly, wishing to divert Marguerite's attention. "How dashing you look in that crimson habit." Marguerite looked embarrassed.

"I expect you are thinking it's rather foolish at my age, but it is my greatest pleasure, and I would be loath to give it up." At the sound of horses, she breathed a sigh of relief.

"At last, look, Miss Margaret, here comes the captain with my son." Margaret saw that she was correct and braced herself for another hefty dose of Charles Dashwood's disapproval.

She was not disappointed. He gravely knelt down beside Margaret, and she would have doubted if he had any other expressions had she not seen him laughing merrily with Miss Parker. It was further evidence to her that it was herself who offended him, although she couldn't understand what she had done to bring about this sorry state of affairs.

"Permit me?" he asked without ceremony, and she nodded for him to examine the injury in his professional capacity.

"I am pleased to say it is not broken," he confirmed at last, much to everyone's relief. Margaret smiled at him, pleased to have her own amateur diagnosis confirmed. Charles did not return her smile and continued to frown as he gave a further diagnosis.

"But it is a bad sprain and likely to become swollen. Dunning, we need to get Miss Margaret to my surgery for treatment. If we can lift her between us into your curricle, then perhaps you would be so good as to drive her there?" Ordinarily, the captain would have bridled at being ordered about by a man out of uniform, but he meekly complied with the doctor's instructions, for once, thoroughly ashamed of himself.

"Of course, it is the least I can do," the captain agreed rather sheepishly, and to her extreme embarrassment, Margaret found herself lifted between them into the curricle and driven to Charles' surgery forthwith.

When Margaret was made comfortable on the consulting couch, Marguerite persuaded the captain to leave her in their charge, feeling rather sorry for him whilst he hovered about anxiously, looking like a fish out of water in the surgery.

"There is nothing further you can do, Captain. She will be in good hands, and we will see her back to Grosvenor Street and explain all to the Dashwoods." He did not protest, and Margaret saw he was as relieved to be released as she was to be out of his presence.

After his departure, she submitted herself to Marguerite, who gently removed her muddied pelisse and battered hat, remaining by her side whilst her son carried out a further examination. This was a great relief to the patient as it would have been too awful to have been left alone with him. Initially rather grave, he now looked positively thunderous, and Margaret was alarmed.

"A very unfortunate accident for a young girl in the midst of her first season. I'm afraid I have to confirm you won't be dancing this side of Christmas. Are you often given to gallivanting around in men's carriages alone?" He fixed her with a such disapproving stare that Margaret saw red.

"No, Mr Dashwood, only those with good manners," she almost spat at him. The fact that she was now conscious of wrongdoing, albeit encouraged by Fanny, did nothing to reconcile her to his implied criticism. How dare he? Marguerite, watching this exchange, was forced to hide a smile at this flash of spirit from his young patient. Not many young women could stand up to Charles with his authoritative doctor's hat on, and his mother noted, in some surprise, he did not retaliate but continued his treatment in silence. Margaret realised her instincts had been right all along, that it was not quite done thing for unattached young ladies to ride around alone with young men in an open carriage. She wondered again about Fanny giving her permission. It was almost as though she was throwing her at the captain. Meanwhile, Charles soaked her ankle in cold cloths followed by a poultice of herbs, finally bandaging it firmly.

"There, I think that will suffice until tomorrow, when I will call on you at Grosvenor Street to dress it again. In the meantime, you must rest and keep it elevated. Are you in pain?" he asked a trifle more sympathetically, and she shook her head, for some strange reason feeling close to tears. It was a few moments before she had enough control of herself to be able to answer him, and he had to repeat his question.

"No, sir, not particularly. Was that arnica you used after the cold compress?" Charles stared at her in surprise.

"Why, yes. What do you know of arnica, Miss Margaret?"

"I have been trying to grow it in Devon, but without a great deal of success," she explained.

"No, well, it is an alpine plant," he sympathised as he busied himself, storing away the herbs and bandages while she rested quietly on the couch. The minutes ticked by, and Margaret was almost asleep when Charles spoke again, and she opened her eyes to see that his mother was no longer present.

"I am finished here, Miss Margaret, so my mother and I will safely see you home. You must put your arm around me so I can take your full weight in order to help you into the coach my mother is hailing." Margaret had no choice but to submit to his support, blushing profusely.

"Thank you, sir," she replied, meekly doing as she was told, not knowing where to look as he took her in his arms.

They were all silent in the coach on the way to Grosvenor Street, each occupied with their own thoughts. Margaret lost no time in putting Captain Dunning firmly out of her mind as he did not deserve her sympathy but was still puzzling over Fanny's actions and Charles Dashwood's perpetual rudeness. Why was he angry with her all the time? What had she done to offend him so? Marguerite Dashwood was also puzzling over Fanny's motives for allowing such a risky outing for her young charge and examining her own conscience, feeling partly responsible for the accident. She had also been amused to witness the interchange between physician and patient earlier and admired Margaret's spirit in not accepting her son's putdown. Charles Dashwood simply couldn't understand why the whole miserable episode made him so very angry. It was nothing to him how Miss Margaret conducted herself. They arrived at Grosvenor Street to find Fanny and John waiting anxiously for them, Charles having sent a brief note of explanation ahead. In great consternation, John rushed down the steps to lend Charles assistance with carrying Margaret into the house. Meanwhile, Fanny questioned Marguerite tersely as to the precise details of the accident. Marguerite was inclined to make light of it, although she was annoyed with Fanny for allowing such an outing in the first place. What was the woman thinking of putting her charge in such a vulnerable position and why had she misled the captain into thinking Margaret was the heiress to Norland? The more Marguerite thought about it, the more she was persuaded that Fanny was the guilty party. A devious woman, if ever there was one, but she answered Fanny lightly enough.

"Aside from a sprained ankle, a muddy pelisse and a battered hat, there is not much harm done. Although, I rather think Miss Margaret will have to miss a few parties and the Christmas ball." Marguerite's calm reassurance seemed to take the wind out of Fanny's sails, whilst John and Charles settled Margaret on the couch. John was mortified that this should happen to Margaret whilst in their care, and he turned to the assembled party vehemently.

"No matter, if Miss Margaret cannot go out in society, then I'm determined society will come to her. I think, Fanny, we will bring forward our Christmas party at Norland. We planned to go there anyway, so two weeks will not make much difference. We can hardly go gallivanting around London with Margaret laid up at home." John gave his wife a furious look, turning away to make sure Margaret had all she needed, missing his wife's mutinous expression entirely. John was angry with himself and even angrier with his wife. Against his better judgement, he'd allowed Fanny to persuade him that the outing in the park would be beneficial to Margaret's interests. Now that it had ended in this most unfortunate way, he could see that she had misled him, and John was becoming suspicious of his wife's motives. He was also aware that Marguerite and Charles Dashwood also strongly disapproved, although they did not say so explicitly.

Captain Dunning was the first visitor at Grosvenor Street the next morning. He did not ask to see Margaret, and Fanny received him in her private quarters as Margaret was occupying the morning room. If Fanny was puzzled he had asked to see her and not Margaret, she did not say so, receiving him with cordiality despite his part in the unfortunate accident. He entered sheepishly, carrying a large bunch of hothouse flowers, his demeanour contrite as he profusely apologised to Fanny for injuring her charge. She listened to his account with growing sympathy.

"Captain Dunning, do not distress yourself so. I have heard all about the accident, and it was not entirely your fault. In fact, it appears to me that Marguerite Dashwood was mostly to blame for riding her horse in such an unladylike way." Fanny had no liking for Marguerite Dashwood, yet another Dashwood of whom she did not approve. She was far too attractive and the gentlemen far too attentive to her. These heavy faults, coupled with a lack of fortune and connections, meant that Fanny disapproved of the lady and considered her to be beneath her notice. The fact that Mrs Marguerite Dashwood had made no effort to cultivate Fanny's acquaintance was also a grievance against her. The captain nodded in agreement, pleased to have so easily convinced Fanny of his innocence.

"There is something in what you say, Mrs Dashwood. My horse would not have veered off if it hadn't been for Marguerite Dashwood, but" – he eyed her accusingly – "I would not have taken Miss Margaret for a drive in the first place if you hadn't led me to believe she would be the next heir to Norland." His eyes continued to bore into her, and she looked away in embarrassment, but aware that she had only given him the smallest of hints, she was not going to admit to being at fault. She quickly recovered herself, laughing up at him mischievously, and the captain, catching the challenging glint in her eye, was further intrigued. She proceeded to defend her innocence as vehemently as he had done.

"Why, Captain, I certainly did not say that. I merely said that John is very fond of Miss Margaret, and as she is the youngest of his sisters, he thinks of her almost as a daughter. Indeed, it is out of his power to make her his heir as the estate is entailed to the male line, and thus Charles Dashwood will inherit Norland." He noted, with admiration, she did not flinch as he gave her another piercing look.

"I am aware of that fact now, Mrs Dashwood, and you have my commiserations. It must be extremely difficult to lose such a great estate to a distant family member." Fanny looked up in surprise at his unexpected empathy. Could it be that the captain had a more serious side? "I must tell you, however, I will not be renewing my addresses to Miss Margaret Dashwood," he continued. "In fact, though extremely charming, she is far too young for me. My tastes run to the more mature woman." At this point, the captain paused to look at Fanny so suggestively she felt herself colouring for the first time in many years. She couldn't meet his eyes as he handed her the bouquet, unsure whether he meant it for her or Miss Margaret. He bowed gallantly and kissed her hand before taking his leave. Fanny sat down with a bump as her legs gave way, so flustered that she was obliged to remain in her sitting room for some minutes to calm down. Reluctantly, she then carried his offering through to Margaret, where she placed them in the window and proceeded to arrange them with great care. This Margaret noticed with surprise as she had never seen Fanny bother with flower arranging, a task usually left to the housekeeper.

"Captain Dunning left these for you earlier," she explained to Margaret, who felt only relief that he didn't deliver them to her in person.

Chapter 8
Norland

A good night's sleep restored Margaret's equanimity, and apart from a sore ankle and the inability to walk without assistance, she had suffered no lasting damage. Refusing to remain in bed, she allowed Lily to dress her informally and was happily reading, ensconced on the couch in the morning room. At this point, Fanny entered carrying the captain's bouquet. Impatient to return to her novel after Fanny's lengthy intrusion, Margaret settled down again to enjoy Mrs Radcliffe, who had been much neglected since her sojourn in London. The approach of visitors interrupted her again, and, stifling a sigh to be distracted from her reading again, she looked up as the two Miss Parkers entered the room. Clearly, the news of her misadventure had travelled fast, and Margaret schooled her features into a smile of welcome. No doubt, they had come to gloat over her misfortune and make the most of any perceived scandal. Miss Parker crossed the room with a touching show of insincere concern and sat down beside Margaret, taking her hand sympathetically. "Miss Margaret, how sorry we were to hear of your accident. We came across Mrs Marguerite Dashwood yesterday evening, who told us everything. How are you today, you poor thing?" Miss Parker asked with feigned concern, one eye on the door, clearly hoping that Fanny would make an entrance. Margaret was amused by this obvious subterfuge and answered her with as much patience as she could muster.

"Tolerably well, I thank you. I do not believe there will be any lasting damage, except to my pride, of course," replied Margaret ruefully, thinking not only of her fall but also the captain's reason for inviting her.

"Yes, quite." Miss Parker sniffed disapprovingly, revealing her true feelings. "It does not show one in the best of light to be tumbling off gentlemen's carriages in public, to be sure." Margaret was annoyed, more especially because she knew Miss Parker had a point.

"Let me assure you, Miss Parker, it's not something that I have ever done before or intend to make a habit of in the future, and it was done with Fanny's full knowledge. It has been pointed out to me that what is deemed correct behaviour in the country may be very different in London. It wouldn't do to be seen as a country mouse," Margaret replied tersely, glaring at her, hoping to snub Miss Parker into silence. Miss Parker did not deign to reply; she merely sent Margaret an incredulous look of disbelief, which made Margaret long to smack her face. She took a deep breath and counted to ten, suspecting Miss Parker's animosity was borne out of her extreme jealousy and that the physician in attendance was Charles Dashwood, but she couldn't resist goading her.

"Well, it is thanks to the excellent care I received from Mr Charles Dashwood that the injury is already on the mend. How fortunate he was close at hand." Margaret smiled smugly at her, seeing her assumption had been correct, and Miss Parker was angry because Margaret's accident had afforded her an intimate moment with Caroline's chosen quarry. Caroline Parker sent Margaret a look of pure hatred but was spared the trouble of further conversation by Fanny entering the room. Margaret was amused to note how quickly Miss Parker moulded her features into a smile and turned all her attention to Fanny. This left Margaret in no doubt of the real reason for Miss Parker's visit: the hope of seeing Fanny and she was just the excuse. Margaret was left to make conversation, as best she could, with Miss Catherine. It proved not to be an easy task as Catherine Parker sat with her head meekly bowed, fiddling nervously with her reticule, refusing to be drawn out.

"And how are you enjoying London, Miss Catherine?" Margaret began tentatively off the top of her head, but before Catherine could pluck up the courage to reply, the door opened, and in came Elinor and Marianne.

"Good Lord, Margaret. What on earth have you been about?" cried Marianne in concern, seeing her sister's prostrate form and rushing to her side.

"No more than you have done in your youth, I assure you, Marianne. It is nothing. Do not upset yourself. All will be well in a day or two." Margaret was quite dismissive of her accident, while Elinor interrogated Fanny as to the exact nature of the injury.

"You make light of it, Margaret, but it is very unfortunate that you will miss the Christmas ball," remarked Elinor in mild disapproval after extracting sketchy facts from a reluctant Fanny, indignant at being cross-examined by someone she regarded as her inferior.

Margaret, seeing Fanny's economy with the truth, undertook to explain her version of the events that led up to the injury, and both her sisters' eyes opened wide with dismay as they turned to look at Fanny in askance. This Fanny completely ignored, continuing her conversation with Miss Parker, oblivious to Elinor and Marianne's disapproval of the assignation with Captain Dunning. Marianne frowned at Elinor in warning, surprised to see her unusually agitated.

"What beautiful flowers, Margaret!" she exclaimed, changing the subject and crossing the room to examine them more closely. "Ah, I see they are from Captain Dunning." She turned to Margaret with a meaningful look. At the mention of his name, Fanny's ears pricked up, and she decided it was the right time to put an end to all speculations regarding the captain, for reasons of her own.

"Yes, the captain called this morning to make his apologies and take his leave for Portsmouth, admitting to me he is quite bored with the London season," Fanny lied. "In fact, we are also leaving London for Norland somewhat earlier than expected, in view of Miss Margaret's indisposition. It is only two weeks in advance of what we intended, and we shall give a Christmas party there," said Fanny, interrupting Marianne's effusions and turning to the Miss Parkers with a smile.

"I do hope that you and your sister can be persuaded to join us for a few days, Miss Parker, that is if your mother can spare you. John told me this morning he has also invited Marguerite Dashwood and her son, so I am sure I could beg a space for the two of you in their carriage." Miss Parker looked as if the heavens had showered her with gold and was so occupied in expressing her delight, she completely missed the dismayed looks that passed between the three Dashwood sisters, but Catherine Parker saw it all. Margaret, who had not been consulted on this change of plan, was delighted to be going to Norland earlier than expected. It was almost worth a sprained ankle for such an unexpected treat, and even the company of Caroline Parker could not dampen her joy on hearing the news.

A day or two later, they set out for Norland, and Margaret was so excited to be revisiting her erstwhile home, she barely gave a second thought to the engagements she would be missing in London. Eagerly anticipating the rediscovery of all her old haunts and the rekindling of old relationships, she planned the first few days. Now able to hobble along without assistance, she had high hopes of a return to full mobility in a day or two. In fact, Charles Dashwood had confirmed as much when he visited the evening after her accident to check on her progress. Examining her solemnly with a practiced eye, he evinced surprise at the speedy healing.

"You are doing extremely well, Miss Margaret, considering the accident was only yesterday. Luckily, you have escaped the swelling I anticipated, but you have the advantage of youth on your side. We may have you dancing again by Christmas yet." He seemed very pleased with the idea, but Margaret presumed this was just professional pride, as he had already demonstrated his complete indifference to her dancing skills. She looked at him archly.

"Perhaps it was opportune that you were nearby, Mr Dashwood, and the treatment applied almost immediately." Margaret was not backward in giving credit when credit was due.

"Yes, I admit that would have helped," he acknowledged without false modesty, continuing to bandage her ankle with care. She tried again to engage him in conversation.

"I hear you and your mother are joining us at Norland, Mr Dashwood." This time, he smiled down at her, and she was struck again by his good looks.

"Yes, I shall be travelling down with my mother in a few days, and we have just heard that we are to escort the Miss Parkers to keep you company." Margaret sighed inwardly and couldn't bring herself to return his smile. *Do not put yourself out on my account*, she thought crossly but managed to reply unenthusiastically.

"I hardly know the Miss Parkers; they are Fanny's guests," she said coldly, but he changed the subject.

"Has the dashing captain visited you yet, to make his apology?" he asked, ignoring her previous statement. Margaret looked at him suspiciously, wondering why he was interested. "I understand from Fanny he called earlier this morning. He remained closeted with her, and I did not see him, so perhaps he was unsure how he would be received. He brought these, however." She indicated the impressive arrangement of flowers with an indifferent wave of her hand. He looked as though he was about to say something but changed his mind at the last moment and turned to look out of the window.

"Pray tell me, Miss Margaret. How would he have been received by the injured party? Do you forgive him?" Charles asked seriously, turning back to look at her, and she was puzzled by his strong expression of disapproval. She knew she had done wrong, but what was it to him?

"Of course, why shouldn't I? Mr Dashwood, I hope you don't blame the captain entirely for the accident. It is true, he was driving too fast, but your mother did appear very suddenly, and the horses were startled by her crimson attire." She felt it was a little unfair to blame the captain entirely, but he shrugged his shoulders.

"It is not for me to judge," he said indifferently. "Fortunately, all's well that ends well this time," he said with more feeling, throwing her another meaningful look, and she was irritated by his continued admonishment.

"Mr Dashwood, you may rest assured, I will not be driving with the captain again, even if he were to ask me, which I am now very confident he will not. I think I can also confess to you in confidence, as a family member, that I didn't really want to go in the first place but was encouraged to accept his invitation by Fanny. The captain also had his own reasons for inviting me, which do him no credit at all." Charles Dashwood received this information with a deep frown.

"What an extraordinary thing!" he exclaimed in surprise, but her explanation seemed to make him easier, and he took his leave with some semblance of cordiality, leaving Margaret to stare after him in puzzlement. What a strange young man he was, to be sure. She felt almost sorry for Caroline Parker. She certainly had her work cut out if she was going to succeed in getting him down the aisle. There was just no making him out.

Margaret expected Norland to be much altered by John and Fanny, but the house was not so much changed that she failed to recognise her childhood home. John must have had more sway with Fanny than she'd thought him capable of. Norland would always be a very fine estate, built in the last century and improved in the present, adding the convenience of modernity to the grandeur of style. Margaret's excitement mounted as the carriage swept up the driveway to the magnificent front entrance door, where all the servants awaited their arrival outside. Margaret was delighted to see Fanny hadn't chopped down the trees lining the drive, as she had once threatened. Again, John's sense must have prevailed. The old cook couldn't hide her delight in recognition of the grown-up Margaret, and the butler, usually so poker-faced, actually smiled. She was sad to see the rest of the servants were now unfamiliar to her, but five years was a long time. Nevertheless, she was overjoyed to be there, and only the fact she could not yet walk far prevented her from exploring the whole park at the earliest opportunity. She did, however, allow herself the luxury of a short excursion to all her nearest haunts, leaning heavily on Lily's arm. Together, they visited the kitchen garden, scented by herbs, even in winter. George, the head gardener and her dear old friend, was overjoyed to see her and immediately escorted her on a tour of the conservatories and potting sheds. There, her memories of Norland were strongest, and she saw herself as a child engrossed with the gardener whilst he taught her much of what he knew. Afterwards, she sat with Lily enjoying the weak winter sun in the shelter of the walled garden until Margaret was strong enough to go a little further. She bade farewell to George with the promise of another visit at her earliest opportunity and continued onwards with Lily until a dear and familiar sight stopped Margaret in her tracks.

"Oh, Lily, look, here is my old treehouse. I dared not hope Fanny would have kept such an eyesore to the avenue, yet here it is quite intact. I suppose young Harry must have played here. I cannot tell you how many hours I've spent up there, acting out childhood fantasies and dreaming of adventures yet to come." Margaret's face was alight with happiness, recalling her childhood in that special place, forgetting for a moment that it didn't belong to her any longer. Suddenly, she felt as cold as the winter landscape, and her involuntary shiver was not lost on Lily, who urged her inside directly.

"Well, miss, that's all very well, but you won't be getting up there today," she scolded, looking up at the treehouse, just visible through the barren branches with something akin to horror. "I should be getting you inside. It is almost dark, and there is quite a chill in the air. We can't have you recovering from a sprain and catching pneumonia. I would lose my place for sure."

"And we can't have that, Lily." Margaret laughed, allowing her maid to lead her inside, where they were greeted by John, who had been searching for them for some time, concerned that they were still outside at such a late hour. His face broke into a smile of relief.

"Ah, here you are, at last. I am sent to inform you that Fanny is tired from the journey and will be taking a tray in her bed chamber, and I have urgent business with my steward. I am sorry to leave you to your own devices on your first evening at Norland, Margaret."

"Please do not concern yourself, John. I will find plenty to amuse myself, and if Lily will tell the cook that I will also have a tray in my room, then we need not trouble the servants further. May I have your permission to use the library in the meantime? There are many old friends within that I should like to be reacquainted with." John was only too happy to comply with her request.

"Of course, my dear, you need not ask. In truth, I will be glad to see it used as the books lie in their own dust these days, too often undisturbed." He turned to leave them but called over his shoulder, "Oh, I almost forgot, we have guests tomorrow for dinner. Nothing formal, just a neighbouring family with whom we have become well acquainted over the years, but I think you will like them, and they will be company for you whilst we are away from London's amusements."

Margaret made straight for the library, glad to have John's blessing to use it whenever she wished. Another favourite haunt, so dear to her in its familiarity. With relief, she saw that Fanny's improvements had not been allowed to stray into that part of the house. Luckily, Fanny was not a great reader and disliked the smell of books, so the library had remained relatively undisturbed in the passing years. Even the oak table, under which she had been so fond of hiding, stood in exactly the same place. With great pleasure, she took down some of the aforementioned childhood favourites but soon found that the elapse of more than five years had elevated her tastes, and she scanned the shelves for something more suitable to her current interests. Her gaze alighted on *Culpepper's Herbal*, but on such a high shelf, she dare not risk climbing on the step ladder with a weak ankle. She was just deciding whether or not to ring the bell when a young footman entered with tea, obviously sent by John for her refreshment. How kind of him to think of her. Fortunately, the footman was glad to fetch the book down, so she spent a very happy time in the company of the great herbalist, glad of the opportunity to apply some of her growing knowledge of the craft. She lost track of the time and was surprised when Lily entered carrying her supper tray. Suddenly very hungry, she turned her attention to the meal, leaving the book on the library table, unable to return it herself to its rightful place, with every intention of continuing its study the following day. This, however, proved not to be possible as fate had other amusements in store for her.

The next morning brought unexpected arrangements, starting with a drive around the entire park, organised by John, especially for her entertainment. Then, in the afternoon, she spent a very interesting interlude in the garden with George until it was time to dress for dinner. That evening, Margaret descended the stairs cautiously, leaning on Lily's arm, wearing a new rose muslin gown. In Lily's eyes, she looked perfection itself as they made their entrance into the drawing room, where the other guests were already assembled. Lily's own rose water, made from the late damask roses in the park, its perfume rich and evocative of summer, followed her into the room. All eyes were turned on her as John bowed formally and made the necessary introductions to the strangers assembled within. "Sir Edwin and Lady Barrington, Mr Steven Barrington and Miss Elizabeth Barrington, may I present to you my youngest sister, Miss Margaret Dashwood?" Margaret curtseyed demurely, observing that Sir Edwin and Lady Barrington were very distinguished and a little older than John and Fanny. Steven Barrington, their son, appeared to be transfixed by her appearance, and Margaret could not help but be flattered at being so obviously admired. It was balm to her wounded vanity after the disapproval of Mr Dashwood and the ignominy of falling prey to a fortune hunter. The young Mr Barrington was a good-looking man of around twenty-five, with the high complexion of someone who spends much of his time outdoors. His sister, Elizabeth, was about Margaret's own age, with a sweet face, and their ready smiles made Margaret like them instantly, pleased to have young people present. John had been right in his assertion that they would be good company for her, and she was already looking forward to making their better acquaintance. At dinner, she found herself seated between brother and sister and took the opportunity of conversing with them further. They were an attractive pair, and Margaret was curious to know more of them.

"My brother said you are neighbours. Do you live very near to Norland?" she enquired of Miss Elizabeth.

"Barrington House is less than a mile away, but the parklands adjoin Norland's, so we really are close neighbours, which means, I'm afraid, there will be no avoiding each other," Elizabeth replied archly, and Margaret laughed.

"Now you come to mention it, I do recall a house, but it was not Barrington House, then."

"No, you are correct, Miss Margaret, my father bought it just after you left, five years ago and has carried out extensive alterations. I think you would hardly recognise it as the same place now, and it was my father who renamed it Barrington House. Perhaps it is presumptuous, but he has long been desiring his own country estate to invest the fortune he has accrued." Margaret was impressed that such an ambition had been achieved and said so.

"I would not presume to judge your father. I am sure he has every right to name what is his, especially as he has virtually rebuilt the house with his own money. I should be very curious to see it if you will be good enough to show me around one day."

"I should be delighted, at your earliest convenience, but I fear we may have to wait a little. I heard about your accident, and Barrington House will still be there when you are recovered. It is a rambling old place, and there is much to see," Elizabeth advised as Steven interrupted impatiently.

"Do you hunt, Miss Margaret?" he asked, without any prior attempt at small talk. Margaret was amused by his direct approach but shook her head ruefully.

"No, Mr Barrington. I rode as a child but have not had the opportunity lately. Sadly, we do not keep horses in Devon."

"Well, we must certainly rectify that. You have the look of an excellent horsewoman," said Steven Barrington admiringly. Margaret was not surprised by his passion for horses; having already observed his strong athletic figure, she thought he also looked every inch the horseman himself. His sister intervened at this point, admonishing her brother for his overly enthusiastic persuasion.

"Oh, Steven, we are in winter. Now is not the time for sport. I'm sure Miss Margaret has better things to do with her time. Besides, do you not remember that Miss Margaret is injured?" chided his sister. Although Elizabeth Barrington was younger and slighter in build than her brother, she was clearly not afraid to stand up to him. Her brother refused to be deterred, however, and continued to sway Margaret.

"What better exercise than riding in the great outdoors, whatever the season? Mr Dashwood will have a horse to suit a novice, I'll wager." Margaret was convinced by his enthusiasm.

"I confess I should very much like to ride again, Mr Barrington, but unfortunately, your sister is right, and I must now wait for a sprained ankle to heal." Margaret was doubtful if her ankle would be strong enough yet, but she found he was not to be out off.

"Oh, yes, I heard about that. No matter, which side is the injured ankle?"

"The right, sir."

"Nothing could be easier. You will mount the horse with your left, and I will be there to guide the horse and help you down. If you are worried about propriety, my sister will join us, of course, which is no hardship for her as she is also a keen rider. What say you, Miss Dashwood? I assure you the fresh air will be most beneficial and will promote the healing of your ankle better than anything." His confidence was infectious, and Margaret found herself already looking forward to it, despite her earlier misgivings. Miss Barrington added further weight to his arguments.

"You had better agree quickly, Miss Margaret, or you will have no peace until you do. Steven is most persistent." Miss Elizabeth laughed. "Horses are his only passion, and he is thoroughly bored with the company of a mere sister."

"But why are you not in town for the season?" Margaret voiced her surprise.

"My father and Steven have no patience with London, and although I should have liked to have gone, my mother is not strong enough to chaperone me to the multiplicity of social engagements. She was ill in the autumn and still suffers with her lungs. Perhaps next season," Elizabeth explained, a trifle ruefully.

Steven's attention was then claimed by Fanny, seated on his other side, clearly expecting him to fulfil his duty to her as hostess. After a few polite sentences, his attention soon returned to Margaret and the all-important subject.

"Miss Margaret, have I persuaded you to give it a try? Do say I have." His pleading look convinced her to accede.

"I confess I am willing to try again, Mr Barrington, and since you brook no refusal, I have only to ask John if he has a suitable mount. Besides, I have motive enough for agreeing as it will be the best way of viewing the park on a regular basis." Steven Barrington smiled his approval of her courage and spirit.

"Do not trouble yourself, Miss Margaret. Leave John to me," he assured her. "My sister and I will ride over and meet you at the stables tomorrow morning. It is confirmed." He shook her hand with a merry twinkle.

The riding lesson was a great success. Mr Barrington, as good as his word, consulted John on a suitable mount for Margaret, and after much deliberation and lengthy discussions on the merits of each of the mounts in the stable, they fixed on a docile little brown mare. Margaret adored Sally on first sight, and fortunately, the skills she learned in her childhood had remained with her. In no time at all, she was delighted to find herself walking confidently around the courtyard without Steven leading. In fact, Margaret was so enjoying being back on the saddle that she was in danger of taking things too quickly.

"I think I could try a short trot!" cried Margaret excitedly over her shoulder to Steven, her confidence growing by the minute.

"Not yet, Miss Margaret!" he cried in alarm, sounding so severe that she pulled Sally to a halt immediately, looking at him in alarm.

"That would not do as your ankle is not strong enough to rise in the stirrup," he apologised in a calmer tone. "Nevertheless, I can see you have complete control over Sally, so we could venture a gentle walk into the park, if that would be to your liking?" he conceded, secretly impressed by her bravado. Margaret sighed. Seeing the sense of his advice, it would not do to reverse the healing that had already taken place.

"Yes, Mr Barrington, that would be quite delightful, and I could show you all my childhood haunts," she concurred happily.

"My brother is right, Miss Margaret; you are a natural horsewoman," admired Miss Elizabeth as they set off into the park, and Steven was quick to blow his own trumpet.

"I am always right when it comes to horses. You should know that by now, Elizabeth."

"You are all modesty, sir." Margaret laughed, overjoyed to be out in the fresh air. The park was not at its best in the winter season, but its stark beauty still struck Margaret with poignant nostalgia. Everywhere they turned, another memory emerged, and she fell into silent introspection until Steven interrupted her reverie in concern.

"Miss Margaret, I hope you are not feeling too fatigued with the exercise," he enquired solicitously, in contrast to his previous boasts, and Margaret was pleased to note that he had a softer side. It was true, Steven Barrington was very sure of himself and forthright, but Margaret was finding his blunt statements a refreshing change from the grave introspection of her cousin and the saturnine charm of Captain Dunning. Elizabeth, his sister, was the perfect foil for her brother, teasing him for his self-importance with such good-natured humour that no offence was ever taken. Margaret could see that genuine affection existed between them and was reminded of the easy relationship she enjoyed with her own dear sisters. They wandered happily in the park for some time, and Margaret was pleased to see its beauty undiminished. By the time they had to return for luncheon, they found they had so much enjoyed themselves that an engagement to meet the next day was enthusiastically made, especially as the weather was set to continue remarkably fine for the time of year.

Thus, three days elapsed before a wet day allowed Margaret to return to Thomas Culpepper, only to find the library and her chosen book already occupied by another. "Mr Dashwood!" she cried in surprise, changing colour. "I did not know you had arrived."

"Miss Margaret." He arose immediately, looking somewhat abashed and made an awkward bow. "Just this moment, in fact. There was something I needed to look up urgently but have become distracted by this intriguing book left out on the table." He pointed to the herbal almanac by way of an explanation. To her great discomfort, Margaret blushed deeper under his scrutiny before replying with some embarrassment.

"I am the one who has been studying Thomas Culpepper, Mr Dashwood, having developed a keen interest in herbs. I've been growing them myself in Devon for some years. I could not return the book to its rightful place as I am still unable to climb." Surprise registered on his face before he remembered his manners and pulled out the chair for her to sit down and continue with her studies.

"Of course not, and how is the ankle progressing?" he asked solicitously, then seeing her hesitation, he endeavoured to persuade her to be seated. "I am so sorry; please don't let me interrupt your studies. I should, in any case, look for the volume I came in search of." She sat down in some confusion, which she tried to cover by polite enquiries.

"Thank you, sir; my ankle is healing well, and I am now able to walk without aid. Was your journey tolerable? How is your mother and the Miss Parkers?" She found she was gushing to hide her confusion. He answered her string of questions with some amusement.

"Firstly, I am delighted to hear the ankle is progressing well, Miss Margaret. I am happy to hear that my prediction of you dancing again soon was probably correct. Secondly, we made very good time on our journey here, thank you. Thirdly, the ladies are well but a little tired so have taken the opportunity to rest before dinner." He regarded her with a smile, and she eyed him uncertainly, not sure if he was laughing at her and unsure how to return to her book in his presence. He saw her hesitation.

"Please, do not let me disturb you. I shall be as quiet as a mouse," he assured her, and Margaret took up her book in an effort to continue reading but found herself unable to concentrate properly, still very conscious of his presence in the library. It was impossible to ignore his movements around the room and wonder what it was he was seeking. At last, it appeared he had found the volume in question and sat down at the other end of the table to peruse a hefty tome. An uneasy silence ensued as they both tried to convince the other they were engrossed until the sky grew dark. The timely arrival of candles put an end to such unsatisfactory studies, reminding them it was time to dress for dinner.

There were nine at dinner that evening as John had invited the younger Barringtons to make the acquaintance of his other guests. Steven Barrington was seated between Margaret and Miss Parker, but to the latter's dismay, John had insisted that Fanny place Charles Dashwood on the other side of Margaret so Caroline Parker could not engage him in conversation without bypassing two guests. As it was out of the question for a lady to behave so, she was forced to talk to Steven Barrington, and Margaret was amused to see Miss Parker was quite out of humour with this unsatisfactory arrangement. Resplendent in bronze satin, she had clearly made an effort with her toilette and was looking remarkably pretty, convincing Margaret still further that it had been a fair assumption that Charles Dashwood was her quarry. Miss Parker's mood was not improved when Steven Barrington, having ascertained her complete ignorance of equestrian skills and any intention of improving them, turned all his attention to Margaret, where he was certain to bring the conversation around to horses.

"Your progress on Sally has been impressive, Miss Margaret, for one who has not ridden since childhood," he enthused. "If the ankle progresses equally well, we will have you trotting before the week is up." This assertion was made loud enough for most of the table to hear and certainly to alert Charles Dashwood, who looked at him in askance.

"I think you had better let me be the judge of that," he interjected with authority, eyeing Steven Barrington so sternly that Margaret felt obliged to intervene in his defence.

"As the owner of the offending joint, I can report it has greatly improved, and I am now walking completely unaided, as I assured you earlier, Mr Dashwood." Nevertheless, Charles Dashwood continued to look stern.

"I was delighted to hear that, Miss Margaret, but walking is one thing and riding is quite another. I am sure you would not wish to risk a relapse," he cautioned, and seeing he was in deadly earnest, she decided not to tease him, no matter how tempting a prospect that was, merely nodding docilely in agreement.

"Then, perhaps you would be good enough to advise me," she conceded meekly, lowering her eyes so he couldn't see the glint of amusement.

"Yes, indeed, Dashwood, we bow to your greater judgement and would not want her taking any undue risks," agreed Steven Barrington, smiling at Margaret conspiratorially, picking up on her amusement. Charles Dashwood ignored him, severely annoyed at his presumption and proprietary manner towards his cousin. He turned to Margaret somewhat huffily.

"I will examine you tomorrow morning, with your permission," he agreed, turning his back on her dismissively to talk to Miss Elizabeth on his other side. Margaret caught sight of Miss Parker's face, quietly seething into her soup and almost felt sorry for her frustration. Her feelings of pity were short-lived, however, because Miss Parker took matters into her own hands, clearly unable to suffer Margaret Dashwood being the centre of attention any longer. She gave a little cry, half stood, then slid elegantly to the floor in a dead faint. Margaret was full of admiration for this perfect piece of play acting as she succeeded in gaining everyone's attention to herself immediately. Most particularly, that of Charles Dashwood, who was by her side in seconds. He picked her up and carried her through to the drawing room, laying her on the couch, waving everyone away as she opened her eyes, closing them again quickly when she saw her success. He demanded smelling salts, which quickly brought her around, and he was relieved to find her pulse normal. Perversely, he still ordered everyone out of the room. The interchange with Steven Barrington had annoyed him, and he wished to exert his authority as a physician. He had not missed the look of amusement exchanged between Mr Barrington and Margaret at his expense and was incensed by their intimacy.

"I am sure it is just the long journey, coupled with the strangeness of new surroundings, proving too much for a delicate constitution. Please return to the table, and I will call if I need any assistance." Charles' professional manner appeared to reassure everyone, and they returned to their seats somewhat easier, but the patient and her physician did not follow their example. To everyone's silent curiosity, they remained closeted alone together for the rest of the evening.

"Mr Dashwood is taking prodigious care of his patient," observed Fanny with a wry smile as the ladies withdrew, unashamedly voicing what everyone was thinking. Margaret couldn't help but agree with her. Clearly, Miss Parker had recovered, so the occasion did not demand the dedicated attention of a physician. There must be another reason, but Margaret could only think of one plausible cause: a desire to be alone together. The gentlemen remained long over their port that evening, showing no desire to rejoin the ladies, and thus the ladies were unusually subdued. Most found an excuse to retire early, Margaret included, wishing to be alone with her thoughts. Surprisingly, she was quite put out by the evening's events, annoyed that Caroline Parker had been allowed to get her way.

"Miss Parker is about as delicate as I am," muttered Margaret to herself as she made her way upstairs.

Nevertheless, Margaret had to hand it to her, she had succeeded in keeping Charles Dashwood's undivided attention to herself for the entire evening. Such consideration on his part could only mean that they were forming an attachment. Try as she might, Margaret couldn't think of another explanation for them to be closeted together for such a long time. Even if there was no such attachment, their actions had given rise to much speculation. It was as if they had compromised themselves on purpose.

Chapter 9
A Discovery

Fortunately, for the continuation of the riding lessons, but much to the chagrin of Charles Dashwood, Margaret's ankle was pronounced almost healed the following morning. When Margaret enquired politely after Miss Parker's health, she detected he was somewhat disconcerted before replying.

"Quite recovered, I believe, although she gave us quite a scare." Margaret noted he did not meet her eye. In truth, he was feeling a little ashamed of himself after the events of the previous evening and could not think what had got into him. He suspected, looking back, his anger had played right into Miss Parker's hands because she had exhibited no real signs of ill health when he examined her. On the contrary, she was the very picture of healthy womanhood. On several occasions, he'd endeavoured to persuade her to return to the other guests, but she had become dizzy again, and he felt obliged to remain by her side. Miraculously, this morning, Miss Parker was quite restored to excellent health, which Fanny lost no time in pointing out to the assembled party with a wry smile in his direction. At this, his mother sent him such a disapproving look, it made him feel ten years old again. In the circumstances, he had no choice but to agree that Margaret could take her riding to a further level, despite his strong inclination to hamper Steven Barrington's plans for a more advanced lesson. Margaret thanked him prettily; having gained her objective, she saw no reason to be churlish.

As a result of her clean bill of health, she decided to take a stroll around the park unaccompanied. Her solitary ramble was bliss after the relative confinement, and she found herself drawn to the treehouse as if by unknown forces, until she stood beneath its branches, looking up in longing. Now that her ankle felt strong enough to tackle the climb, there was no reason not to attempt it, and she'd just made it safely inside when the sound of voices approaching caused her to look out of the spy hole. Seeing Marguerite Dashwood accompanied by her son, she decided to remain hidden from view, unwilling to bear the brunt of the doctor's icy disapproval of the risky climb she had just undertaken. She watched from her elevated position as they proceeded to pass beneath the treehouse to a wooden seat located on one side of the tree that concealed Margaret. Then, to her utmost dismay, Margaret found herself forced into the role of an accidental eavesdropper. From her lofty spy hole, Margaret could just see Marguerite's face, but Charles had his back to her, hiding his expressions. She saw Marguerite turn to her son with a frown clouding her lovely face.

"Charles, you know that I am not usually given to interfering, but I feel it is high time I asked you a very serious question. What are your intentions exactly to Miss Parker?" His mother came straight to the point.

"My intentions, Mama?" Charles sounded horrified, and Margaret wished she could see his face. Marguerite sighed with impatience at his attempt to dissemble, aware that everyone present had noticed his behaviour to the lady yesterday evening, and it had given rise to suspicions in all of the guests. Marguerite had heard the whispered speculation, quickly hushed at her entrance.

"Yes, Charles," she said wearily. "Please don't pretend to misunderstand me, even you must see that Miss Parker's intentions to you are clear enough. Don't feign that you haven't noticed, encouraged her even. Whatever induced you to remain alone with her for the remainder of yesterday evening?" His mother was clearly very concerned and continued to state her case firmly. "It was noticed, Charles, and remarked upon by Fanny, who pointed it out to the rest of the party, as if she needed to. It was really quite scandalous of you, and I own, I was quite shocked that you could be so lacking in propriety." Charles hesitated before replying to his mother in placatory tones.

"Mama, Miss Parker is a sweet, pretty girl, but I haven't thought of her in any serious way. She does not have the qualities I would look for in a wife. Besides, Mama, I am a doctor, and she was weak and in need of my help last night." Margaret could hear that his glib reassurances did not convince his mother, who continued her relentless interrogation.

"Really, Charles, Miss Parker is no more weak than I am, but now you come to mention it, I would be interested to hear the qualities you do most prize for your future wife." Margaret saw her quizzical look.

"Sense for one," he answered decidedly and without hesitation.

"Sense? I see. Well, Charles, you may rest assured, it is also a quality that a sensible girl will look for in a husband. Therefore, if it is your wish to attract a woman of sense, you need to show some sense yourself. Like attracts like." Margaret heard the sarcasm in her tone. "Be careful what you are about, Charles," she warned. "Girls have been known to order their wedding clothes for less encouragement than you have given Miss Parker. She may not have the kind of sense you are talking about, but she is no fool, and her artful guile may have already led you to go too far." Margaret saw Charles shake his head vehemently.

"I think you exaggerate, Mama, but I promise to take more care in future," he soothed her, but to Margaret, he sounded rather perturbed by his mother's warning. Margaret knew her to be a sensible woman, one who would never interfere without good reason. She herself had also considered there may be an attachment between Charles Dashwood and Miss Parker, and his explanation also seemed inadequate to her. If it was true that he felt nothing for her, Margaret hoped he would heed his mother and cease his attentions to Miss Parker, which she felt sure were being misinterpreted by the lady.

Mother and son continued to sit together in silence for a minute or two, then Marguerite turned to her son with a serious expression before introducing a different subject.

"Charles, I must ask you if you have given any thought to the other matter that John discussed with you when you first learned of the Norland inheritance." Her expression was candid, and he hesitated before replying wearily.

"As you are well aware, Mama, I did not expect the Norland inheritance. I am a physician, first and foremost, and my practice is in London, so I cannot see how I can play the country gentleman. Although, now having seen Norland for myself, I grant you, it is a very fine estate. With regard to the matter to which you refer, I will not be dictated to by anyone, and I alone shall choose the woman I marry." Margaret could hear, even from her elevated position, he was becoming quite incensed.

"Of course, Charles, that is quite understandable, and no one could blame you," his mother agreed placatingly. "I wouldn't have expected anything else of you, but surely, now that you have seen more of the young lady in question, you may have had second thoughts." He remained silent, and she tried again.

"I see that a country life at Norland may not be quite to your taste at present, but please remember that John is not an old man. Thus, the likelihood of you having to claim your inheritance in the near future is slight. Add another few years and you may feel very differently. I ask you, Charles, to remember your ambition to set up an herbal apothecary. Would this not be the very place to begin such a venture? In the meantime, I would advise you to be amenable to your new family connections. As for Miss Margaret, I can tell you honestly that I think she is charming. You tell me that you prize sense above all other qualities, and she has that in abundance. Sense in every form, especially that of humour as well as beauty, makes the best of combinations in a wife. If I'm not much mistaken, men may talk of other qualities but most require a little beauty unless the lady is very rich. You could do a great deal worse. It's true she has no money, but I do not think that need be of concern to you, especially now." It was all Margaret could do to stay silent, stifling her gasp of shock with her fist. He answered his mother drily.

"Here endeth the lecture, I hope, Mama. Anyway, I thought Captain Dunning had stolen a march on me in that respect, and if not, there is another waiting in the wings; Steven Barrington is hovering hopefully." Margaret was surprised to hear the bitterness in his tone.

"Charles, a lovely girl like Margaret Dashwood will always have young men hovering about her. You should not be afraid of competition. Faint heart never won fair maid. As for Captain Dunning, she was only flattered to be singled out by such a man. What young woman would not be? But it is in my power to assure you that his attentions to Miss Margaret are entirely over. He was under the mistaken impression that John intended to make her his heir and had no knowledge of your prior claim."

"Your network of spies never fails to amaze me, Mama. Pray tell me, how did you come by that information?" Charles drawled ironically.

"Do not be facetious, Charles," she chided, unwilling to tell him she'd heard it from Margaret herself. "The captain has paid me a couple of visits since the accident in the park." She lowered her eyes modestly, but his laugh was mocking.

"So the gallant captain is a fortune hunter, is he? I cannot say that surprises me. Although I am surprised at you, Mama. I'd credited you with better taste." Marguerite shook her head unashamedly, refusing to be admonished by her son.

"Be sensible, Charles. His fortune is all lost on the gaming tables, so what else is he to do as the second son? The captain and I have become friends, but you can rest assured we are very discreet, and neither of us has any intentions beyond that. Even a woman of my advanced age needs a little dalliance now and again, and we are both old enough to know better than to take it seriously.

Besides, he has been quite honest with me, in that he needs a rich patroness, and I know I am not his only amor. He has hinted at the interest of another lady who is rich enough to keep him in the manner to which he has grown accustomed. We digress, however. I must insist on knowing your current opinion of Miss Margaret Dashwood, Charles. I hope you are too sensible to take against her merely because John Dashwood wants you to make her your wife." Margaret strained to hear his answer with bated breath, but she was destined to be disappointed. It seemed an age before he stood up, offering his mother his hand.

"It is becoming a little cold. Shall we walk again, Mama?" Without waiting for a reply, he helped her up, and they walked away, thus making his answer inaudible, to Margaret's complete chagrin. She remained in the treehouse for a long time, pondering all she had learned, absolutely mortified at John's suggestion for her future. She knew he was trying to make amends, but that was surely carrying matters too far. Of course, she now saw why Charles Dashwood had been so cold to her from the start, and who could blame him when John was trying to force an arranged match between them? Margaret squirmed at the thought. How could she ever look him in the face again? It was too much to be borne. Several more minutes ticked by before Margaret could think clearly, but she had to admit she would have dearly loved to have heard his answer to his mother's last question.

When she finally descended from the treehouse, Margaret made her way to the library, passing the open door of Fanny's private sitting room on the way. Fanny was taking tea with the Miss Parkers, and her strident voice could clearly be heard.

"My dear Caroline, you can quite depend upon it; he will make you an offer before your visit to Norland is up. Why, he is absolutely besotted. We all saw that he refused to leave your side last night. He made his devotion to you quite clear, and everyone is speculating about it this morning." Fanny sounded so convinced that Miss Parker was about to become betrothed to Charles Dashwood that Margaret would almost have believed it herself had she not just heard his conversation with his mother. Miss Parker's simpering tone followed Fanny's clamorous statements.

"Oh, Mrs Dashwood, do you really think so? I have no fortune to speak of, you know," she admitted.

"Nonsense, child, Charles Dashwood does not need to marry for money, and with your pretty face, you will never lack for suitors. Besides, I have witnessed his attentions to you from the beginning, and I am never wrong in these matters." Fanny was adamant and not to be gainsaid.

"I would like it of all things but mostly because we shall then be family, Mrs Dashwood," said Caroline in an obsequious tone, guaranteed to oil the way into the heart of her benefactress, and Fanny did not disappoint.

"I own, it will be delightful for me to have your company here, my dear. Mr and Mrs Charles Dashwood will have to be often at Norland for him to learn the running of the estate, so you will be my instant companion." Fanny was clearly overjoyed by the picture she painted.

"What a cheering prospect, Mrs Dashwood, to be always near at hand," Caroline flattered obligingly.

"My dear Caroline, that picture will become reality very soon; you mark my words." Fanny's reassurance was then interrupted by the incredulous voice of Miss Catherine Parker, who dared to interject at this point, clearly unable to believe her ears.

"Did I hear you correctly that Caroline is to be married to Mr Charles?" she queried in a loud squeak that spoke her disbelief. Caroline rounded on her aggressively.

"Hush, Catherine, someone will hear you. What do you know of such things?" she admonished her sister dismissively. Too late, Margaret realised she had been eavesdropping for the second time that day and hurried away in shame. She couldn't help thinking that Mrs Marguerite Dashwood's instincts had been entirely correct and that her son was in much deeper than he thought. Despite his previous denials to his mother, he must be more serious about the lady than he admitted. If not, Margaret hoped he could stand up to the determination of Fanny and Miss Parker in unison against him. She had only been a child at the time, but if her mother and sisters were to be believed, Fanny had single-handedly cheated them out of the Norland inheritance; therefore, achieving a match between Miss Parker and Mr Dashwood would be a small fry for her.

Marguerite Dashwood remained alone in the park after her son took his leave of her, feeling relieved she'd had the courage to mention her concerns to him. She knew Charles' independence of spirit, and it was not often she interfered, but her worry about Caroline Parker had been so great, she'd had no choice. This time, he'd taken the hint rather well for once, and Marguerite was reassured. She shook her head sadly, knowing it was her son's independence of spirit that had led to John's undoing. His pointed suggestion that her son marry Margaret had not been well received, to say the least. It was most unfortunate because if John hadn't prematurely stepped in, it was highly probable that Margaret and Charles would have worked it out for themselves. They were clearly made for each other, and her instincts told her Charles was, belatedly, coming to realise this. His answer to her pointed question had lacked clarity, but she knew enough of Charles' character that, had he been dead set against Miss Margaret, he would have no hesitation in saying so.

Nevertheless, he had bitterly resented John's interference, so he ignored Margaret to the point of rudeness and dangerously encouraged Caroline Parker, all in a fit of pique. Marguerite had witnessed it all in increasing distress. Stubborn and hot-tempered, Charles was now unable to admit he was in the wrong, thus complicating his affairs beyond belief.

Marguerite had met a lot of 'Caroline Parkers' during the course of her life and knew that Charles was in great danger of being compromised. She hoped it was not too late for him to extricate himself from her ambitious clutches. Even more worrying was that the girl seemed to have Fanny Dashwood's backing, and Marguerite saw that Fanny was a lady used to getting her own way. What Marguerite couldn't understand was why Fanny was supporting Caroline Parker in this matter. The girl had neither connections nor money, and both of these assets seemed to be profoundly important to Fanny Dashwood. It just didn't make any sense.

In his mother's opinion, Charles and Margaret were a perfect match, and she agreed with John that their marriage would be an equitable way of making amends for the entail of the Norland Estate. She had been struck by Margaret from the moment of their first meeting, finding her completely unspoiled and utterly charming. It was a relief that she was recovering so well after her accident as Marguerite considered herself to be partly to blame. In her excuse, she rode in the park every day and rarely encountered anyone at that time on Sunday morning; nevertheless, she was resolved to take greater care in the future. A visit from Captain Dunning on the morning after the accident had taken her completely by surprise. Apparently, he was fresh from Grosvenor Street, where he had delivered flowers to the invalid, and on the spur of the moment, he'd decided to make sure she was not suffering from shock. Marguerite hid a smile, well aware that Harley Street was hardly on his way home, and clearly, she was not the type to suffer from shock. She was not fooled for a second, knowing exactly why the captain had called on her, but she was not averse to a discreet flirtation with a handsome man, some years her junior. There was no harm in it, provided it hurt no one. After all, the captain was not married, and neither was she.

Chapter 10
An Unexpected Departure

After a sleepless night, Margaret saw the futility of speculating on the possibility of an attachment between Charles Dashwood and Caroline Parker. Time would tell, and she couldn't influence matters, hardly being able to take up the subject with him herself. It was fortunate that her sisters arrived at Norland that day to distract her attention with all their news. A larger party was greatly desired, and Margaret was very thankful that her sisters' lively conversation concealed her introspective silence at dinner. She was at leisure to listen and observe undistracted. That evening, Charles Dashwood was seated at the other end of the table, between Catherine Parker and Marianne, and Caroline Parker was seated next to Steven Barrington. Margaret heard her trying, without much success, to engage him in conversation. She observed Charles discreetly from a distance as he turned to Miss Catherine in a kindly effort to draw her out. Unbelievably, considering how shy she was, it appeared that he succeeded because Margaret saw her answer him in an unusually animated manner. Whatever she had to say went on for several minutes, and the more she spoke, the graver Charles became. So much so, he said nothing further during the entire dinner. Margaret speculated curiously about the subject of their conversation later whilst the ladies waited for the gentlemen to join them in the drawing room. When the door opened to admit the gentlemen, she saw that Charles immediately sought out his mother, drawing her aside for a few words. With growing dismay, Margaret noticed that her countenance changed colour at what he had to impart. An earnest conversation took place between them, and shortly afterwards, he excused himself to Fanny and left the room, much to the consternation of Caroline Parker, who watched his departure with a deepening frown. Extremely curious but completely puzzled, Margaret only knew something serious had happened, that much was clear, and Caroline Parker knew nothing about it.

For the satisfaction of Margaret's curiosity, it was fortunate she found herself alone with Marguerite at breakfast, as none of the others had yet come down. She was unusually quiet and thoughtful, so Margaret ventured to begin the conversation and couldn't resist questioning her about her son's hurried departure.

"I hope your son hasn't had bad news, Mrs Dashwood?" she enquired tactfully, arousing Marguerite from her reverie, who shook her head in denial, perhaps a little too quickly.

"No, Miss Margaret, not at all. Thank you for your concern. It's just the usual circumstances. He has been called away by a patient." Margaret thought her answer was a little too glib.

"I hope it's nothing serious, Mrs Dashwood," Margaret further probed in concern, giving her the benefit of the doubt.

"No, not serious, although the patient in question often believes it to be requiring Charles' attendance, as these matters often do. His richer patients insist on seeing him personally. The consequences of being a lone practitioner and having the reputation of the most skilled obstetrician in London, I'm afraid." She sighed in resignation.

"Will he return today?" Margaret persisted, finding she was suddenly quite desperate to know.

"He was not sure how long it would take, perhaps a few days." She smiled ruefully.

"I'm sorry. You will miss him," Margaret sympathised, hiding her disappointment as Marguerite laughed.

"Do not feel sorry for me. I am used to other ladies taking priority over my son. His patients always come first, as indeed they should," she explained stoically, her pride in her son's professionalism entirely apparent to Margaret.

"He seems a most conscientious young man," Margaret acknowledged, sure there was more to his departure than his mother had revealed. Something had occurred to upset him yesterday evening, and Catherine Parker had something to do with it. Knowing her sisters had an engagement with old neighbours, Margaret didn't like to think of Marguerite alone with Fanny and the Miss Parkers, an idea suddenly occurred to her.

"Do you have any engagements this morning, Mrs Dashwood, because I am to ride with the Barringtons, if you would care to join us? I know you to be an accomplished horsewoman."

Marguerite's lovely face brightened at the prospect.

"How thoughtful of you, Miss Margaret. I confess I should have great pleasure in accepting your offer if a suitable mount can be found in the stables here." Margaret was quick to reassure her on that point.

"John has large stables, so I'm very sure that can be accomplished. I will go and find out what can be done whilst you make yourself ready, Mrs Dashwood. Leave it to me."

"Please call me Marguerite," she called after her. "There are so many Mrs Dashwoods."

The Barringtons were already eagerly waiting for her at the stables when Marguerite and Margaret joined them. She noted with amusement that Steven Barrington was rendered speechless by the sight of Marguerite Dashwood, decked out in the crimson riding habit she'd been wearing in the park, a high-crowned, plumed hat completing the ensemble. His admiration knew no bounds, as she mounted the liveliest stallion in the stables and proceeded to walk him calmly around the forecourt. Reluctantly, he withdrew his gaze to help Margaret into the saddle, and they walked their horses out into the park together. Margaret turned to Marguerite with enthusiasm.

"I have only been riding a few days, somewhat hampered by the sprain, but today I have been given permission by your son to trot," she gleefully explained as Elizabeth Barrington showed her how to rise in the side saddle, and Marguerite noted she copied her example with ease.

"Well done, Miss Margaret," she congratulated. "Indeed, it was a nasty fall, but you have recovered very well. The great advantage of youth." She smiled ruefully, pleased to see Margaret was a natural horseman and quite at home in the saddle. Steven and Marguerite soon broke into a gallop, unable to contain themselves any longer, whilst Margaret and Elizabeth followed behind at a more sedate pace. It soon became clear that Elizabeth was also smitten by their new companion.

"Mrs Dashwood is the most dashing creature I ever beheld. I thought her beautiful last night at dinner, but today I see she has the vigour of a much younger woman," observed Miss Elizabeth in stunned admiration as she stared after their departing backs. Margaret nodded in absolute agreement with her friend.

"Yes, it's hard to believe that she is the mother to Charles Dashwood, but the resemblance between them is unmistakeable; you must have noticed it, Miss Elizabeth."

"Yet, she doesn't look more than mid-thirties, if that much and so elegant. There is something about the French, don't you think? A certain *Je ne sais quoi*." She laughed at her little joke.

"Mr Charles Dashwood is indeed the very image of her and a very handsome young man but a rather more serious conversationist, at least with me. It appears he only has eyes for the Miss Parkers. Why only last night, Miss Catherine Parker seemed to engross him more than I could, although not for the want of trying, I might add." Elizabeth looked archly at Margaret, but she looked away, unable to join in the humour, before replying indifferently.

"I dare say he is handsome, but I think you will be disappointed when you know him better. His manners are too serious for flirtation of any sort." Elizabeth, however, was not to be put off and persisted in her enquiries, much to Margaret's discomfort.

"The future heir to Norland must be worthy of a little of my attention, surely. As I am not to go to London, I must make the most of every opportunity that comes my way." She laughed teasingly, but Margaret was spared from answering by the return of the other riders, who joined them at a pace. Margaret saw Steven Barrington was looking quite put out and wondered what had occurred to upset him.

"My apologies, ladies. Sadly, I have just remembered a prior engagement with my father and must return to the house, although I'd much rather stay." He glanced warmly at Marguerite and Margaret. "Will you come with me, Elizabeth, or shall I return for you later? Should I send for the groom to accompany you two ladies back to Norland?" he enquired solicitously, but his sister intervened.

"Oh, Steven, your head is so full of horses, you forget everything else," she chided. "I will come with you now and pour oil on the troubled waters between you and Papa. You know how he hates to be kept waiting. It will save you the trouble of returning for me. I am sure Margaret and Mrs Dashwood are not in need of a groom's protection and are quite capable of finding their way home safely." She grinned at the other ladies, and Margaret laughed.

"Of course we can, Mr Barrington. Do not disturb yourself on our account, and it is nearly time for luncheon, in any case. Rest assured, Mr Barrington, we will be quite safe in the park and be each other's protection on the way home." She was secretly pleased at the prospect of another tête-à-tête with Marguerite.

Margaret and Marguerite made their way slowly back to Norland in easy companionship. "Do you stay long with John and Fanny?" Marguerite enquired curiously.

"Yes, I return to London with them after Christmas, and I will be their guest for the rest of the season," Margaret replied, a trifle sadly, Marguerite thought.

"Forgive me, Miss Margaret, may I speak plainly?" Marguerite turned to look at her so earnestly that Margaret was surprised.

"Of course, Marguerite, I wouldn't have it any other way." Margaret smiled encouragingly at her, wondering what was coming next.

"That prospect does not seem to make you very happy. Why not stay with Mrs Brandon?"

"I would prefer that, of course, but it's not straightforward. When John first inherited Norland, he promised our father on his deathbed that he would look after my mother and her daughters, but he was later persuaded otherwise. I think you can guess by whom." Marguerite nodded her assent, having already made a fair assessment of the lady's character.

"It was my growing knowledge of Fanny Dashwood's character that caused me to ask the question," she admitted, and Margaret nodded in understanding, continuing to explain her predicament.

"When young Harry Dashwood died, I really think John wanted to make amends, and as my sisters are both well settled, his benefice fell to me. He offered to launch me into society at his expense, and my mother would not brook a refusal. I must now find a suitable husband, for what else is there for a penniless girl like me?" She turned to Marguerite with a hopeless shrug, and she nodded sympathetically.

"Yes, we ladies do not have a great deal of choice, either we find a husband or become an old maid, which is not an enviable prospect. But do not despair of making a love match as your sisters have done, Miss Margaret. I myself had little choice but to marry Charles' father at the young age of fifteen. My mother and I were in such straitened circumstances, it was the only option, but it turned out for the best in the end. He was a kind man, and I grew to care for him, although he was rather older than I. In fact, much the same age gap that exists between the colonel and Mrs Brandon, and they are happy, are they not?"

"Yes, indeed they are, and that is a very good example of a happy ending to a sad beginning. Marianne was cruelly disappointed by her first love," Margaret explained, knowing she could trust in Marguerite's discretion, and Marguerite was quick to reassure her.

"It will be the same for you in the end, I am sure of it, but hopefully without the sad beginning." Margaret smiled ruefully at her.

"Although I haven't made a very good start, first the prey of a fortune hunter and then injuring myself so I cannot go out in society at all." Margaret sighed, and Marguerite laughed.

"If you are referring to Captain Dunning, he is a devil, though a handsome one, I grant you. Do not despair, however; you will be surprised to learn that the dramatic style of your physical injury has not done you any disservice amongst society. No, indeed, I have it on good authority that the ton is quite piqued by curiosity. No doubt, the rumour was first spread around by someone without good intent, but the effect has been quite the opposite from what the perpetrator intended. London is very curious to meet with Miss Margaret Dashwood again." Margaret stared at her in such disbelief that Marguerite's laugh rang out.

"It is true. You will see when you return," Marguerite assured her, then her face fell as she looked into the distance.

"I think we should proceed more quickly to the stables. See, there are the Miss Parkers, just leaving the house, and they are headed in this direction." Margaret looked to where Marguerite was pointing and saw that she was right. The Miss Parkers were, for once, in animated discussion, or rather, Miss Caroline seemed to be berating her younger sister relentlessly. Margaret also felt a very strong aversion to meeting them, enjoying having Marguerite to herself.

"I do not think they have noticed us, so if we proceed to the stables in haste, we may still avoid them," agreed Margaret, unwilling to spoil a pleasant morning by an encounter with Caroline Parker.

"Forgive me, Margaret. I find myself about to be impertinent again. Why does Mrs Fanny Dashwood prefer the company of Miss Caroline Parker to John's own sisters, who are vastly superior beings?" Margaret sighed as she thought back over the many disagreements between her family and John's wife. How could she begin to explain such long-standing animosity?

"I'm afraid it's a very long story, Marguerite. Perhaps I can be persuaded to tell it one day." With that, Marguerite had to be content.

Margaret was greatly reassured by her conversation with Marguerite Dashwood, cheered by the older woman's words of sense. There was every reason to hope that Marguerite's optimism was justified; after all, she was a woman of the world and had much experience in these matters. It was true that the season had hardly begun, but how surprising to learn that she, Margaret Dashwood, was the subject of society gossip. Of course, Captain Dunning was the kind of man who would always attract gossip. It did not take long before her suspicions fell on Miss Caroline Parker as the initial source of the rumour. It had been clear from the outset there was no love lost between them, and Margaret was now aware that Charles Dashwood was the reason. Instinctively, Caroline viewed her as a rival, although Margaret did not understand why she should think so. In dismay, she remembered seeing the Parker sisters that morning, and she wondered why Caroline had been so angry with her sister. Miss Catherine had appeared so very upset; Margaret felt rather guilty that she and Marguerite had not gone to her rescue. Poor Catherine was little more than a child, and it was difficult to imagine how she could have so angered her elder sister. Caroline belittled the younger girl so frequently that it was no wonder she lacked confidence. It was obvious to Margaret that Marguerite Dashwood had no liking for Caroline Parker either; that much had been made clear by her warning to her son and her avoidance of the Parker sisters that morning. Her chamber door opened, and Margaret found herself interrupted by the very person who occupied her thoughts as Caroline Parker entered without knocking.

"Here you are, Miss Margaret. I have unearthed you at last," she exclaimed rudely. "Considering this is my chamber and I was not in hiding, it is hardly surprising that you have found me, but since you are here, what can I do for you, Miss Parker?" Margaret enquired coldly, and Caroline Parker forced a smile.

"I believe you saw my sister and I arguing this morning, and I wanted to explain. You and Mrs Dashwood seemed to run away from us earlier." Her tone was accusatory, but she wore a fixed smile.

"I confess, I did see it, but you do not need to explain yourself to me." Margaret ignored her accusation and discouraged her confidence, distrusting her motives, unsure she could believe any explanation Miss Parker could offer anyway. Caroline Parker was not deterred by Margaret's lack of enthusiasm, clearly determined that Margaret should hear what she had come to say.

"I did not want you to think me unkind to poor Catherine, but she can try one's patience so with her naive ways. She views the world in black and white and does not think before she opens her mouth. Unfortunately, this thoughtlessness can sometimes cause a great deal of trouble." Margaret was exceedingly puzzled by her statements and wondered where they were leading.

"Indeed, Miss Parker. Go on." But Caroline did not elaborate further.

"I knew you would understand, Miss Margaret." With that, she left the room before Margaret could question her further. Obviously, Miss Catherine has said something she shouldn't have, but why Caroline felt the need to come and explain this to her in person remained a mystery to Margaret. She puzzled over this unexpected visit for some time. It was not like Miss Caroline Parker to show her any attention, let alone seek her out. Finally, Margaret came to the conclusion that Caroline had meant it as a warning for her not to take anything Catherine Parker said too seriously.

Later that afternoon, Margaret was occupied in the library when Miss Catherine Parker entered, looking flushed and harassed, and it was clear she had been crying.

"Miss Margaret, I wondered if I would find you here. I feel sure that I can trust you, so may I speak to you in confidence?" She was obviously quite upset by something, and Margaret bid her sit down, taking her hand in sympathy.

"Of course, Miss Catherine, you need not ask," Margaret assured her kindly, all the while wondering what on earth was coming next. Miss Catherine, chest heaving, got up and paced the room as if unsure how to continue, turning to Margaret in hesitation.

"I saw you this morning riding with Mrs Dashwood, and I know you saw us; that is, you would have seen Caroline arguing with me. My sister accused me of stupidity and breaking her confidence. She was very angry with me." Catherine hesitated again.

"Go on," encouraged Margaret.

"Caroline and Fanny believe that Charles Dashwood will soon make a proposal of marriage to Caroline. Are you of that opinion, Miss Margaret?" Catherine blurted out in a rush to Margaret's astonishment.

"I confess I know nothing of the matter, except that Mr Dashwood does seem partial to Miss Parker's company." Margaret felt bound to acknowledge it, but Miss Catherine shook her head vehemently.

"Well, I do not believe it, so last night I thought I'd sound him out," she confided to Margaret, who was becoming more curious by the second. She was also astounded that this shy little mouse had found the courage to tackle Charles Dashwood. Margaret knew, to her own cost, he was not the easiest of men to talk to.

"What did you discover, Miss Catherine?" By now, Margaret was all ears.

"To my severe disappointment, nothing at all. I asked him if he was about to make a proposal to Caroline, and he fell completely silent on the subject and neither confirmed nor denied their attachment, but I do not believe he loves her, Miss Margaret. They think I'm stupid and I don't understand, but I see the things they don't, so busy as they are with their scheming. I think Mr Charles Dashwood loves another, and Fanny and Caroline are seeking to entrap him. What should I do?" she entreated, and Margaret gave her advice decidedly. Miss Catherine was no match for her sister and Fanny, so she would do better to keep out of it, in her opinion.

"I advise you to do nothing, Miss Catherine. Charles Dashwood is a grown man and should be quite capable of looking after his own interests." Margaret was certain that no good would come of a confrontation. Miss Catherine Parker would not be able to stop the scheming of Fanny and her sister, so she might as well save her breath. Catherine, still dabbing her eyes with her handkerchief, looked at Margaret in relief.

"Thank you, Miss Margaret; you have removed a great weight from my shoulders, but please don't tell anyone. I should be in such trouble." Margaret was greatly relieved to see her advice had been of some comfort to the younger girl and sincerely hoped it had deterred her from an unpleasant confrontation.

"Please rest assured of my absolute discretion, Miss Catherine. I shall not give you away." Catherine Parker's visit left Margaret more concerned for Charles than ever. She did not understand his attentions to Miss Parker, bearing in mind his own words to his mother yesterday and was also puzzled by Miss Catherine's declaration of him loving another. If that was the case, why entangle himself with Miss Parker? Nothing made sense. She was beginning to share the concerns of Marguerite, that he may now be in too deep to extricate himself from Caroline Parker's clutches, supported as she was by Fanny. Fanny's reputation within the family was hard to ignore, and Margaret knew from her own experience that what Fanny wanted, Fanny usually received.

The much-anticipated day of the Christmas Ball had arrived, and all the resident guests enthusiastically volunteered to assist Fanny with the festive arrangements for the house. The ladies were set to work internally, while the gentlemen were commissioned to find the finest holly and Christmas foliage from the surrounding woods. The stately old house was a bustling hive of activity, much as it had been in the days when Margaret had lived there as a child. It was reported that the cook was in high dudgeon and her assistants trod in fear of objects being launched at any time. The other maids gave the kitchen a wide berth and busied themselves cleaning silverware and polishing glasses, whilst the housekeeper hovered around ticking off lists and supervising. Margaret was delighted to volunteer her services for the task of arranging flowers, with a willing assistant in Marguerite Dashwood. Marianne and Elinor were busy hanging the woodland offerings over pictures with the help of the footmen, a task that seemed to involve much laughter and merriment. Fanny and the Miss Parkers were together, as usual, occupied in supervising the placing of numerous Christmas candles in the dining room. Margaret was overjoyed to learn that her mother had arrived in the early hours from Devon and was resting after her long journey. She had not brought Kitty as the child had a slight fever, and it was deemed best to leave her in the care of the housekeeper. Elinor and Edward would be returning to Devon for Christmas in a couple of days, in any case. Mr and Mrs Robert Ferrars were expected at any time, and Margaret understood that the rest of the guests would be arriving that evening. So far, nothing had been said of Charles Dashwood's return, and Margaret intended to ask his mother whether he was expected to attend. In fact, it was with this in mind, she begged for Marguerite's assistance with the flowers. To Margaret's chagrin, she was not able to mention her conversation with Catherine Parker to Marguerite, feeling herself bound by her assurances of absolute discretion.

"You really do have a considerable talent for flower arranging, Miss Margaret," complimented Marguerite as they finished the first vase, a giant creation supplied from Norland's own greenhouses. The gardener was zealous in making sure they were abundant at all times of the year, and Margaret replied enthusiastically.

"If I do, it's because I love them so, especially those that grow in the wild. Although, at the moment, we must make do with the hothouse. Still, these are lovely and perfect for Christmas. The gardener has been employed here for many years and knows the estate well. He and I are great friends, and it was he who taught me about horticulture. Do you expect your son to return for the occasion?" Margaret slipped in innocuously, at last finding the courage to ask the question that had been hovering on her lips for the last hour. Marguerite smiled to herself at this little display of indifference, seeing through her at once.

"As a matter of fact, I am glad to say that I do expect him. He sent me word that he hopes to return this afternoon, but as I know to my cost, a physician is at the mercy of his patients, and babies are no respecters of the festive season. We must wait and see." Marguerite was noncommittal, and Margaret had no choice but to be content with that. She dare not ask more, much as she would have loved to, so she contented herself with an innocent observation.

"I expect you must wish to see him settled in life. A wife could help him when he is much occupied with his patients." Then, remembering John had put her name forward for the position, she blushed profusely and became entirely engrossed with the rose she was placing at the time. Thus, she did not see Marguerite observing her closely.

"The right wife would," she agreed. "But I have often observed that gentlemen are ready enough to choose a pretty face over sense, and I cannot suppose my own son to be any different," she continued with a sigh, pretending not to notice Margaret's change of colour. She is referring to Miss Parker, Margaret thought and surmised that the mother and son must have had further words on this subject. More than ever, Margaret believed the announcement of their engagement to be imminent, but the arrival of Mr and Mrs Robert Ferrars put an end to further discussion and signalled time for luncheon.

The flower arrangements were done, an exquisite profusion of red and white roses embellished with forest greenery from the park. Margaret was delighted with the results of their labours and retired to her chamber to read. She felt awkward and in the way downstairs, without a specific task and was glad of the opportunity for a little solitude before it was time to dress for the evening. Unable to understand why she was feeling so anxious, it would be beneficial to have a little time to compose herself. It was most unlike her, but she was unable to concentrate, and hearing two carriages arriving, she was glad to observe from her window the arrival of Sir John and Lady Middleton and Mr and Mrs Palmer. The tense waiting period was nearly over, and everyone who was expected at Norland had now arrived. All except Charles Dashwood. It would be a sad disappointment for Caroline Parker if he was unable to leave his practice, but as Margaret was just beginning to realise, it would be equally sad for her. She tried again to settle down to her book with a sigh of impatience. The next thing she knew, it was dark and Lily was lighting the candles.

"Evening, miss," she twinkled, very much looking forward to dressing Margaret for a special occasion.

"Goodness, Lily, is it that time already?" Margaret sat up, rubbing her eyes, feeling much better for a nap, as Lily busied herself laying out the gown and accessories they had chosen for the evening. Fanny no longer involved herself in these matters, much relieved to be released from this tedious responsibility. Lily had proved entirely competent, as Fanny predicted, leaving her free to look after her own concerns. After much excited deliberation, the two girls had decided on the cream silk, which was so admired at her first London ball. A Christmas celebration demanded a higher standard of dress, in Lily's opinion, and Margaret agreed, recognising the maid's very good taste. Just as Lily was adding the finishing touches to Margaret's hair, her mother arrived, elegantly attired for the evening in burgundy.

Margaret was overjoyed to see her; they embraced each other fondly after the long absence as Lily looked on with some sadness. She had never known her mother.

"Mama, I'm so very glad to see you. How was your journey? Not too arduous, I hope," Margaret questioned her mother eagerly, and Lily was warmed to see the great affection between them. When Margaret introduced her to her mother, she sank into a low curtsey, impressed that Miss Margaret's mother remained such a handsome woman.

"You look very fine, Mama. Is that a new gown?" Margaret was also happy to observe her mother was looking extremely well, and the gown suited her perfectly.

"Yes, I thought the occasion warranted the extortionate expense, and I didn't want to look like the poor relation. Fortunately, Elinor no longer oversees my expenditure." She winked at her daughter, knowing she would remember the days when Elinor had kept a close watch on their expenditure. Mrs Dashwood was quick to return the compliment, casting an experienced eye over Margaret's ensemble.

"You look very fine yourself, Margaret. That is an exquisite gown, and I really admire the way you've done my daughter's hair, Lily. You've made her look so sophisticated. Is that a new fashion? We are so behind in the country," Mrs Dashwood admitted ruefully. "You must teach me how to do it myself."

"I would be glad to, ma'am, but I must admit Miss Margaret's curls took some getting used to," Lily answered, meeting Mrs Dashwood's eyes with a wry smile. Lily added a few finishing touches to the perfect ensemble and stepped back to critically appraise the result. At last, she pronounced Margaret, and mother and daughter were allowed to go downstairs together to find many of the party already assembled. Elinor and Marianne rushed to greet them.

"Mama, what a joyful occasion, all of us together again!" Marianne cried in happiness.

"How lovely all my daughters look tonight!" Mrs Dashwood exclaimed, proudly admiring Marianne in pale blue silk, and Elinor in rose. "What a handsome trio I've been blessed with, to be sure."

"Well, that is no surprise considering our provenance." Elinor laughed, linking her arm affectionately with her mother's. "Come and talk to Edward, Mama; I see he is bringing us refreshment."

Standing together as a family group, they watched as the new arrivals were announced into the ballroom. Margaret's anxiety was calmed by her mother's presence at her side. First came Mr and Mrs Barrington, followed by their offspring, looking very elegant. Then came the vicar and his shy young wife, whom Margaret had only seen once in church. Several more neighbours followed whom Margaret wasn't acquainted with, then, to Margaret's surprise and chagrin, Captain Dunning was announced. She felt herself flush with embarrassment, remembering their last unfortunate meeting and wondered why he had been invited. She sincerely hoped that it was not on her account because that would be too distressing for words. Just as she thought all the guests were assembled, a latecomer was announced to be Mr Charles Dashwood, and her heart missed a beat whilst her eyes flew involuntarily to Caroline Parker. She did indeed seem gratified at his entrance, and reluctantly, Margaret had to admit she was looking extremely pretty in a pale yellow gown with her dark hair piled high and dusted with jewels. She and Catherine were standing with Fanny and John, so Charles had no choice but to make his way through the crowded room to address the hosts first. Margaret's eyes followed him jealously, painfully aware of how handsome he looked in his evening attire. Her thoughts were interrupted by her mother touching her elbow.

"The new heir to Norland, I presume," enquired Mrs Dashwood of her daughter, giving her a misty expressive look.

"Yes, Mr Charles Dashwood, Mama," replied Margaret with feigned indifference.

"A handsome face but not an easy man, by all accounts," Mrs Dashwood observed dispassionately. Margaret made no reply but thought that her mother had made a pretty fair assessment of his character at first sight.

John gave the signal for the dancing to begin, and the musicians ceased to play background music to begin their lively dance repertoire. Marianne and

Elinor eagerly left them to join the dancers as, suddenly, Charles Dashwood appeared before Margaret. With a bow, he enquired if she was engaged for the first dance, but it was several moments before she was able to answer him, so acute was her astonishment.

"I am not engaged, sir," she stuttered, at last, taking the arm he proffered and allowing him to lead her out, conscious that her heart was fluttering so alarmingly that she thought he must hear it. Recovering herself enough to look up, she couldn't help noticing Caroline Parker's disgruntled face as she stood on the sidelines, glowering at them. Unfortunately, she was not dancing, there being more young ladies than gentlemen present. Fanny was also watching them suspiciously, her sour expression evident from the other side of the room. Margaret chose to ignore their baleful looks, turning her attention to her partner. "I am glad, sir, that you were able to return in time for the ball." Margaret smiled up at him, gaining the courage to speak at last. Although she was tall, Charles topped her by more than an inch.

"Fortunately, matters were resolved in time, and I was able to leave a very demanding patient safely delivered of a healthy boy," he explained happily, returning her smile with evident pride.

"How charming for the parents! They must be overjoyed!" Margaret exclaimed. "What a satisfying profession you have, Mr Dashwood. I should so like to be able to contribute something useful to the world, but it is impossible for a woman to find fulfilment in a professional way." He seemed surprised by her comment, and it was several minutes before he replied.

"I admit, when the outcome is as satisfactory as this pregnancy has been, then one could not hope for more, but that is not always the case. Sometimes the opposite is true. The important thing is to be certain that you have done the very best for the patient." He looked down at her, holding her eyes for such a long moment as Margaret blushed in confusion.

"Your mother must be so very happy to see you here again," she commented when she had recovered herself again.

"I hope she is not the only one," he said with feeling, and Margaret wondered if he was referring to Caroline Parker, although it was puzzling why he wasn't dancing with her at this very moment. Perhaps John had interfered again and suggested he dance with herself first as their particular guest of honour. It wouldn't be the first time he tried to throw them together.

When Charles returned Margaret to her mother, she was immediately approached by Steven Barrington, who had been waiting impatiently. As they joined the line of couples, she was surprised to see Charles Dashwood leading out Miss Elizabeth Barrington, but she supposed Miss Parker to be already dancing. Later, she saw this was not the case when she saw Caroline, still at Fanny's side. How very strange; perhaps they have had a quarrel, she conjectured as they finished the dance, and Steven enquired solicitously.

"Will you dance the next, Miss Margaret, or would you like me to procure you some refreshment?"

"I confess, the latter, Mr Barrington, if you would be so kind," she replied gratefully, and he escorted her back to her mother's side, where she made the introduction to her curious mother and explained his connection to their hosts.

"Delighted to make your acquaintance, Mrs Dashwood. May I say what a fine rider your daughter is making?" Mrs Dashwood smiled graciously, happy to hear her youngest daughter complimented by the fashionable young gentleman.

"I am so glad she has the opportunity to try it again, and may I thank you for teaching her, Mr Barrington. I remember your house and its previous occupant. It was a fine old place, but he was an old skinflint who would never spend a penny on renovation. I am delighted to hear that your father has given it the attention it deserved. You see, I know everything about you, Mr Barrington. Margaret is a lively correspondent, telling of her progress on horseback and the great pleasure she takes in it. Thank you once again for giving her the opportunity."

"No trouble at all, Mrs Dashwood; it has been my pleasure," he replied, looking at Margaret warmly.

"Perhaps you and your daughters could visit us one day soon, then I could show you the improvements my father has undertaken personally." He bowed.

"We should all be delighted, Mr Barrington." Mrs Dashwood gave him her hand, and he bowed over it chivalrously.

Mrs Dashwood was extremely gratified to note that at least two of the young men present admired her youngest daughter. It was reassuring to see, with her own eyes, that Margaret's season was still a success, despite her removal from London. She had been horrified by the unfortunate accident and was only slightly mollified that Margaret was not seriously hurt. Frowning, she remembered she had yet to tackle Fanny about that. Turning away from the young couple, she saw John approaching them in the company of a young man not yet known to her.

"John, may I thank you and Fanny for a marvellous party? We are all enjoying ourselves immensely," Mrs Dashwood said warmly. "It was so kind of you to invite me to Norland for Christmas." Margaret was glad that her mother took over the conversation, having watched the two men approach with some suspicion, conscious that John had tried to pair her off before.

"Mrs Dashwood, Margaret, may I present my neighbour, Mr Frederick Harris?"

"If you are not engaged, Miss Margaret, may I have the next dance?" He bowed bashfully, first to her mother, then to her. Although Margaret really preferred to sit with her mother, she took pity on Mr Harris, seeing as he was rather shy.

"I am not engaged, sir," she admitted, allowing him to lead her out to join the set. During the dance, she was pleased to discover Mr Harris owned the pretty farmhouse they passed often whilst riding, and Margaret was elaborate in her approval of its beauty and situation, nestling in the downs.

"Of course, I have heard of you, Mr Harris. Elizabeth Barrington has spoken to me often of you and your mother. Miss Elizabeth explained that the farm has been in your family for generations and that you are a very great friend. She also told me it was you and your mother who alerted the Barringtons to the neighbouring estate to Norland being for sale." Margaret was surprised to see him change colour but couldn't think of what she had said to embarrass him. At length, he recovered himself enough to reply.

"I am so glad you approve of my home, Miss Dashwood. Perhaps you and the Barringtons would do us the honour of a visit when you next ride in our direction. Miss Barrington has also spoken of you, and I know you to be firm friends." She could see he was very eager for her acceptance.

"I should enjoy that very much, Mr Harris, and I am very sure it could easily be arranged. We could ride over on the next fine day." She was genuinely pleased to accept his invitation. At that moment, the dance brought Margaret face-to-face with Charles Dashwood and Mr Harris opposite Miss Caroline, whose humour seemed to have much improved. Then, to her acute embarrassment, the dance carried her face-to-face with Captain Dunning, but when she saw he was partnering Fanny, astonishment quickly eclipsed every other feeling.

Margaret had never seen Fanny dancing, but today she was as spritely as a woman half her age, her happy smile contributing to the blooming appearance of youth. The complete alteration in Fanny's demeanour and looks was as unfathomable as it was astonishing. In amazement, Margaret watched them together for as much as the dance would allow and saw Fanny was as animated as a girl in her first season. Her eyes flew involuntarily to where John was standing with the colonel, but his expression was sanguine, and it was clear he didn't see anything unusual in his wife's behaviour.

Later that evening, when Steven Barrington escorted Margaret into supper, she was further surprised to see Captain Dunning's continued presence at Fanny's side. She watched as Fanny paused by Charles Dashwood and so pointedly asked him to take in Caroline Parker; he couldn't very well refuse. His face was hidden from Margaret, but she thought she detected a moment's hesitation before he complied with Fanny's wishes, as good manners dictated. To Margaret's profound dismay, she found herself seated at table with them, so she had no choice but to observe their behaviour to one another at close quarters. The atmosphere was strained as Charles was silent and Miss Parker appeared cross, and Margaret could think of nothing to say to lighten the mood. With relief, she looked up to see the Barringtons and Frederick Harris preparing to join them. Elizabeth was the first to break the awkward silence by turning to Frederick Harris with a smile.

"How does your mother, Mr Harris, and why do we not have the pleasure of her company tonight? I hope she is not unwell," Elizabeth asked politely. He returned her smile, his eyes softening fondly, leaving Margaret in no doubt of his feelings Elizabeth.

"She is well enough, thank you, Miss Elizabeth, but not inclined to leave the house in the evening, especially during the winter months." Then Margaret heard him repeat the invitation he had made to her earlier.

"Winter is challenging for all of us, Mr Harris, especially the elderly," Elizabeth replied sympathetically. At this point, Steven interjected.

"Although we are extremely fortunate that this December has been exceptionally mild, making it possible to take outdoor exercise nearly every day. Thank you for the invitation. It's a fine idea, Harris, and I will make it my business to arrange it very soon," Steven observed enthusiastically, and Charles appeared to wake up.

"And on that subject, how does my patient?" he interrogated. "Not suffering too much from all this riding about the countryside, I hope." Margaret was relieved to hear him speak, even though it did sound a little like an admonishment, and she was pleased to be able to give him a positive answer.

"Very well recovered. I thank you, Mr Dashwood. It is as if the accident never occurred, but I suspect the skill of my physician had something to do with that." Margaret smiled at him warmly, catching sight of Caroline's furious face out of the corner of her eye. Blushing guiltily, as though she had been caught in the act of flirting, she turned away.

"Mr Dashwood, we are all delighted that you could return for the party," Caroline gushed, touching him lightly on the arm in a proprietary manner, but he did not reply.

"Will you remain now for Christmas?" She tried again, this time with a direct question that demanded a response.

"My plans are not yet certain," he replied coldly, turning to Elizabeth Barrington on his other side.

"When you ride out again, may I be permitted to join you? I have already ascertained that John has a suitable mount, and the exercise would be very pleasurable after the confinement of London."

"Of course, Mr Dashwood, the more, the merrier," Elizabeth replied with her ready laugh. "As you have heard, we have a plan to visit Mr Harris and his mother on the next fine day. Why don't you join us, sir? I am sure Frederick can have no objections." She turned to her friend with a pretty smile, and Frederick gave her a look that spoke very eloquently of his agreement. Reluctantly, he tore his gaze away from Elizabeth's face and turned to Charles Dashwood.

"Of course, Mr Dashwood, as Elizabeth says, the more, the merrier, and I invite you all to stay for luncheon. My mother will be so pleased to have company," insisted Frederick Harris, and Charles shook his hand.

"Obliged to you, Mr Harris. I am pleased to accept your generous invitation."

Caroline said nothing, knowing she was excluded as she did not ride, but her unusual silence did not last for long. Obviously, she had been reassessing her position with regard to learning equestrian skills, and she turned to Steven with a seductive smile.

"Mr Barrington, I believe I was a little hasty the other evening at dinner when I told you I did not ride and had no intention of doing so. I see now that I should not have criticised what I had no knowledge of. The truth of the matter is, I've never had the opportunity, but I see now, the exercise is most beneficial. Could I possibly induce you to help a complete novice, such as myself, to have the confidence to try it?" Her voice was contrite and her expression humble as she glanced up at him through her lashes. Her ruse succeeded because Steven Barrington looked at her as though he was seeing her for the first time.

"My dear Miss Parker, you had but to ask. Nothing would give me more pleasure. In fact, Miss Margaret is going on so well, she is now more than ready for a more challenging mount, leaving our dear little Sally for you to begin on. What do you say, Miss Margaret? Do you agree?" Margaret was annoyed, having become very fond of the little mare but considered she had no choice in the matter.

"Why, of course, Mr Barrington," she replied civilly, hiding her irritation with Caroline's scheming. "Sally is the perfect horse for a novice. As you say, I think I am confident enough now to ride one of the larger mares." Margaret recognised any refusal on her part would look churlish and petty. Despite her irritation, she could not help observing Caroline Parker was not easily beaten, and Margaret acknowledged a reluctant respect for her perseverance.

The party continued in full swing until the early hours as no one seemed in a hurry to leave. It was gone three in the morning when Margaret finally retired, yawning loudly as she climbed the stairs. Fatigue had caught up with her, but when she opened the door to her chamber, she found her mother waiting up for her instead of Lily. Mrs Dashwood was quick to explain her presence, seeing the look of surprise on her daughter's face.

"I dismissed young Lily as she looked fit to drop, and I promised her that I would help you undress for bed. Are you so very tired, my dear, as I would like to talk to you." The lateness of the hour meant it must be something important, so Margaret submitted to her request without question.

"A little tired, but after such a lively evening, I could not sleep immediately, in any case. What did you want to say to me, Mama, that couldn't wait until morning? You must be tired yourself."

"Not really, probably because I slept most of the day. It was indeed a lovely party, but are you aware that you have captured the interest of two young gentlemen, Margaret? You have grown into a beautiful young woman, and Fanny has added the polish I could never have given you in Devon." Mrs Dashwood came straight to the point such was the relationship between mother and daughter.

"I am sure you exaggerate, Mama," protested Margaret, blushing, used to her sisters claiming the limelight in such circumstances.

"No, if I'm not much mistaken, Mr Charles Dashwood seems quite smitten with you, also Steven Barrington in his rather ebullient way." She was adamant. "How fortunate, both are worthy young men with excellent prospects." Clearly, her mother had been busy making a few discreet inquiries about Steven Barrington. Margaret had been present when her mother questioned him about Barrington House but assumed it was a disinterested enquiry.

"Mama, I think you exaggerate. Steven Barrington admires me because I enjoy riding, and horses are his only passion. As for Charles Dashwood" – she hesitated – "I hardly know where to start," Margaret admitted and proceeded to unburden herself to her mother, telling her about the conversation overheard from the treehouse and John's attempt at matchmaking. Mrs Dashwood listened in increasing astonishment to all her daughter had to impart.

"So you see, Mama, John's interference turned Mr Dashwood against me from the start, and he barely spoke a word to me when we first met. Matters have thawed a little between us, but I expect his engagement to be announced to Miss Parker immanently." Margaret sighed heavily, noting her mother's stunned silence, relieved when she spoke at last.

"Goodness, how unfortunate. I credited John with more sense. Well, it is certainly true that I didn't know either gentleman until tonight, but I have lived a long time in this world, and I think I can recognise when a gentleman is attracted to a lady, even if that lady is my daughter. My only question to you now is, how do you feel about these two gentlemen, Margaret?" Margaret stared at her in surprise, not knowing how to answer, and Mrs Dashwood embraced her daughter, seeing her discomfort.

"My dear, I have said what I came to say, and it is now very late. Why don't you sleep on it? I often find the answer that alludes me before bed is on my pillow in the morning. Good night, my dear. Sleep well." With that, Mrs Dashwood left the room, leaving Margaret to toss and turn for several hours. Just before dawn, she fell into a troubled sleep and did not wake until late in the morning.

Margaret Dashwood was not the only lady to toss and turn that night; Marguerite was also finding sleep elusive. With increasing pleasure, she had witnessed Charles' changed behaviour to Margaret, and it was clear to his mother he was beginning to appreciate her worth at long last. Marguerite cursed John roundly for his precipitate interference, because without that, all might have been settled between them by now. Unfortunately, John was not very wise, as witnessed by his choice of a wife. Neither Margaret nor Charles had characters that could be forced into a match. Anyone could see that except John, it would seem. Nevertheless, Marguerite knew she was not the only one to have noticed Charles' attentions to Margaret. Marguerite saw that Caroline, who watched his every move jealously, had also observed this change. The worrying thing was that she had Fanny on her side, encouraging Charles to dance with Caroline and obliging him to take her in to supper. For reasons that Marguerite couldn't quite fathom, Fanny wanted Charles to marry Caroline, and this was cause for extra concern for his mother. Although Charles might evade Caroline's determination, with Fanny as an ally, it could be exceedingly difficult for him. Caroline, with Fanny's backing, would be a formidable force to be reckoned with. She pondered discussing her concerns with John. Ultimately, he was the one who'd caused all the problems with his interference, albeit inadvertently. Presumably, he still wanted to achieve an alliance between Margaret and Charles. Marguerite wondered if he was aware of Fanny's determination to thwart him in that regard and marry Charles to Miss Parker. Marguerite thought, probably not, as he seemed not to notice his wife at all, and if he thought of Miss Parker, he merely saw her as a distraction for his wife. Marguerite decided it would be better not to involve John in her worries. It was doubtful if he could do anything to help, and it could complicate matters still further.

Fanny's behaviour was puzzling Marguerite altogether, not just because of her championship of Caroline Parker but because Marguerite had also noticed that Captain Dunning was paying Fanny particular attentions, and she appeared to welcome them. Although both parties thought they were being discreet, it was obvious to Marguerite's experienced eye. Certainly, John Dashwood had not noticed, or if he had, he was not at all perturbed by the flirtation between the captain and his wife. In fact, he seemed to have been so much occupied with his extended family that he did not notice his wife at all. Marguerite had danced with the captain herself, and he had been as charming and attentive as ever, but when she voiced her surprise at seeing him at Norland, he had been very evasive. His brief explanation had simply not rung true to her. If he was to be believed, he was on route to London from Portsmouth and had been invited to call in at Norland on his way. He had not revealed who had invited him specifically, and Marguerite suspected it must have been Fanny. He was not a particular acquaintance of John's, and they were not even members of the same club, as far as Marguerite was aware. Marguerite also reflected that Captain Dunning seemed to make quite a habit of calling into places on his way home, even if, in reality, they were not on his way at all. Her astonishment was considerable when he singled Fanny out, leading her out to dance twice and taking her to supper. It was also remarkable how Fanny became illuminated in his company, which Marguerite had never witnessed before, and she wondered what was going on between them. She remembered how the captain had talked to her about a wealthy patroness, but surely he hadn't meant Fanny Dashwood. Fanny was certainly wealthy, but Marguerite couldn't believe she would open herself up to such impropriety. Fanny was a married woman, and such a liaison would be entirely improper. Even such a rogue as Captain Dunning could not contemplate it, could he? Surely, Fanny would not risk her reputation, having such regard for the opinion of society. It was puzzling, indeed. Taking everything into account, however, it was obvious to Marguerite that their relationship had progressed beyond that of a hostess and her guest. If her suspicions were correct, then Marguerite had to admit she was shocked, and it had been a long time since she had been that.

Chapter 11
More Departures and a Welcome News

Lily was so eager for a full account of the party that her curiosity got the better of her judgement and she brought Margaret her morning chocolate rather earlier than usual. She was destined to be disappointed, finding her mistress unusually pale and uncommunicative, and Lily was dismayed to see her lying so still in bed. She scuttled around picking up scattered accessories and hanging up the discarded ball gown with great care, taking as long as she dared in case her mistress rallied.

"Shall I help you to dress, Miss Margaret?" Lily tried a direct question, but Margaret barely acknowledged her presence.

"Very well, miss, I will leave you to rest and return in an hour or so." Lily had no choice but to leave her alone, although she was still burning with curiosity. Wrapped up in her thoughts, Margaret didn't notice the maid's departure. She had done as her mother had asked and searched her heart to find her true feelings for the two young men. It had taken no time at all to realise that for Steven Barrington, she felt nothing but friendship. Of that, she was certain, but she had to acknowledge her feelings for Charles Dashwood might be changing rapidly. In fact, so rapidly that she had trouble keeping up with them herself. Recognising she had long been taking a very keen interest in his concerns and remembering her heart fluttering alarmingly when he entered the ballroom, she was fooling herself if she pretended to be indifferent to him any longer. There had been an undeniable frisson of excitement between them during the dance last night, and it finally dawned upon her that she was in love with Charles Dashwood. It had been coming on so gradually, she hadn't realised it at first, but now she had to face the truth. His initial indifference had certainly dampened any interest she might have felt at first meeting, but that first spark of attraction had not been entirely extinguished. Their first dance had been a disaster, and she'd tried to push all thoughts of him from her mind. It clearly hadn't worked, and the propensity to blush profusely whenever he was near was proof of his profound effect on her. She was not usually in the habit of blushing around young men. That she had lost her heart was a most uncomfortable realisation, more especially because she believed that he was honour bound to another. If he had changed his mind, it didn't make him any less obligated. His attentions to Caroline Parker had been marked from the moment they met, and why pay such attentions to a girl he had no feelings for? She remembered the conversation overheard in Fanny's sitting room when they were talking about an engagement as a settled thing. There must be an understanding between them; there was no other explanation. Pleading a headache, she remained in her room for the rest of the day, only rising when Lily came to dress her for dinner. Lily went about her business in silence, seeing her mistress was still pensive and unwilling to talk but was worried something serious had happened. What could possibly have occurred to cause this change in her mistress, who is usually such an optimistic person and never casts her down for long? A couple of dabs of rouge brought back the roses to Margaret's cheeks, and Lily was satisfied she sent her down for dinner looking more like herself, on the outside at least.

Even én famille, they were still a party of twelve, so if Margaret was more silent than usual, she felt safe to assume it would go unnoticed. She needn't have worried as the talk around the table was mostly about the afternoon's riding lesson for Caroline Parker. Apparently, Steven Barrington had taken her at her word, and the first lesson had not only taken place already but, by all accounts, been a resounding success. It appeared Caroline had taken to the sport like a duck to water, and Margaret couldn't help feeling rather irritated. Although she knew this was uncharitable of her, it was difficult to believe that the fastidious Caroline could be such a competent horsewoman in just one day. Was there no end to her resourcefulness in the pursuit of personal gain? Nevertheless, Steven Barrington was fulsome in his praise for the fearlessness of his new pupil, whom he obviously regarded with new and admiring eyes. Margaret looked at Charles Dashwood to see if she could read his feelings, wondering how he would react to Caroline being admired by another young man. Moreover, one she had been alone with all afternoon as Miss Elizabeth had been resting at home after the ball. As ever, he gave nothing away, his expression remaining inscrutable. Fanny, who missed nothing, had observed Margaret studying Charles and her unusual silence over dinner, and she eyed her disapprovingly, retorting loudly enough for the whole company to hear. Her sarcastic tone was unmistakeable.

"Ah, Miss Margaret, may I congratulate you on your recovery? It is a pity you missed a great many of our acquaintance this morning, who wished to bid you goodbye." Fanny's disapproval was evident to everyone, and John stared coldly at his wife, but Margaret didn't rise to the bait.

"I am also very sorry not to have been able to say goodbye, Fanny, but I really did feel quite unwell this morning," apologised Margaret, noting that Fanny's contented demeanour of the night before had quickly degenerated into her usual sourness. It was hard to imagine she was the same woman who had been dancing happily with Captain Dunning last night. Fanny was about to speak again, but John frowned at her in warning, immediately taking the part of their young guest against his wife.

"Sir John and Lady Middleton did set off exceedingly early, Fanny. You were not even up yourself. They wanted to be at Barton Park in time for Christmas Eve, and it is three days' drive. Mr and Mrs Palmer left even earlier for the same reason as they needed to prepare for Christmas with little Thomas in Somerset. Very few were up to see them off, so do not disturb yourself, Margaret. It was a very late night and, therefore, not surprising you were fatigued after your exertions. No doubt, we shall see them all again soon enough." John, unlike Fanny, was sympathetic and didn't hesitate to defend Margaret from his wife's unwarranted criticism. Fanny threw him a look of dislike, which he completely ignored.

"Mr and Mrs Robert Ferrars have also left us for London," Fanny continued, changing the subject as though John had not spoken. "They will spend Christmas with our mother, who, most unfortunately, is quite unwell. I do hope it's not serious as it is very unlike her to succumb to illness. From tomorrow, therefore, we shall be bereft of almost all of our visitors." Fanny looked regretfully at Caroline Parker, who wiped an imaginary tear most obligingly. Margaret observed this deft piece of playacting with wry amusement and all but laughed out loud when Caroline replied in a suitably downcast tone.

"Dear Mrs Dashwood, we have so enjoyed our visit and are extremely loathe to return home tomorrow," said Caroline, still dabbing her eyes prettily, completely unaware she was the subject of some amusement. Margaret caught Marianne's eye and had to hold her napkin over her mouth to stifle a loud giggle.

"Yes, indeed," concurred Elinor, quickly intervening, noting Margaret's stifled laugh and wishing to divert Fanny's attention away from her sister, who'd been on the receiving end of her rancour quite enough for one evening. "I must thank you again, Fanny and John, for inviting us. Edward and I have greatly enjoyed our visit and have been happy to see dear Norland again. We must also take our leave of you tonight, as it is our intention to be back in Devon by Christmas." Margaret smiled her thanks to her sister for the timely diversion, thinking how sorry she would be losing their company. She had known all along they were to leave, but now that the time was almost upon them, she felt sad they wouldn't be staying for Christmas at Norland. It would have been like old times. It was welcome news, however, that the Miss Parkers were to return home as well. Margaret had forgotten this, and her eyes flew involuntarily to Charles Dashwood, to see how he would bear the separation from his beloved Caroline, but his full concentration had returned to his dinner. Mr Barrington, on the other hand, was eloquent in expressing his regret at her departure and sincerely hoped they could continue their lessons another time. Caroline lost no time in pursuing this advantage and devoted a great deal of her attention to Steven throughout the evening, all the while gauging Charles Dashwood's reaction to her flirtation out of the corner of her eye. Margaret, who was also watching, could not detect anything but complete indifference in his countenance.

The tedious meal dragged to a close, and the drawing room beckoned the ladies. Marianne went straight to the pianoforte and proceeded to entertain them with her musical skills. Fanny, as usual, sat with the Miss Parkers, discussing the events of the night before and basking in Caroline's flattery, which was clearly audible throughout the room. Marguerite Dashwood and Mrs Dashwood were in a cosy tête-à-tête, reminiscing about old times and talking about their husbands, trying to ascertain why there had been a falling out between them. Thus, Elinor, seeing Margaret alone in the corner, took the opportunity of crossing the room to join her for a private talk.

"Margaret, I couldn't help noticing you were very pensive at dinner," she began in concern. "Are you still feeling unwell? You mustn't mind Fanny; she positively delights in being vexatious. It's what she does best, but it's not a good idea to antagonise her further, even if Miss Parker's playacting is so transparent." She smiled wryly at Margaret, but Margaret could see she was genuinely worried, despite her little jest, and sought to reassure her sister.

"No, Elinor, I am quite well, and you know I pay no attention to Fanny. It is not in her power to upset me because I do not value her opinions, and one cannot help but admire Miss Parker's ingenuity," Margaret observed with some irony, ignoring Elinor's main question. Elinor, however, was not to be put off, perhaps more so because it would be her last opportunity before leaving Norland, and she sensed all was not well with her little sister.

"Then what is the matter? It's no use denying it, I can see something is wrong."

"Oh, Elinor, where do I begin?" wailed Margaret, secretly relieved to be able to talk through her concerns again. She poured forth everything she had told her mother the night before, and Elinor listened without interjection until Margaret came to an end. Her eldest sister was not at all surprised, as she had suspected for some time that Margaret was not as indifferent to Charles Dashwood as she professed to be. In her experience, the path of true love rarely ran smoothly.

"I note, Margaret, you do not clearly state the nature of your feelings for Charles Dashwood," she enquired in an even tone when Margaret had finished her account, but Margaret shook her head in anguish.

"I hardly know myself, Elinor, as they have been changing so very rapidly. I thought about him last night, as Mama bid, and I realise my feelings are stronger than friendship, but is that love, Elinor? I just don't know." Although Margaret thought she was in love, she still had doubts. Elinor nodded in sympathy, smiling at her sister reassuringly.

"I will acknowledge that I, for one, have grown to like him over the past few weeks. He is a little serious, perhaps, but a sensible wife could change that. As to his choice of intimate companion, we will have to wait and see. Believe me, I do understand the anguish you are going through as I have been through it all myself. I advise you to take courage from that, Margaret, as my story ended well, despite all odds. I also counsel you to be guided by his behaviour and his alone. Only then will all become clear. We can surmise what Miss Parker's intentions are and the lengths she will go to fulfil them, but we must trust in the intelligence of Charles Dashwood. He doesn't strike me as a fool. Remember the time when I thought I'd lost Edward to the guile of Lucy Steele and the agony I endured until she married Robert? Unfortunately, we ladies are not at liberty to dictate the pace of courtship, and it is not seemly for us to ask direct questions of young men. Sadly, we are destined to be the passive ones and must allow the gentlemen time to come to us, and that waiting is never easy." Margaret had to acknowledge the truth of Elinor's statements and was grateful for her sister's good sense, promising to heed her sound advice. Elinor squeezed her hand encouragingly.

"I am sure all will turn out for the best, Margaret. Now I must leave you and go and talk to Mama as it is my last evening." Rising, she kissed her sister, leaving Margaret to her thoughts, which were soon interrupted by the very person who occupied them. Charles Dashwood sat down in the seat recently vacated by Elinor and regarded her with concern.

"Miss Margaret, how does my patient? I see you are pale. Are you still unwell?" he asked solicitously.

"I am well, sir. Just a little tired after last night's exertions," she assured him but could not meet his eye, unable to suppress another self-conscious blush. He gently took her hand to feel her pulse, and finding it normal, he smiled.

"Then, I prescribe early to bed and a good night's rest, and tomorrow you will be as right as rain. I wish all my diagnoses were as simple as that." He laughed awkwardly, trying to elevate her pensive mood, but she was still unable to meet his eye, fiddling nervously with the lace on her gown.

"Do you know, Mr Dashwood, I think I will take your advice," she replied, suddenly feeling utterly exhausted. "Please excuse me, I will say goodnight to everyone and go straight to my chamber." With that, she took her leave of the assembled company after a special goodbye to Elinor and Edward, promising to return to Devon in the spring. Elinor squeezed her hand sympathetically.

"Try not to worry, Margaret. I am confident the gentleman will make the right choice," she whispered encouragingly in her ear. Margaret was convinced she would not sleep, but despite her conviction, sleep came quickly and was long and sound.

Just as her doctor predicted, in the morning everything looked brighter, and Margaret arose in a more optimistic frame of mind. In the breakfast room, she found Fanny and the Miss Parkers, who had enjoyed a farewell breakfast together. They were on the point of departure, and she was relieved to have missed it. Nevertheless, she said all that was proper and hoped, insincerely, they would meet again soon in London. Her mood lifted further when they left the room and she sat down to enjoy the luxury of a hearty breakfast. It was the twenty-first of December, and Christmas was almost upon them, but Margaret couldn't help feeling that Norland was entirely devoid of Christmas spirit, especially now that Elinor and Edward had gone. Fanny prided herself on being the perfect hostess, providing every fashionable consideration, but somehow she'd managed to make the festive season soulless. They were now down to a party of eight, but surely more could be done to make it a joyful occasion, much like the Christmases she remembered. She went in search of Marianne to ask for her help with Christmas music. Christmas carols would be cheering and add some jollity into the long evenings. Her sister was in her usual place at the pianoforte, practising a complicated but mournful dirge, and Margaret eyed her with some impatience. Sometimes, Marianne rather overdid the melancholic heroine.

"Marianne, do please play something a little more cheerful," she begged. "It is Christmas, although one could be forgiven for forgetting that fact here. Look, I've unearthed these music sheets of Christmas carols in the library. Why don't you play them and I will do my best to sing in tune? I'm determined to revive the festive spirit and liven us all up," Margaret chivvied her sister, who eyed the carols with little enthusiasm.

"Please, Marianne," Margaret begged. "We are all feeling a little flat after the ball and could do with cheering up."

"Oh, very well, if you insist." She sighed, taking the sheets from Margaret. "You look better this morning, Margaret." Marianne favoured her with a long, inquisitive look. "Pray tell me, what was the intense conversation with Elinor all about?" Margaret sighed. She'd thought Marianne was too occupied with her music to notice the tête-à-tête between them last night. There was nothing for it; she must now repeat the whole story again to Marianne. Thus, the tale was told for the third time. Margaret knew it would not do to have secrets with her mother and elder sister, to the exclusion of Marianne. They were a close-knit family, despite their differences in character. Marianne was all astonishment.

"Goodness, Margaret, what a dark horse you are!" she exclaimed in wonder. "This is quite a revelation. We all thought you didn't like him, although I suspected you did protest too much." Margaret looked away in embarrassment.

"I didn't at first, or at least, I pretended I didn't. He was unpardonably rude to me, but now I can't blame him for being offhand after what John proposed to him." Marianne nodded in understanding.

"No, I suppose not; it was extremely presumptuous of John and very unwise, although I daresay he meant it for the best. His interference has had the opposite of what he intended. Anyone can see that you and Mr Dashwood are not the types to submit to an arranged match. He is handsome, that I will acknowledge, but Margaret, oh so serious and not at all romantic." Marianne sighed over these heinous deficiencies.

"It may be that romance is not as important as we were once led to believe." Margaret was thinking of Willoughby. "Perhaps other, more lasting qualities are the basis of a happy marriage," she finished, thinking of the colonel and Edward, who possessed these qualities in abundance. Marianne nodded in agreement, also thinking of the fecklessness of Willoughby's character.

"You are right, Margaret. I bless the day I met the colonel, although once I thought him too old. He is the kindest and best of men. I do not deserve him."

"You do, Marianne, and although the colonel would be the first to say that he is the one who doesn't deserve you, neither case is true. You both deserve each other, and you are very fortunate in that regard," Margaret said a little wistfully, and Marianne's heart went out to her little sister.

"And you will be too, Margaret, you'll see, but one thing is certain: you can't go and tell Charles Dashwood of your change of heart. Elinor is right in that. You must let his behaviour be your guide. I also agree with Elinor and Mama in that I cannot believe he is attached to Caroline Parker, which must convince you, Margaret. Both your sisters and your mother doubt any attachment between them. Why, they are completely different characters and have nothing in common at all. I agree, there is a very strong parallel with the former relationship of Lucy Steele and Edward, and the similarities between the characters of Mrs Lucy Ferrars and Caroline Parker are obvious to me now. They are both utterly ruthless in the pursuit of money and position and care little how they obtain their ambitions. It is also no coincidence Fanny has made a protégée of them both. Flattery is a weapon they both use to advantage, and Fanny is very susceptible to that." At that point, Margaret interrupted Marianne's outpouring, reminded of Fanny's patronage.

"Which is what is so worrying, Marianne, the fact that Caroline is Fanny's current protégée. They are working together to ensnare him."

"I see what you mean, but you must have faith that all will turn out well in the end, as it did for Edward and Elinor." Marianne saw that Margaret still looked very doubtful.

"Another thing, I concede you are absolutely right about the carols. It is Christmas, and we will have a jolly sing song tonight, if only to annoy Fanny with our vulgar performance," she conceded with a wink at Margaret, making her laugh as the door opened.

"What will annoy Fanny?" Mrs Dashwood asked in concern as she entered the room and embraced her two daughters.

"Music, Mama, lively music. Margaret and I have a plan to cheer up our evenings," Marianne explained to her mother, still laughing.

"Oh, music, is that all you are plotting? That, I will allow, but I cannot have you two deliberately making our hostess uncomfortable." She tried to look stern, but their jollity was infectious.

"No, indeed, Mama, Fanny does that well enough for herself. Surely, not even Fanny can have any objections to carols at Christmas?" Margaret reassured her mother, who knew their lively dispositions too well. Satisfied, she turned to Margaret, glad to see the roses back in her daughter's cheeks and her spirits returning to normal.

"I see you have fully recovered, Margaret. I didn't bother you yesterday, but have you thought about the subject we discussed after the party?"

"Marianne and Elinor know all about it, Mama, so you needn't be obtuse. Yes, I have given the matter some thought, and I can tell you that I do admire Charles Dashwood, and that is all I will admit to. We must all wait patiently and see how it develops from there." Margaret was adamant, and her mother wisely let the subject drop.

"Very well, my child, there is no need to rush things. We will do as you ask and wait and see." She turned back to Marianne, suddenly observing her middle daughter didn't look quite herself.

"Now, it is you looking a little pale this morning, Marianne. Are you quite well?"

"Yes, Mama, only a little tired. I admit, it has been rather a strain being at Norland again. Everywhere, there are memories of dear Papa and our former lives here together."

"Indeed, Mama, everyone forgets this used to be our home," agreed Margaret with feeling, acknowledging that Marianne did look rather tired now that she came to think about it.

The Christmas carols were a great success, more especially as dinner was a subdued affair following the loss of several guests and their hostess was particularly out of sorts. Without Miss Parker and her constant supply of flattery and admiration, Fanny felt listless and bored with the remaining company, with which she had little in common. John, the colonel and Charles Dashwood remained longer over their port as if to escape the tedium of the drawing room, but when they eventually joined the ladies, an unexpectedly lively scene presented itself. As usual, Marianne was seated at the pianoforte, but instead of her normal choice, she was playing Christmas music and around her stood Margaret, Mrs Dashwood and Marguerite Dashwood, all singing along in harmony. Even Fanny was tapping her foot in time to the rousing music. Charles Dashwood was entranced and immediately went over to join them. To the delight of the female singers, his fine baritone added the depth needed to compliment the three sopranos superbly. Then, he and his mother were persuaded to sing a duet, much to the delight of their audience. Halfway through their song, Marianne suddenly faltered at the piano, swaying a little giddily.

"Please forgive me," she said, lifting her hand to her forehead, attempting to stand but falling to the floor in a dead faint. Margaret gasped in horror, as there was no doubt that this swoon was genuine. For a second or two, nobody moved until Colonel Brandon picked up his wife and carried her to the sofa, whilst everyone moved to assist him at once.

"Stand back, stand back, give her some air," he ordered with military authority. "Dashwood, pray come and advise me. What is the matter with my wife?" Charles went to his side immediately, dismissing everyone from the drawing room whilst he proceeded to examine Marianne.

"Give me time to ascertain what is wrong with her," he insisted to the departing company.

"I need no assistance, but her sister's, who should remain for the protection of Mrs Brandon's modesty." He threw Margaret a meaningful look, and she took the hint, ushering everyone out of the room. Whilst Charles began his examination, she stood and watched him with her sister, in silent concern, before he looked up and smiled with satisfaction.

"Miss Margaret, I believe you may now fetch the colonel." Margaret hurried from the room to do his bidding and was pleased to see Marianne propped up on the sofa when she returned with the colonel, who looked questioningly at Charles. He was quick to reassure him, pouring Marianne a glass of wine before handing one to the colonel and Margaret. "Let me assure you that there is absolutely nothing to worry about. It is the most natural thing in the world. In fact, may I be the first to congratulate you, Colonel, as you and your wife are expecting your first child?" he explained happily, grinning widely from ear to ear, clearly delighted to be the bearer of such joyful tidings. At first, the colonel stood stock still as if unable to believe his ears, then he rushed forward to embrace his wife as Margaret and Charles discretely left the room. Outside, they were accosted by Mrs Dashwood, who received the news that Marianne was pregnant with tears of joy. It was with some difficulty they were able to persuade her to give the happy couple a few minutes alone together. At length, the colonel threw open the door and bid them all return to his wife's side, and Mrs Dashwood was the first over the threshold.

"My dearest Marianne, how positively wonderful! Colonel, I'm so happy for you both!" cried Mrs Dashwood in ecstasy. Margaret found herself so overjoyed she could hardly contain herself and shook the colonel's hand repeatedly, expressing her delight over and over again. Fanny alone did not return to congratulate the Brandons but sent her maid to say she had retired, thus leaving John to say all that was proper on her behalf. This he did with some embarrassment, aware of her rudeness, calling for a bottle of his finest claret to offer a toast to compensate for his wife's absence. He need not have worried as nobody missed her presence. Finally, the colonel insisted that Marianne had exerted herself enough for one evening and helped her up to bed. John also excused himself, and Mrs Dashwood, unwilling to let Marianne out of her sight, followed her and the colonel upstairs, hovering on the landing, in case there was anything she could do to help.

Thus, only three guests remained in the drawing room, and Marguerite was quick to replace Marianne at the pianoforte. She discarded the festive melodies, opting instead for a quiet concerto, taking full advantage of this unexpected opportunity of leaving Charles and Margaret to talk alone. Margaret was full of eager questions for him.

"Is it quite normal to faint in the early stages of pregnancy, Mr Dashwood?" Margaret demanded, her shyness overcome by worry for her sister now that the initial excitement was over. He reassured her as best he could.

"You must not concern yourself, Miss Margaret. It is not unusual, and Mrs Brandon had perhaps overexerted herself at the pianoforte tonight." Margaret had to agree with him on that point.

"Yes, Marianne is a very enthusiastic musician. In fact, she does nothing by halves."

"Nevertheless, she will need to take care of herself from here onwards, Miss Margaret." He regarded her seriously. "May I take you into my confidence as I do not wish to alarm your mother and the colonel at this stage?"

"Go on," Margaret urged with wide eyes, now even more concerned for her sister.

"I think you are a sensible young woman, and Mrs Brandon will need to be encouraged to rest, perhaps more than her restless nature will allow. In my opinion, this pregnancy will not be an easy one, especially in the early stages, although I hope, for Mrs Brandon's sake, I am wrong. I will, of course, have a word with the colonel tomorrow, but you may have more influence with your sister. Wives tend to be of the opinion that their husbands fuss over them unnecessarily."

"What makes you think Marianne will have a difficult time in the early stages?" Margaret couldn't help questioning his diagnosis, extremely alarmed for her sister.

"Experience, Miss Margaret, simply that. I can see that Marianne has a delicate constitution and a sensitive nature."

"It was not always so, Mr Dashwood, but an episode of ill health in the past has left her with a weakened constitution," Margaret explained.

"I confess, I guessed as much. Perhaps an affair of the heart that did not match up to her romantic expectations." He looked quizzically at Margaret, and she nodded, surprised at his intuitive guess.

"Something of that sort, Mr Dashwood; more I cannot reveal, as it's not my story to tell. You may rest assured, however, I have heard and understood your instructions, and Marianne will want for nothing," she reassured him, a plan forming in her head, and he nodded, smiling his approval.

"I knew I could rely on you, Miss Margaret," he said, taking her hand in gratitude and making her heart miss a beat. Margaret's feelings were divided between alarm for her sister and pleasure at the compliment he gave her.

Chapter 12
London

Christmas at Norland came and went in such an unremarkable way that it bore no resemblance to the Christmases Margaret remembered from childhood. The New Year, which would normally have demanded a dance, at least, was celebrated equally quietly because of an unexpected turn of events. Mrs Ferrars' sudden illness had sadly proved fatal, and she died of a seizure two days after Christmas, leaving the whole family plunged into mourning. Mrs Dashwood reluctantly set off for Devon, instinctively wishing to remain with Marianne but feeling unable to prolong her stay at Norland in the current circumstances. Charles Dashwood returned to the care of his London patients, promising to call on Mrs Brandon the moment she returned to town. On the fourth of January, Margaret returned to Grosvenor Street in the company of Fanny and John, whilst the Brandons left for Bath Square, giving a place in their carriage to Marguerite Dashwood. It had been clear to Margaret, during the interim period, Charles Dashwood had been correct in his prognosis. Marianne, unlike Elinor, was not going to have an uncomplicated pregnancy. On the contrary, she had been listless and suffering from nausea so badly at times, she had not left her bedchamber.

Margaret was greatly concerned for her and said as much to Fanny and John in the carriage on their way back to Grosvenor Street.

"Dear John and Fanny, I fear that I will offend you by declining to trespass on your hospitality further. I cannot remain with you at Grosvenor Street any longer as I will be needed in Bath Square. When I accepted your offer to launch me this season, no one could have foreseen this change of circumstances. The unexpected demise of Mrs Ferrars has also altered your situation, and you are now in mourning for your mother, Fanny, and must have long been desiring my absence. I quite understand that it would not be acceptable for you to chaperone me to the rest of the parties and balls of the season. Please allow me to express my gratitude for everything you have done for me, but my sister is in need of my assistance, and that must be my first consideration." Margaret's tone was adamant, not least because it was a way of ending her stay at Grosvenor Street on legitimate grounds. She could see that John was very disappointed but had no choice but to acknowledge the truth of her statements. It was undeniable that it would be improper for Fanny to chaperone Margaret in the current circumstances. Fanny was delighted, although she remained silent, continuing to stare out of the carriage window but not before Margaret caught sight of her triumphant smile reflected in the glass window. She turned back to Margaret, once she had rearranged her features into a more sombre expression.

"Of course, Miss Margaret, we quite understand your sentiments and that you must be with your sister at this time," she confirmed. "I am sure we are both in agreement." She looked at John, but he didn't reply.

"What you say is true. It would not be seemly for us to escort you to parties and balls in the circumstances." John looked miserable but could not gainsay his wife, and Margaret thanked them both graciously for their forbearance. Fanny saw her opportunity, turning immediately to John with a suggestion, taking full advantage of the moment.

"Perhaps we could invite the Miss Parkers again, my dear? That would compensate us for the loss of Miss Margaret. I believe dear Miss Parker would be willing to sacrifice all the entertainments of the season for an invitation from me." Margaret smiled to herself, thinking how right Fanny was. There was nothing Miss Parker wouldn't do to further the connection between herself and certain members of the Dashwood family. John was clearly shocked by her proposal and said so.

"Fanny, you would think of having guests to stay at Grosvenor Street with your mother so recently deceased?"

"Really, John, I am surprised by your objection. What could be more appropriate as Miss Margaret must leave us, than to invite the Miss Parkers to keep me company? Of course, I would not think of chaperoning them to balls, nor would they expect it in the circumstances, but their cheerful company would keep me from melancholic reflection at the loss of dear Mama. Surely, you do not expect me to be entirely alone?" Fanny threw in for good measure. Unfortunately, John was unable to think of a reason to deny her request, especially as he felt guilty of neglect, but Margaret saw he was less than enthusiastic about her proposal.

Margaret, however, was delighted at the turn of events, not because of her sister's temporary indisposition but because it meant she was able to quit Grosvenor Street with good reason. It was the perfect excuse for putting an end to her enforced stay at Grosvenor Street and Fanny's irksome company without giving offence. She felt sorry for John, who had done his best to make her feel welcome. Nevertheless, he had achieved his object handsomely and made amends for his lack of assistance on her father's death. No expense had been spared on equipping her for the season, and she would always feel grateful to him, but it was time for her removal to Bath Square. Her one regret was Lily, who was really upset to see her go and loath to miss out on the opportunity of dressing her young mistress for the rest of the season.

"Oh, miss, I do understand; really, I do, but I wish I could accompany you to Bath Square." Margaret heard her laments with sadness but was powerless to do anything about them.

"I'm afraid Fanny will never allow that, Lily; besides, if she has her way, you will soon have two other young ladies to dress," Margaret consoled her, while Lily expertly packed Margaret's belongings into bandboxes and valises for their imminent transportation. Lily sighed heavily.

"Yes, miss, I have been informed the Miss Parkers are to be invited, but that will be no consolation. If you remember, I am already acquainted with the Miss Parkers. Mrs Dashwood made me wait on them at Norland when I was not occupied with you," said Lily unenthusiastically. "Besides, I do not think there will be balls and parties now that Mrs Ferrars is dead," she wailed. "Although I am certain of one thing: that Miss Caroline Parker will keep me busy. She positively delights in having someone to order around. Will you have your own maid to look after you in Bath Square?" Lily enquired wistfully.

"No, Lily, no such luxury, I'm afraid. I must go back to shifting for myself. I dare say I will share my sister's maid on special occasions, and you have taught me so much in the last few months that I am confident enough to fend for myself again. In any case, I don't think there will be balls and engagements until Marianne is considerably better, but I will bear it as best as I can, and so must you. Take heart, Lily, something will turn up for someone with your qualifications, and if Fanny is too perverse to give you a reference, then you can come to me." Margaret was resolutely cheerful, shaking Lily's hand affectionately before she went downstairs to take her leave of Fanny and John, relieved to see that Lily had brightened a little at the prospect of finding employment elsewhere. John was very kind, but it was clear Fanny could barely contain her impatience for her to be gone, smiling triumphantly as she gave Margaret her hand in farewell. It transpired that Fanny had lost no time in inviting the Miss Parkers, and the carriage that arrived to transport Margaret and her belongings to Bath Square also brought the Miss Parkers and their luggage to Grosvenor Street. Margaret was surprised to see them so soon but studiously ignored the look of venom Miss Parker bestowed on her before her departure. Fanny was on the steps to greet them in person, overjoyed that matters had taken this turn for the better. Unbeknown to Fanny, however, Margaret was equally overjoyed to be on her way, her happiness only marred by her pity for Lily.

The Miss Parkers had hardly arrived at Grosvenor Street when Fanny ordered Lily to wait on them, and she went reluctantly to their chamber to do her bidding. She was not looking forward to being at the beck and call of Miss Parker again. The lady was clearly unused to the luxury of having a maid and tended to abuse her position shamefully. Lily was not impressed by the Miss Parkers, who gave themselves airs beyond their station. Miss Caroline was imperious and demanding and Miss Catherine uncommunicative and sullen. It was a sad exchange for Miss Margaret. While Lily hung their gowns in the closet, she couldn't help noticing they were of poor quality, having been designed for show rather than wear. She sniffed in contempt, thinking some of Miss Caroline's gowns were positively vulgar in the low cut of the neckline. What was her mama thinking of? It was true that they were both pretty enough in their way, but their upbringing sadly let them down. Lily made no allowances for them being poor as Miss Margaret was also poor and there was a world of difference in the way she conducted herself.

She looked up as the young ladies entered the chamber and noted, with great indignation, they began making themselves at home immediately in the chamber so recently vacated by Margaret. They were clearly delighted to be in such grand surroundings, exclaiming over the quality of the furnishings and fingering the plush curtains. Lily continued about her business, whilst the Miss Parkers took no notice of Lily's presence. Or, most likely, they thought it of no consequence that a mere maid overheard their conversation. Miss Catherine was the first to speak, as if she had something on her mind.

"What will you do, Caroline, if he really prefers Miss Margaret? How can you hope to make him alter his opinion?" Miss Catherine enquired of her sister earnestly, and her sister replied with some impatience, as if repeating a lesson to a child.

"Oh, Catherine, what a bother you make over nothing! Fanny told me just now that she will speak to him at the earliest opportunity and tell him that she considers his attentions to me too marked to be ignored. She has promised to impress upon him that he has given rise to expectations he is expected to fulfil and he cannot go about trifling with young ladies' affections. In short, she will appeal to his better nature as a gentleman, and Fanny is skilled at getting what she wants." Caroline smiled conspiratorially at her sister, who looked horrified.

"But consider, sister, is that a wise course of action if he really loves another? If Fanny forces his hand, it cannot bode well for your future happiness together." Catherine argued, making Lily think she had misjudged the younger sister by tarring her with the same brush as the elder. Caroline shrugged her shoulders with complete indifference.

"Really, Catherine, you know nothing of the world and are not qualified to judge in this matter. Surely, you remember the old adage, that all is fair in love and war. What care I that Charles Dashwood loves Miss Margaret? What has love got to do with anything in a marriage contract? The important thing is that he will be impelled by Fanny to do what is right for me. Marriage is simply about the acquisition of an establishment, and, for me, I would prefer that establishment to be Norland. Consider, Catherine, such a fine estate and a house in town. What more could a girl wish for so? I'm certainly not going to allow the small inconvenience of his affections for Miss Margaret to stand in my way, if indeed they do exist. I cannot say I've seen any evidence of an attraction between them." Caroline saw that her sister still remained unconvinced. "Simply put, my dear sister, if Charles Dashwood can be persuaded to make me an offer, then I will accept him, of course."

Lily was appalled but not greatly surprised by Caroline Parker's mercenary view of marriage and felt distinctly sorry for Mr Charles Dashwood.

Catherine was silent, clearly shocked by her sister's statements but unable to think of anything else that might induce her sister to give him up. Although, she deplored her sister's reasoning in a way she understood. Mama had gone to great lengths to impress upon them that this was their one and only chance and they had to make the most of it, making it abundantly clear she had used up every ounce of credit to equip them for the season and rent the London house. Caroline was only acting as instructed and making the most of her opportunities. Catherine sighed, contemplating her dismal future as an old maid, constantly scolded by her parents for being a failure. Not having Caroline's brazenness, she couldn't create opportunities where none existed, and it simply was not in her nature to compromise young men into making her an offer. It just wasn't her way. Meanwhile, Lily stored up the information to give to her young mistress at the earliest opportunity.

Chapter 13
An Unexpected Windfall

Fanny had just time to greet the Miss Parkers in person before setting off in the carriage for the reading of her mother's will, which was delayed specifically until her return from Norland. She was not looking forward to such a tedious duty, and she would much rather have spent the morning gossiping with her dear friend, Caroline, but Fanny felt obliged to attend, if only for the sake of appearances. It was just a formality as her mother had dished out the money years ago, and Fanny had long been aware the house was to go to Robert. Robert had already inherited the money that was Edward's birthright when Edward refused to give up Miss Steele. If Fanny wondered at the irony of this situation, she had never once pointed out to her mother that it was her favourite son, Robert, who had actually married Miss Steele. Despite this, his mother had not been able to reverse the decision to disinherit Edward. Such was her anger with her eldest son, she had settled all upon Robert irrevocably and could not turn back the clock, even if she wanted to. The fact that Robert's marriage had been far worse, in terms of want of connection, than Edward's to Elinor Dashwood seemed to have completely escaped her mother's notice. There it was; Fanny knew that Robert could do no wrong in his mother's eyes, and there was no changing that now she was dead. Poor Edward had sent word from Devon he would not be attending the reading, having no reason to expect anything from his mother at this late stage. His duty to his hard-hearted mother had gone as far as attending her funeral, although neither Elinor nor Kitty made the journey. In the end, it had just been the three of them present at the old lady's interment.

The forbidding house was plunged into even greater gloom by the recent demise of its severe proprietor, and Fanny's spirits sank as she crossed the threshold of her childhood home. Although the building was older than the house at Grosvenor Street, Mrs Ferrars had refused to spend a penny on its improvement, meaning nothing had changed in two generations. Despite the efforts of the servants, to Fanny, it smelt strongly of decay. Robert would have his work cut out if he were to make it a fashionable residence, and he was welcome to it, thought Fanny with a shudder. An elderly servant, wearing a sombre expression, showed her into the morning room, where she was awaited by Robert and the family lawyer, who was shuffling his papers impatiently at her late appearance. After greeting them both perfunctorily, Fanny sat down for the reading of her mother's last will and testament, anticipating nothing but boredom, having received all monies due to her on the occasion of her marriage to John. At least, that is what Fanny had always thought. The old lawyer droned on, and Fanny was nearly asleep when he announced that Mrs Ferrars had an additional fortune she'd kept secret until now. Fanny's ears pricked up at this announcement, and Robert dropped the pen he was twisting with an audible gasp.

The lawyer was amused to find he suddenly had the full attention of the two younger Ferrars children, and it delighted him to observe Fanny's irritation when he paused and cleared his throat. He proceeded to explain that this additional sum was to be divided between Robert, Fanny and Edward. Edward, the eldest but his mother's least favourite, and out of favour because he'd engaged himself to Lucy, then married Elinor against his mother's wishes, was left the sum of five thousand pounds. Although this was not exactly stated in her mother's will, it was quite clear she meant Edward to know she had never forgiven him, right up until the end. It hadn't crossed her mind that Edward could be absent at the reading of her will. To Fanny, her only daughter, she bequeathed fifteen thousand pounds, to be drawn up in such a way as to keep it entirely independent of her husband. Fanny, although speechless with surprise, couldn't help a wry smile at this. Mrs Ferrars' inherent distrust of men, instilled in her by an aggressive father and an ill-tempered husband, had endured until the very end. Finally, Robert, her favourite and the only man she could bear, was also to receive fifteen thousand pounds, as well as the house, which he had been expecting.

Robert jumped up from his seat and cheered loudly, completely ignoring the lawyer's look of distaste at this disrespectful display of emotion. Fanny remained silent, her head reeling, trying to take in the magnitude of this unexpected legacy.

"Well, well, the miserly old skinflint," crowed his mother's favourite child, vastly pleased with the turn of events, as the lawyer sniffed in disgust.

"Poor Edward," said Fanny, finding her voice at last. "To only have five thousand pounds. Mother carried her resentment to the grave." Robert did not agree with her sentiments and had no hesitation in giving his opinion of his elder brother's prospects.

"Not at all, my dear sister. What would Edward do with more money? I'm sure he has none of the expenses of a man of fashion, and our mother understood that. Now, he is to have five thousand pounds, which he didn't expect. Besides, my dear sister, Edward has not taken the trouble to attend, so he will never know that our share is much greater. Do not waste your sympathy on Edward, Fanny; he will be vastly contented. What need could he have, in Devonshire, for anything more?" Fanny observed that Robert continued to be selfishly dismissive of his elder brother's claims. She was not so sorry for Edward, however, that it would induce her to part with any of her share of this unexpected windfall.

"Very well, brother, we will keep this to ourselves and tell no one of the additional money. Let them all think we each inherited five thousand pounds."

Robert then proceeded to inform her that he had no intention of keeping the family mausoleum and would sell it immediately to the highest bidder. This was done in the hearing of the family lawyer, who knew it had been the darling wish of his mother that her favourite son would live there. Sometimes it was very hard for Fanny to understand why her mother had been so besotted with her younger son.

Driving home in the carriage, Fanny calculated that, together with the sum settled on her when she married John, which had accrued interest while mostly left untouched, added to this new inheritance of fifteen thousand pounds, she was now a very rich woman. Her fortune amounted to the considerable sum of thirty thousand pounds, and due to her mother's latent distrust of the male sex, it was entirely independent of her husband. This was a circumstance so utterly unexpected that Fanny's head was still reeling. She prided herself on being level-headed and calculating, but this unexpected legacy had taken her completely by surprise. Despite her confusion, she had already come to one decision: that she was not going to tell her husband of this unforeseen turn of events. Robert had agreed to secrecy; in fact, he had suggested it himself. The two younger Ferrars siblings had no real loyalty to anyone but themselves.

She tapped her umbrella smartly on the roof of the coach as a signal to the coachman to pull over.

"I wish to walk a while in the park," she curtly informed him as she got out. "Please drive the coach back to Grosvenor Street, and I will return on foot in an hour or two." If the coachman was surprised at this unusual behaviour on the part of his mistress, he dared not say so. He merely nodded respectfully and drove off. Fanny watched the coach turn the corner before setting off in the opposite direction of the park. A short walk took her to a pretty terrace of modern houses in a less fashionable part of town. Hesitating for just a moment, she knocked smartly on the door of the shabbiest. Shortly afterwards, the door was opened by a male servant, who knew better than to show any curiosity at the unexpected arrival of a female visitor. Nearly two hours later, Fanny emerged, somewhat flushed in the face and a little agitated in manner. Despite the lateness of the hour, she resolved to walk home in order to give herself time to compose herself.

Chapter 14
Bath Square

Although Margaret was overjoyed to be in Bath Square, she missed the elegant proportions of the Grosvenor Street House. The rented house was rather smaller, and the room allotted to Margaret was half the size of her previous abode and rather plain. She chided herself for having become spoiled, especially when remembering her cramped bedchamber at Barton Cottage. Margaret was the only one of the Dashwood girls who had never quite become used to their change in fortune, and she still missed Norland more than anyone. This was not surprising, as she had yet to leave the family nest. Her sisters had their own establishments to look after and thus took all their attention. Norland had been blessed with so many interesting nooks and crannies, providing ample opportunity for hiding herself away. Nevertheless, she was somewhat ashamed to be hankering after the old ways and would never have admitted it to her mother or sisters. It was the main reason she spent so much time out of doors as it was impossible to feel cramped in the open air. Latterly, she also missed the luxury of having a personal maid, especially one as talented as Lily, and their easy friendship.

All the same, Margaret could not regret her decision to leave Grosvenor Street as Marianne's health had not improved and Margaret was in constant attendance on her sister. Marianne felt so ill, it was no hardship to keep to her room, and there was no necessity to persuade her to rest. Whenever he could spare the time, the colonel read to his wife in the hopes of keeping up her spirits. Margaret was frequently called on to sit with her sister when he had to go out on business, although she would have willingly done so more often.

"Oh dear, Margaret," repined Marianne on one such occasion, the morning after her arrival. "You are not here as a nursemaid to me but to make the most of the London season. We cannot have you as the proverbial 'desert flower'." Margaret did not hesitate to reassure her sister.

"You know I care naught for that. The most important thing is your health and the safe delivery of your child. Although, I must admit, it was quite a surprise to find out that you are pregnant. Had you no symptoms before?" Margaret gently bathed her sister's flushed face with lavender water, ignoring the implication that she must be out in society in order to make a good match. Marianne shook her head emphatically

"No, not until the night I fainted at Norland. I have often missed my courses before so thought nothing of it. I have been so long in conceiving, I suppose I gave up looking for it to happen." Marianne clapped her hand to her mouth as another wave of nausea shook her, and Margaret fetched the basin, offering words of consolation.

"I have heard that the sickness does not last full term, so, with luck, it will soon subside." She wiped Marianne's face again with the cool cloth, as she fell back against the pillows, exhausted. Her pallor was so alarming that Margaret considered calling for the doctor early. She was expecting him to visit that morning anyway, but before she could ring the bell, he was announced by Marianne's maid. Margaret's heart missed a beat as Charles Dashwood entered the sick room, but she jumped up from her sister's bedside in relief.

"Mr Dashwood, I am so very glad to see you!" cried Margaret, making way for him to go to her sister. "Marianne is no better, as you can see. The sickness is almost constant, which means she is receiving very little nourishment." Charles sat down by Marianne to take her pulse, and Margaret watched his skilled bedside manner, admiring the way he quickly put her sister at ease whilst he carried out his examination. Surprisingly, he then turned to Margaret as if speaking to an equal.

"Some physicians would advise bleeding at this stage, but I am not one of them, Miss Margaret. This nausea seems bad, but it will pass, and in the meantime, Mrs Brandon must take as much nourishment in liquid form as she can manage. Miss Margaret, can I trouble you to ask the cook to make a batch of chicken broth, and I will make up an herbal tonic that will help with the sickness."

"Of course, Mr Dashwood. What herbs will you use?" Margaret asked curiously, very conscious that she seemed to hold his trust.

"Mint will form the main component, I think," he replied absently whilst continuing his examination, taking his time before pronouncing his judgement to the ladies.

"The child is the right size and all appears healthy, so there is nothing to concern yourself with, Mrs Brandon. Rest as much as you can, and you will soon be up and about again. The sickness does not usually last beyond three months, and childbearing is a natural occurrence, not an illness, although it may not seem so at the moment." Marianne nodded ruefully.

"That is all very well, Mr Dashwood, but I had hoped to attend the concert tomorrow night with Margaret. I cannot have her cooped up with me when she should be making the most of her time in London," Marianne lamented, again becoming upset to be the reason that Margaret was missing engagements. Charles Dashwood smiled down at her reassuringly.

"If that is your only worry, Mrs Brandon, then let me put your mind at rest. My mother and I are to attend the concert tomorrow, and we would be delighted to escort Miss Margaret." Marianne smiled at him in gratitude.

"Mr Dashwood, how kind of you. I confess that is the perfect solution!" she cried in relief, and he turned to Margaret, to see her looking extremely embarrassed.

"Then we will call for you here at seven o'clock, Miss Margaret. If that is agreeable to you?" Margaret thanked him sincerely, really happy she would now be able to attend the concert, especially as the programme was very much to her taste.

"I should be delighted to accompany you and your mother, Mr Dashwood." She smiled at him shyly and was surprised when he smiled back.

"Very well, then it is settled. I will send over the tincture this afternoon. Until tomorrow, ladies." He gave them both a small bow, but Margaret detained him, feeling compelled to add something.

"Before you leave, Mr Dashwood, permit me to say, I have also found camomile to be of great help with nausea with the added effect; it is calming to the nervous system." She braced herself for ridicule, but none came. Charles Dashwood merely bowed again and took his leave.

"Until tomorrow, Miss Margaret," he repeated, and later that day, two packages arrived from Charles Dashwood for Marianne: a tincture of peppermint to be taken before the chicken broth and a tincture of camomile to be taken before bed.

Not for the first time since her arrival in Bath Square, Margaret felt the loss of Lily's sound advice and experience. She changed her mind numerous times, having already pulled three gowns from the closet. If it hadn't been for the timely arrival of Marianne's maid, she would have been in danger of keeping the Dashwoods waiting. They fixed on a white muslin embroidered with the palest of blue spots, to be covered by a warm pelisse as the mild weather was over and January had turned very wintry indeed. Snow was falling lightly as the carriage left Bath Square, but thanks to the assistance of Marianne's maid, they arrived at the concert room in good time and were able to procure good seats near the front with an excellent view of the orchestra. Charles sat between them and explained the meaning of the pieces to her as the majority were sung in Italian, of which Margaret had no knowledge. It appeared there was no end to his talents, and Margaret was very conscious that French was all she had learnt in the schoolroom. His understanding of Italian was impressive, and she complimented him on his skills, but he modestly explained that a doctor must learn Latin, which is the key to many European languages.

"Of course, Mr Dashwood, now I understand; it is so with plant names. I hadn't thought of that." Just then, the performance began, and they turned their attention to the music. Margaret, though spellbound by the performance, was nevertheless acutely aware of Charles Dashwood's presence beside her. Inexplicably, this seemed to heighten her appreciation of the heavenly music, and she was extremely sorry when it came to an end.

During the interval, Charles escorted the ladies to the crowded refreshment room, and Margaret looked about her curiously as her heart sank.

"Look, there is Fanny and the Miss Parkers!" exclaimed Margaret in surprise at seeing them out and about as Fanny was in deep mourning. Fanny simultaneously spied the Dashwood party and was equally surprised and dismayed that Margaret had deserted Marianne so soon after her arrival. She was also seriously displeased to see her in the company of Charles Dashwood and resolved to do something about it immediately, raising her hand to beckon them over imperiously. Margaret rose to the bait, seeing Fanny's disapproving scowl, feeling obliged to join them, if only to explain her presence at the concert.

"Pray excuse me for a few minutes, I must pay my respects to Fanny." She turned apologetically to her companions.

"We will all pay our respects to Mrs Dashwood and the Miss Parkers, Miss Margaret. Come, Charles," said Marguerite determinedly, rising from her seat, having noted Fanny's expression and unwilling to let Margaret face Fanny alone. Caroline Parker smiled ecstatically at Charles as they approached, but Margaret saw he did not return her enthusiasm, merely greeting all the ladies with a cold little bow. Caroline did not trouble herself to speak to Margaret, and Fanny merely nodded to her and Marguerite without any pretence of warmth, having no liking for either.

"How does your sister, Miss Margaret? I had not thought to see you out so soon," she queried with a look of disapproval, always quick to imply criticism, but Margaret was ready for Fanny's slights.

"Unfortunately, my sister is still unwell, but the colonel is with her tonight; thus, Marguerite kindly invited me to join them for the concert," replied Margaret without mentioning Charles' hand in the invitation, knowing instinctively it would be misread by Fanny and her companions. Fanny raised an eyebrow before turning her attention to Charles, whom she greeted with a little more animation, drawing him aside so the rest of the party could not hear their conversation. The polite exchanges of the others went unheard by Margaret, who was straining every muscle to hear what was passing between them, burning with curiosity as to what Fanny could possibly have to say to Charles so privately. The more Fanny said, the more his face darkened, until he looked positively thunderous.

When they eventually returned to their seats for the second half of the concert, Margaret was acutely aware that Charles was not attending at all. Margaret, too, found herself unable to concentrate, wondering what Fanny had said to upset him so. He continued in silent introspection all the way back to Bath Square, and nothing could draw him into the conversation. Margaret tried to catch Marguerite's eye, but she, too, was withdrawn, clearly affected by the strained atmosphere. Margaret was dismayed beyond belief and excessively disappointed to be deprived of hearing his translation of the second half. It had been a most unsatisfactory end to the evening, and she knew Fanny was to blame.

The following day, Margaret was seated in the morning room, in the process of writing to her mother and Elinor, when Marguerite Dashwood was shown in. They had become firm friends during their stay at Norland, and Margaret was very pleased to see her again so soon. "How does your sister, Miss Margaret?" she first enquired solicitously.

"Unfortunately, she is no better and still keeps to her room. The sickness is almost constant at this stage," Margaret replied, sure this was not the reason for her visit as her son would keep her abreast of Marianne's state of health. Watching in surprise as her guest rose and paced the floor for a few moments, she then turned to Margaret in some agitation.

"Miss Margaret, I confess I had hoped to find you alone, as I have had some distressing news. May I confide in you?" She sat down again, twisting her wedding ring nervously, before speaking again. Margaret was alarmed, unused to such displays of emotion from the older woman, and she answered her question in concern.

"Marguerite, you know you may rely on me to be discreet, and you have my full attention for whatever it is you wish to say," she reassured Marguerite, seeing her hesitation.

"I hardly know how to begin. It appears my foolish son has compromised himself with a young lady, and I am sure you can guess her identity." Marguerite sighed in frustration.

"Are we talking of Miss Caroline Parker?" Margaret's heart sank.

"Indeed, we are, Miss Margaret. Fanny accuses him of trifling with Caroline Parker's affections, and I know, to some extent, it is true. I warned him of it myself, but he wouldn't listen. It seems, Fanny and the Miss Parkers have all been expecting him to propose to Caroline at any moment. You must have noticed Fanny draw him aside last night, and that is what she had to say to him. Needless to say, Charles does not return Caroline Parker's affections, but I fear he may have gone too far to withdraw honourably." Margaret bit her lip uncertainly before replying, wondering how much knowledge she could reveal at this stage.

"I confess, I did know of this as Catherine Parker let slip that Caroline expected his proposal, but this was also borne out by what I saw for myself. I am afraid to say that his behaviour to Miss Caroline did appear preferential, even to me." Margaret felt obliged to point this out, in fairness, despite her abhorrence of the situation. Marguerite nodded.

"It is true; I cannot deny it, Miss Margaret, there is something in what you say, but he assured me yesterday that he doesn't care for her at all." Marguerite paused, also considering her choice of words to explain her son's behaviour. "It's all such a terrible muddle. It appears what started as a ruse to show his independence of choice has caught him up in the most compromising way." Marguerite was clearly very distressed at the thought of her son wasting his life on a woman he didn't care for, and Margaret decided this was not the moment to enlighten her that she knew why Charles had felt such a ruse necessary.

"Oh dear, this is a predicament indeed, if what you say is true. What will he do, Marguerite?"

"Charles first learnt of his mistake at Norland, having further compromised himself there. Miss Catherine Parker is so innocent that she took it upon herself to congratulate him on his forthcoming engagement to her sister. Needless to say, he was horrified and came straight to me. I advised him to absent himself without delay, and that is what took him from Norland for several days before the Christmas Ball. We thought that his absence would lessen her expectations, but that has not been the case. Unfortunately, Fanny confirmed this last night, but I'm sure she has had a hand in keeping Caroline's hopes burning bright. Apparently, Charles has made the lady very unhappy! Although I can scarcely believe she is capable of any deep feeling." Margaret could not help but agree. If Miss Caroline's emotions could be described, then anger might be more appropriate than unhappiness. Her pursuit of Charles Dashwood depended more upon Charles' prospects than any great affection for him. She did not voice her opinion and waited in uncomfortable silence for Marguerite to answer her question.

"I am very sorry to say, Miss Margaret, he intends to propose to Miss Caroline Parker. What else can he honourably do?"

"I am very sorry for it, Marguerite," Margaret answered truthfully, in some distress. "It is a great shame to marry without affection, but in all honesty, I do not think there is an alternative course of action open to him."

Fanny Dashwood was feeling quite jubilant. How right she had been to bide her time until opportunities occurred. All things come to she who waits, she thought triumphantly. The irksome Margaret Dashwood had left Grosvenor Street and was safely ensconced in Bath Square with the Brandons, which meant that Fanny was free of her challenging company and prying eyes. Fanny felt sure that Margaret had been watching her and judging, as she felt judged by all of the Dashwood ladies, and she had long been desiring to be rid of her. Indeed, she had made several attempts to convince John that Margaret would be better off with her sister, but he wouldn't hear any of it. In the end, her removal to the Brandons' house in Bath Square was achieved without Fanny's interference, and John had been forced to let her go. This had given her the opportunity to invite the Miss Parkers in Margaret's stead, and John couldn't very well protest, as she had been deprived of the company of his sister through no fault of her own. She knew she could completely rely on Miss Caroline's loyalty, whatever happened, and, at this time, it was of great importance to Fanny that she had such an ally in her home for more reasons than one.

Almost at the same time when Marianne Brandon discovered herself with child, Fanny was also confirmed to be pregnant. At first, it had been a terrible shock that her affair with the captain had resulted in this outcome. Of course, she had taken no precautions, believing implicitly she was beyond the years of childbearing. Nevertheless, the more she thought about it, the more she was reconciled to it. As yet, she hadn't informed the captain about the child, and no one knew anything about their liaison, of which she was certain. She had given the captain enough money to ensure his loyalty and would continue to reward him handsomely for his discretion.

The difficulty she now faced was how to handle John. It was true, John was not the cleverest of men, but even he would not believe the child was his if they hadn't shared a bed in several years. She had a desperate plan, but if this failed, then she would have to make a clean breast of it. If John did not acknowledge the child, there would be a terrible scandal, and John was most particular about his reputation.

In addition, she had a trump card. This was the only chance left for John to retain the Norland inheritance, which, she knew, was very dear to his heart, but if neither of these two considerations had any weight, then Fanny had two other fish to fry. She was rich, and John had come to rely on the interest her fortune produced, despite the fact he had to gain her permission for the release of any monies. Nevertheless, he knew they were a back stop in case of an emergency. Fanny had also kept John in the dark about the other inheritance, clever enough to know she must keep some ammunition in reserve. It was always wise to keep some powder dry. In fact, the more she thought about it, the more she felt there was a very good chance of all being well.

Chapter 15
Unexpected News

Mercifully, over the next few days, Marianne's health improved slowly, and she was able to leave her chamber more regularly. Now, past three months into term, the nausea had ceased, as predicted, and the tinctures Charles Dashwood prescribed seemed to be doing their work well. One morning, over breakfast, she turned to the colonel with a request. "My dear, I think I am well enough now for us to give a little soiree. We really ought to have Fanny and John to dine; after all, we have deprived them of their guest, and I wish to thank them for inviting us to Norland for Christmas." He turned to her with an affectionate smile.

"Of course, my dear, if that is what you wish. I can see your health is much improved, and perhaps a little company would do us all good."

"I think I shall also invite Marguerite and Charles Dashwood, and I suppose we must have the Miss Parkers as they are staying with Fanny, although I would rather not. What do you think, Margaret? Can we exclude them?" Up until now, Margaret had been silent on the matter Marguerite discussed with her the day after the concert, but she couldn't let her unsuspecting sister invite Charles and Caroline together. She decided it was the right time to enlighten the Brandons of the full circumstances. In open-mouthed surprise, they listened to all she had to say before Marianne interjected in dismay.

"Good grief, Margaret. What a to do! It is my opinion, Caroline Parker is a calculating young woman and has completely drawn him in. What on earth induced him to choose her to flirt with? Any other girl would not have taken him seriously on so small a pretext. Caroline Parker and Fanny have joined forces and have him completely duped." Marianne voiced what Margaret had been thinking but dared not admit; however, the colonel was not so certain. His sympathies naturally lay with the young lady in these situations because of the seduction of his ward, Beth, at the hands of Willoughby.

"We cannot know that for certain, Marianne." He shook his head in disapproval of his wife's uncharitable outburst. "If he has given rise to expectations he did not intend to, then I pity him, but he must behave honourably towards the lady. It is the only gentlemanly thing to do in the circumstances. Perhaps it will all turn out well in the end. She seems a very good sort of girl," the colonel pronounced, and not for the first time in her life, Margaret observed how easily even the best of men could be fooled by a pretty face. Marianne was not sorry for her condemnation of Miss Parker's methods, but she didn't want to upset her husband.

"Very well, my dear, have it your way, but as we have not heard anything of the engagement, he may not have asked her, and perhaps he will not," Marianne speculated, clearly hoping it might never transpire, and the colonel agreed.

"Probably not; I agree that we would certainly have heard of it by now, as you say, Marianne. I believe Miss Parker would have ensured that the news was spread about. Indeed, it is in her interest to do so, especially if she considers her reputation to be tarnished in any way. Nevertheless, it could be excessively awkward to invite them here together. In my opinion, we should restrict our invitation to Fanny and John only, using the excuse that you are only well enough for a small family party. The Miss Parkers will understand, and I am sure they are capable of amusing themselves for one evening. Fanny and John will be able to update us with the latest news on the subject." The colonel's suggestion was a sensible one and was immediately agreed upon by the two sisters. Marianne duly sent Fanny a note, inviting them to dine the next day and swiftly received their acceptance. Marianne read her note aloud to Margaret in some dismay.

"Fanny and John are delighted to accept, and they have some interesting news to impart. That's it then, Margaret, Charles Dashwood has proposed to Caroline Parker, and we shall hear all about it tomorrow." She looked at her sister searchingly. "Pray tell me, Margaret, what are your feelings on the subject, bearing in mind our last conversation at Norland?"

"Marianne, we agreed we would let Mr Dashwood's behaviour be my guide, and his behaviour has led to this outcome. I must accept it, and so must he, whatever our secret wishes to the contrary." Margaret was determined to be stoical, however much she had hoped for another outcome, and Marianne admired her for her show of strength.

"You are certainly more like Elinor than myself, Margaret, but perhaps that is for the best in the circumstances," Marianne acknowledged with a sigh, thinking of her past mistakes.

Fanny and John arrived the next evening with an air of importance about them, but it was not until they were all seated around the dining table that they made their announcement. Margaret had been very surprised to see a change of behaviour in John towards his wife, fussing around her on arrival and making sure she was comfortable in a most unusual way. Margaret wondered what could possibly have occurred between them to effect such a change.

"You said you had some news to impart, Fanny. Pray do tell us, as we are all in suspense," Marianne began the conversation, looking at Fanny and John expectantly, and John cleared his throat importantly.

"Colonel and Mrs Brandon, Margaret, Fanny and I have some wonderful news to tell you," he said, looking at his wife fondly and taking her hand. "Fanny is expecting a child." For several seconds, no one spoke, shock registering on all their faces, but it was the colonel who recovered first, rising from the table and shaking John's hand with great cordiality.

"My dear, John and Fanny, please accept my sincere congratulations. This is wonderful news, indeed." By that time, Marianne and Margaret had recovered themselves enough to also offer their congratulations, although these were more subdued than the colonel's effusions, both still numb with disbelief.

"I have more good news," said Fanny when the excitement had died down. Now it comes, thought Margaret, bracing herself to hear the news of Caroline Parker's engagement to Charles Dashwood.

"This very morning, Mrs Lucy Ferrars gave birth to a healthy boy who is to be named Robert after his father. Our mother would have been so overjoyed." More congratulations flowed, and the colonel, on the strength of this double celebration, rang the bell for the butler to bring a bottle of his best claret.

"A toast to the newborn and the yet unborn." He raised his glass to the happy couple. When the excitement died down, Marianne couldn't rest until she knew for certain whether Charles Dashwood was engaged. She was determined that Margaret must not be kept in suspense any longer; it would be too cruel.

"I am sorry not to have invited the Miss Parkers as I know they are your guests, but the colonel thought it would be too much for me as this is my first social engagement since my indisposition." Marianne hoped by introducing the subject of the Miss Parkers, Fanny would remember to tell of the engagement, but Fanny had nothing to say on the subject.

"Please don't concern yourself, Marianne; they quite understood and have taken the opportunity of paying a visit to their mama this evening to tell them our good news and beg that Caroline can make a prolonged visit to us during this time. She really is a treasure; nothing is too much trouble, and I simply cannot do without her," gushed Fanny, looking pointedly at Margaret, who quickly hung her head to hide a smile of relief. If Miss Parker was to stay with Fanny for the ensuing months, then she was unlikely to be engaged to Charles Dashwood. She would have far too much to attend to if there was to be an immanent wedding to be able to devote time to Fanny, and as the fiancée of Charles Dashwood, she would have no further need for her patronage. Margaret looked up, catching Marianne's wide-eyed, questioning stare. She shook her head and shrugged her shoulders, as puzzled as Marianne.

"May I recommend the services of Charles Dashwood to you, Fanny? His tinctures have quite cured me of the acute sickness I was experiencing," said Marianne enthusiastically, but Fanny shook her head in askance.

"I have no wish to cast any doubt on his professional ability, Marianne, but I hardly think he would be the appropriate choice in the circumstances. My being with child could considerably change his prospects, so it may be construed that he would have a conflict of interest," Fanny replied reprovingly, and Marianne looked uncomfortable as she caught Fanny's meaning.

"Of course, I had not thought of that. You mean, if your child is a boy, then he will inherit Norland and not Charles Dashwood, although I hardly think he would allow that prospect to make him professionally negligent," Marianne defended him without reservation.

"No, I did not mean to imply that it would. Nevertheless, it would be very awkward to have him as my physician in such circumstances. In any case, I have been given another reliable recommendation by Lucy and have already employed him to look after me." Fanny was dismissive of Charles Dashwood, and Marianne chose not to pursue the conversation further. Margaret had also failed to see immediately how this news would affect Charles Dashwood. Of course, his prospects of inheriting Norland were diminished from certainty to a fifty-fifty chance. She couldn't help wondering if Caroline Parker was a gambler.

It was lucky for the extent of Margaret's curiosity that it was only three days later, on the thirty-first of January that the first of the New Year's assemblies was to be held. Margaret could only contain herself on the basis she would have the chance of speaking with Marguerite at the function. She had considered taking the drastic step of calling on Marguerite herself, but her courage failed at the thought of encountering Charles Dashwood. Dressing with unusual care, she chose the second of the ball gowns Fanny ordered for her, a pale lilac silk, its first outing. This was the one gown Margaret had chosen for herself, attracted by the delicate nature of the fabric, and she had to admit it was a success, despite Fanny's misgivings about the vulgarity of the colour. Marianne's maid, with much trial and error, had painstakingly tried to imitate Lily's skills with Margaret's hair, and tonight, Margaret was pleased to see her efforts had been rewarded. Her hair was piled high and studded with tiny jewels, with striking effect, and this view was endorsed by Marianne when she entered her sister's chamber to see if she was ready.

"You look absolutely charming, Margaret. What an elegant gown!" she cried admiringly, somewhat taken aback by her little sister's sophisticated appearance. If Charles Dashwood were present this evening, he would surely be unable to resist her.

The Brandon party arrived at the assembly in good time, seeing no need to make the fashionable entrance so vital to Fanny. In fact, they attached far more importance to the surety of obtaining convenient seats for Marianne's sake. Margaret ensured her sister was made comfortable before she allowed herself the luxury of scrutinising the assembled company. Spying Marguerite across the room, talking to a stranger, Margaret waved in greeting, trying to catch her eye. With great relief, she saw Marguerite excuse herself immediately and come towards them. She stopped to make polite conversation with the Brandons for a short while, enquiring particularly after Marianne's health, before asking Margaret to take a turn with her in the conservatory. Margaret promptly concurred, and the two of them made their way to the conservatory, arm in arm, oblivious of the admiring stares that followed their progress across the ballroom.

"You look very charming tonight, Miss Margaret," her friend complimented. "But I have news. You will not believe it, my dear, but Charles has been saved at the eleventh hour from a disastrous match."

"I wondered that we hadn't heard anything, Marguerite, but hardly dared hope that he had escaped." Margaret was all ears as Marguerite explained everything in a whisper, conscious the conservatory was also busy. Margaret was incredulous, unable to believe her ears.

"I don't understand," was all she could reply, feeling stunned, and Marguerite shortened her explanation to one sentence.

"Charles proposed to Caroline Parker and was refused." Margaret still stared at her in disbelief, as it was the last news she'd expected to hear.

"Refused? I cannot believe it. We were given to understand Miss Parker was counting on him in every way." Marguerite hastened to reassure Margaret of the veracity of her statements, despite their implausible nature.

"Nevertheless, he was refused. It seems she was not prepared to take on the latest uncertainty of his prospects caused by Fanny being with child. Of course, you will not be surprised that this was not the reason she gave Charles. She merely informed him that she had no intention of leaving Fanny until she was safely delivered and had no thought of matrimony at the present."

"If that is so, then he has had a very lucky escape, but Marguerite, it is just as we thought, Norland was the object of her desire and not the man." Relief was the uppermost of Margaret's emotions, but relief for him or herself or both, she was not entirely sure.

She still couldn't quite understand why Caroline Parker had refused Charles Dashwood. Surely, a fifty percent chance of being the mistress of Norland was better than no chance at all. It was not as though she had any other options open to her, being without fortune and connections. Something else must have occurred, of which Margaret was certain.

"Is your son here tonight?" she asked, looking around hopefully, but Marguerite shook her head sorrowfully.

"No, I'm afraid not, Miss Margaret. I tried to persuade him, but he thought it best to absent himself from society for a few days and let things blow over. Although, I must be honest with you, his vanity has been badly wounded. Even if he didn't wish to marry Caroline Parker, he believed she wanted him for himself, and it has been a shock for him to learn the desire to be Mistress of Norland was uppermost in her mind. He has learnt a hard lesson in courtship and has gone away to lick his wounds." Margaret didn't know how to answer her, remaining silent and pondering everything Marguerite had said whilst struggling with acute disappointment that Charles Dashwood was not present at the ball. Marguerite saw her turmoil and sought to change the subject.

"Enough of Charles. He has been a very silly boy, but I daresay he will get over it in no time, but for the present, we must leave him to smart. On another matter, Miss Margaret, what is your opinion of Fanny and John's news? To me, it appears nothing short of miraculous to have conceived at her age, after nine years without issue." Margaret was spared the necessity of a response by the appearance of Lieutenant Carter, seeking her hand for the next dance. She allowed him to lead her out with very mixed emotions, sincerely relieved that Charles Dashwood was not to marry Caroline Parker but unaccountably hurt that he was not present tonight. The rest of the evening went by in a flash. She danced a great deal and laughed a lot, but all the while, her mind was occupied by the magnitude of change brought about by unpredictable circumstances. She agreed with Marguerite entirely that Fanny's pregnancy was miraculous, in more ways than one. Margaret always tried to think well of people, including Fanny, however difficult that might be. Still, an uncharitable suspicion began to form in her mind, and try as she might, she couldn't extinguish it.

Chapter 16
An Exchange of Letters

Dearest Mama and Elinor,

I write to you both under one cover because I know you will pass on this letter to Elinor after you have read it, Mama, and I have no secrets from either of you. I am sorry to have kept you waiting for this communication, but circumstances have been changing so rapidly that no soon as I begin one letter but I must tear it up and start again. Even though I have now grown used to the faster pace of London life, I now find myself in a whirl at the speed with which events have changed the course of several lives.

By now, you will have heard the astounding news that Fanny is with child. John and she are beside themselves with joy, not least because this is a chance to retain Norland within their immediate family and cut out Charles Dashwood from the inheritance. Forgive my plain speaking, but I do not see the point of beating about the bush. Another direct consequence of Fanny's pregnancy is that Caroline Parker has refused Charles Dashwood his offer of marriage. I remember we were all in agreement that Caroline Parker is a fortune hunter, so marriage to a mere physician would not suit her at all. Although I confess, I don't entirely understand the motives for her refusal because there still remains a fifty-fifty chance he will inherit, and as far as I can see, she has no other options. Perhaps I am wrong, as there must be another reason she has refused him. You will have heard from Marianne all the circumstances that led up to his proposal, so I will not bore you by repeating those events here. Suffice it to say that his mother is beside herself with joy at this unexpected turn of events and the deliverance of her son from one such as Caroline Parker. I am scarcely less so but dare not hope beyond that as he continues to absent himself from society. I hear you both reminding me I must let his behaviour be my guide.

On the matter of Fanny's being with child, the truth is, I am in need of your counsel. The more I think about it, the more I am sure there is something very odd about Fanny's pregnancy. As you know, I was a guest at Grosvenor Street for several months, thus it was possible for me to observe John and Fanny's behaviour to each other firsthand, and the estrangement between them was obvious. If you remember, Mama, I even wrote about it to you. Most of the time, they went their separate ways except for appearance sake, meeting only to dine. Even that formality may just have been because I was a guest in the house. I hardly dare put pen to paper about my scandalous suspicions, but I must unburden myself. I simply don't believe that this is John's child. I know I can speak of my worry to you both in absolute confidence and you will not judge me harshly. Please advise me on my course of conduct. What should I do about it, if anything? It would be fruitless to talk to John. Whatever the truth of the matter, he has decided to acknowledge the child as his and, therefore, the potential heir to the Norland Estate.

Your loving daughter/sister,
Margaret.

PS. I should add that I am not the only one to be suspicious. Marguerite Dashwood first put the idea in my head, and I think she knows something she is not revealing. I should also say that I have not discussed this matter with Marianne because I don't want to worry her in her delicate condition.

Margaret's mood improved after she had written the letter. She missed the sound counsel of her mother and Elinor, and it was cathartic to get her worries off her chest. It was very hard to believe that Fanny could have taken a lover, but this was the only explanation. Margaret suspected she was very unhappy about Charles Dashwood inheriting Norland and could do nothing to prevent it. Except this. Desperate measures for a desperate plight. John must surely know the child is not his or at least have his suspicious, unless Fanny has somehow fooled him. Poor Charles Dashwood to be disinherited by an imposter, but then he had never sought the inheritance, and Margaret had heard that from his own lips. Moreover, the potential loss of it had spared him from a disastrous union with Caroline Parker. Although, it seemed the male ego was a fragile thing. He had not wanted to marry Caroline but, perversely, has been wounded by the realisation that she only wanted him for his fortune. Margaret hoped he would soon get over it and recognise that not all women were tarred with the same brush as Caroline Parker.

Margaret decided to pay a morning call on Fanny, feeling strongly that the occasion demanded it. Despite her misgivings about the father of Fanny's child, she was family and would be its aunt. On arrival at Grosvenor Street, Margaret was shown into the morning room to find only the Miss Parkers present. She was quite taken aback when Caroline Parker smiled cordially in welcome.

"Good morning, Miss Margaret. How delightful to see you. I'm afraid you have just missed Fanny, who has taken the carriage, and we do not expect her back soon." Caroline Parker informed her politely. "But do sit down and take tea with us. Catherine, please ring the bell." If Margaret was astonished by Caroline Parker's change in manner towards her, she did not show it and decided to accept the invitation in the hopes of learning more.

"I am sorry to find Fanny out, but thank you, Miss Parker. I would be pleased to take tea with you. How is Fanny? I hope she does not suffer as Marianne did?" Margaret enquired politely, and Caroline went to great lengths to reassure her on that head.

"Oh, no, I am pleased to be able to reassure you on that head, Miss Margaret. Mrs Dashwood is the very picture of robust health. One could almost say she is blooming. Motherhood seems to agree with her, and it is especially wonderful news after the great sadness that occurred in this family."

"Indeed, Miss Parker, it is wondrous news," Margaret agreed readily. "I am so pleased that she does not suffer the terrible sickness Marianne endured, and let us hope it continues. It is well known that motherhood over the age of thirty can be a little precarious, so Fanny should take every care." Margaret was genuinely concerned for Fanny, and Caroline nodded sympathetically.

"Yes, how right you are to be concerned, Miss Margaret, but Mrs Dashwood is in the best of health and will have the best of care," Caroline replied happily. "She has asked me to stay with her until the child is delivered, and Mr Dashwood cannot do enough for her at present. She complains of being thoroughly spoiled, although I think she is actually relishing the attention." Margaret was shrewd enough to recognise that Caroline's extended invitation to Norland could probably explain why she had refused Charles Dashwood. Assured of a home with Fanny for more than six months, who knows what other opportunities may arise for her? And she must know, in her heart, that Charles Dashwood didn't really care for her.

Nevertheless, she was surprised at how communicative Caroline was that morning. "Perhaps you could encourage her to rest more, Miss Parker, especially in the early months," Margaret advised, thinking of Fanny gallivanting around London at that very moment alone in the carriage.

"I could not agree more, Miss Margaret, but Mrs Dashwood would not be persuaded to remain at home this morning, saying she had an important engagement that couldn't be delayed," Caroline defended herself, catching Margaret's meaning. "We are to leave for Norland the day after tomorrow, and Catherine will return home to Mama. Fanny would only explain that she had someone in particular to take her leave of. That is all I know, but I'm certain she will return very soon if you would care to wait."

It was evident to Margaret that Fanny had not confided in Caroline, so she decided not to wait for Fanny. Taking her leave of the Miss Parkers, she also recognised that Caroline's changed behaviour was because she was no longer a rival. Caroline's pursuit of Charles Dashwood was now over, and as Margaret had rightly guessed, jealousy had been the cause of her previous incivility. Fanny's conduct was a mystery. She must have had someone very important to say goodbye to in order to take the carriage out alone in her delicate condition.

Margaret returned to Bath Square, her mind full of suspicion, to find a letter waiting for her.

My dearest child,

It relieves me greatly that you are with Marianne at this time and that you no longer have to suffer at Fanny's hands. I am also very glad to hear that Marianne is well enough now to leave her room and go out into society. It would have been a great pity if you had sacrificed your opportunities in London for the sake of your sister, no matter how important the reason.

On the other matter, Elinor and I were just as astonished as you when we received John's letter announcing Fanny to be with child. It does seem as though they have been blessed by a miracle, and that is what we must believe. If John has recognised this child, then we must do the same. No good will come from harbouring suspicions, no matter how convinced we are of their foundation in truth. We must trust that sins of such magnitude have a way of coming to the surface on their own. I advise you, therefore, to do nothing and rise above idle speculation. It never does to be uncharitable.

With regard to Charles Dashwood, I am pleased he has escaped from an unfortunate match, but I could never see he paid any particular attention to Caroline Parker. In my opinion, it was more in her mind and much encouraged by Fanny. He did the right thing and was refused, most probably because of the change in his circumstances, but we don't know that for certain. It is best to be slow to judge if we are to expect the same charity from others. Perhaps Miss Parker realised how unhappy she would have been married to a man without any real attachment to him or he to her. Maybe she had other irons in the fire, so to speak; only time will tell. We do not know her intimately, and, again, I advise you not to judge. In any case, it appears the chapter is closed. Miss Parker has moved on, and so must he. Give him time, Margaret, and things will mend. He has had a most unfortunate experience and is probably suffering from the potential loss of Norland and a general distrust of womankind. No doubt, he is also ashamed of his own conduct, which seems to have been rather foolish.

Things go on much the same here in Devonshire. Tom bid me tell you that the garden is just starting to come to life after the January frosts. The bank of snowdrops is a delight, and the camellia is in full flower. Take heart that your gardens will be in safe hands and you will be back for spring, which is a time I look forward to very much.

Give my love to Marianne and advise her to take every care.

Your loving
Mama.

PS: Elinor has some very good news to tell you, but I will leave that to her.

Enclosed with her mother's letter was a short note from Elinor.

Dearest Margaret,

Mama and I have discussed the contents of your last letter at great length, and we are both of the same opinion, so I will not repeat her advice to you. Do nothing, bide your time and watch. There is nothing to be gained by taking action now, when time may heal all things. In the meantime, take every opportunity of enjoying yourself in London as this chance will not come again.

Now for my news. I know you will be very pleased to learn that Mrs Ferrars remembered her duty to Edward at the end of her life in her final will and testament. It appears that not all the money was settled irrevocably upon Robert, and Edward is to inherit five thousand pounds. I cannot tell you what a difference such a large sum will make to our lives, and we are eternally grateful for this unexpected legacy. All my little economies will be over, and we can now afford to live in the style that Edward deserves and has been brought up in. The legacy is even more important now that we have more happy news to impart. I am delighted to tell you that, by Christmas, you will have another little nephew or niece to welcome into the family. We are both overjoyed, of course.

We all look forward to the spring when you and the Brandons return, but I too am glad you are with Marianne at this moment and that she has recovered enough to chaperone you about.

Kitty and Edward send you their love.

Your loving sister.
Elinor.

PS: I have also written to Marianne to tell her of our happy news.

Margaret's heart leapt at Elinor's news. It made up for her own disappointments, and she was very excited to hear there was another little Ferrars on the way. She knew what a difference the extra income of five hundred pounds a year would make for them, especially with another mouth to feed. Although she could not help suspecting that if Edward had received five thousand pounds, then his siblings had very likely received more. It was not in Elinor's nature to be suspicious, however, and she was clearly very thankful for the additional sum so unexpectedly bequeathed to Edward. It was also a relief to Margaret that her mother's and sister's advice was to take no action and bide her time. She would try to do as they bid and give Fanny the benefit of the doubt. Innocent until proven guilty, and after all, she had no proof beyond feminine intuition. It was also true that her acquaintance with Caroline Parker was of short duration and she had no right to judge her motives. After all, Margaret had seen a different side of her only that morning. She went to see if there was anything she could do for Marianne and found her preparing to do some gentle exercise in the park.

"Why don't you come with me, Margaret? Then I can leave my maid behind. I'm sure she has enough to do without following me around." Margaret went to put on her pelisse, as the day was fine, but a chilly wind was blowing, making her fuss around Marianne solicitously.

"I hope you are warm enough, Marianne; it wouldn't do if you caught a chill. You know how susceptible you are after that time in Somerset."

"Don't fret, Margaret; you are as bad as the colonel. It is on Mr Dashwood's advice that I take a little gentle exercise daily. He reminds me on every visit I am not ill. There now, you can see for yourself how well wrapped up I am," said Marianne, holding up her muff and pointing to the fur tippet as proof. Margaret caught her breath.

"You have seen him, then?" she could not help asking. "How did he seem?" Marianne shrugged.

"He seemed just as normal as a physician to a patient. We didn't discuss anything but the state of my health and that of the baby. I dared not bring up the subject of Miss Caroline unless he began it first, which, to my chagrin, he did not. I sent for you, Margaret, but was told you were closeted in your room, reading letters and asked not to be disturbed." Margaret turned away in some confusion.

"Yes, a letter from Mama and a note from Elinor. They both send their best love and beg you to take care of yourself, but I think you know the rest."

"Of course, I know all about the legacy and that there is to be a new baby. Naturally, I am delighted for Edward and Elinor. I have long been worried by their relative poverty and my inability to persuade them to accept help from us. It is a great relief that Mrs Ferrars remembered her duty to Edward at the end. Although, I daresay Robert and Fanny received more." Margaret nodded in agreement.

"My thoughts exactly, Marianne."

"Now, suppose you tell me everything, Margaret, what other news is there? What did they say of Fanny and Charles?"

"They expressed surprise, of course, and relief that Charles had not been caught by Caroline Parker." Marianne sent her sister a look of disbelief.

"Margaret, I may be with child, but it hasn't addled my wits. You can talk to me about your suspicions of Fanny, you know." Margaret could hear her sister was vexed to be excluded on the grounds of her delicate condition, so she decided to come clean.

"You are right, Marianne, I do suspect that John might not be the father of this miracle child, and I wrote to Mama and Elinor about my suspicions." Margaret decided that Marianne must have the whole truth rather than risk upsetting her further. Marianne nodded with satisfaction, pleased to have her own suspicions confirmed.

"What did they advise?"

"You know Mama and Elinor. They are more charitable than we are, Marianne. Both pointed out that as John has accepted the child, there is nothing to be done, and we have no proof of anything different." Marianne nodded knowingly.

"In that case, Margaret, I am no more charitable than you are. I also think it is most unlikely to be John's child, but I agree with Mama and Elinor, there is nothing to be done about it unless we have irrefutable proof. One can't go around making accusations of that sort without grounds." It was a relief to Margaret that Marianne also suspected Fanny of duplicity, and she was cheered they could now talk about their doubts openly.

"Mama and Elinor advised we should watch and wait in both matters, Fanny and Charles Dashwood, alike. I have new information to report, however, as I called on Fanny this morning. Firstly, I found Fanny out of the house, having taken the carriage despite her delicate condition, apparently saying goodbye to someone important. I should tell you, Miss Parker informed me of their imminent intention of going off to Norland. Secondly, that Caroline Parker has mended her manners to me. What do you make of that, Marianne?"

"That the person Fanny was saying goodbye to is the father of her child and Caroline's former coldness to you was borne out of jealousy." Marianne's sharp intellect went straight to the point.

"My thoughts exactly, Marianne," Margaret agreed. "I also think it is good advice to watch and wait."

"Yes, I agree. For the moment, we can do nothing more. We will keep our eyes and ears wide open for clues of any sort. I do not believe in coincidences," Marianne replied, but Margaret wished to sound her out on their other topic of conversation.

"Marianne, were you surprised that Caroline Parker refused Mr Dashwood?"

"I confess, I was, but there is no denying his prospects have diminished, Margaret."

"Even so, Marianne, they are still better than hers. What are her options? I do not see any other young men queuing up for her hand. Surely, it's better to be married to Charles Dashwood, an eminent physician, than end the season unengaged." Marianne nodded in agreement.

"I have to acknowledge the truth of that, but from what little I've seen of Caroline Parker, I suspect she has a second option lined up, and Fanny had something to do with it."

"Just what Mama said, but who or what could it be?" Marianne shook her head.

"I do not know. Again, we must watch and wait, Margaret, and I'm sure all will be made clear." Margaret nodded thoughtfully as Marianne changed the subject.

"I am so delighted that Edward's mother did the right thing in the end. It will make all the difference to Elinor and Edward." Marianne was acutely aware of Elinor's strict economy in housekeeping, even though it was a skill long acquired after the loss of Norland. It has been a great source of unhappiness to Marianne that her sister was reduced to such a small living, whereas she had married into Delaford. Although, to give credit where credit was due, Elinor managed without complaint.

Chapter 17
Further Clues

A note arrived from Fanny the following morning, officially informing the Brandons and Margaret they were leaving for Norland. Thus, the two sisters decided it was incumbent on them to call on Fanny and John to bid them farewell. Unusually, Lily answered the door, having seen them approach from an upstairs window, running downstairs ahead of their knock and pre-empting the butler. It was the opportunity she'd been long waiting for: to speak to Margaret alone. Lily knew she would be severely castigated later, but what she had to impart was worth the risk. Her face lit up at the sight of them.

"Miss Margaret, Mrs Brandon, I'm that glad to see you both!" she cried in delight, stopping Margaret from following her sister into the morning room.

"Miss Margaret, please wait a moment as I have something important to tell you," she whispered urgently by way of explanation. Marianne looked over her shoulder in surprise but wisely left them together and continued on to Fanny's sitting room alone.

"Go on, Lily, you have my full attention," said Margaret, greatly curious, and Lily urgently whispered to her the gist of the conversation she'd overheard between the two Miss Parkers. She couldn't help noticing that Miss Margaret changed colour before replying. "Thank you, Lily. You know, of course, that Miss Parker refused him?"

"Yes, indeed, Miss Margaret, and I was never so surprised. More especially, after what Miss Parker said to her sister, I thought she'd stop at nothing until she had him at the pulpit. But it was more Miss Catherine's words I wanted you to hear." Lily looked earnestly at Margaret, but she shook her head in disbelief.

"Yet he has said nothing to me, Lily." If truth were known, she was rather tired of hearing from other people that Charles Dashwood loved her. If he really did love her, then it was high time she had it from the man himself. He really was most infuriating. Nevertheless, she turned to Lily with an affectionate smile.

"Thank you for telling me, Lily, but until he declares himself, we cannot move further forward. I must go now, or they will be wondering what I am doing out here in the corridor for so long. Thank you again, Lily." Margaret gave her a grateful hug, and Lily watched her go in concern. She had come to know Margaret Dashwood very well over the past few months, and if Charles Dashwood didn't move swiftly, then he would lose the opportunity.

Fanny and Marianne were alone in the morning room when Margaret joined them, and she was astonished to hear them conversing like old friends. Of course, at long last, they had found a subject in common. In the past, Marianne had barely exchanged more than a few words at a time with Fanny. In all their long acquaintance, they had found nothing to say to each other, but now they had pregnancy in common and, thus, a whole host of symptoms to compare.

Just as well, Margaret thought, as her head was full of the conversation with Lily and she sat in silence contemplating this new information. In any case, there was nothing she could add to the subject her sister and Fanny were discussing. Despite her show of indifference to Lily, she was not unmoved. It was amazing to Margaret that Catherine Parker had plucked up the courage to confront her intimidating sister, daring to voice that Charles Dashwood loved another. Until now, Margaret had only her own feelings to go on and those of her sisters and mother, who were hardly impartial observers. Catherine was an outsider and had no motive for saying such a thing, unless she had a very good reason to believe that it was true. Why else upset her sister? Margaret knew Caroline Parker could be vituperative if crossed, but Fanny's suspicious tone soon interrupted her thoughts.

"Miss Margaret, you are very pensive this morning. Is anything the matter?" A lull in the conversation had suddenly brought her silence to the attention of Fanny's sharp eyes.

"No indeed, Fanny. It was only that you and my sister have so much to discuss at present and it is a subject to which I cannot contribute," Margaret quickly explained, hoping it would satisfy her and prevent further prying questions. "I understand that you are returning to Norland soon?" Happily, she succeeded in changing the subject because Fanny became full of their plans to refurbish the nursery.

"Well, Marianne, did you learn anything interesting from Fanny whilst I was talking to Lily?" Margaret asked on their way home.

"No, she would hardly reveal anything intimate to me, but there was one thing that struck me as unusual. I did notice a large flower arrangement in the window when I first entered the room, and when I remarked upon its beauty, Fanny actually blushed. In fact, it felt like déjà vu. I couldn't help going over to take a closer look, and it was then I saw the bouquet was exactly like the one that Captain Dunning left for you on the day after the accident in the park. Fanny must have been conscious she'd changed colour because she said something about the heat of the fire, but it was not hot in the room to my mind."

"Yes, now you come to mention it, Marianne, I did register the flowers but thought no more about it. You are right, however; it was very similar to the bouquet the captain left for me as an apology for the accident. The style of arrangement was exactly the same." Margaret and Marianne exchanged significant glances.

"Not only similar, it was the same florist. I discreetly examined the card, but there was no inscription." Marianne confirmed her sister's suspicions, and Margaret looked shocked.

"Surely not, Marianne. Fanny and Captain Dunning, it is beyond belief. Even Fanny would not do such a thing." Marianne shrugged, remembering his overtures to her on several occasions despite her being married to the colonel.

"Yet he is an outrageous flirt, so I don't suppose there would be any scruples on his part. I think we may have hit upon something, Margaret."

"What should we do, Marianne? We can't voice our suspicions simply on the strength of a bouquet. It may well be just coincidence."

"I told you, my dear sister, there is no such thing as a coincidence of this nature, but I agree with you, we can do nothing at present. As you say, an arrangement of flowers is not proof. Anyone could use the same florist, but something tells me that this is a significant clue, which means we have discovered Fanny's secret. Frustratingly, we still can't do anything yet, so must watch and wait, as Mama and Elinor advised."

"Do you think we should tell them of our suspicions, Marianne?"

"Not yet, I think. They would be very shocked to think Fanny could be so duplicitous." Margaret agreed but was greatly relieved that Marianne appeared to have forgotten her private conversation with Lily. What was the use of discussing Charles Dashwood further? It was time for him to act.

Back at Bath Square, Margaret retired to her bed chamber to think over the morning's revelations, going over the occasions she had seen the captain and

Fanny together. They stood before her in her mind's eye, like an artist's impressions. Fanny and the captain at Hannover Square, when he asked permission for the drive in the park, talked for an unusually long time in the most animated way, certainly much longer than the occasion demanded. Then, there was the captain's unexpected appearance at the Norland Christmas party, when Fanny danced with him twice and allowed him to escort her into supper. Margaret recalled Fanny's lively demeanour on that night in stark contrast to her usual sourness. Intuitively, she knew they were right in suspecting Captain Dunning, but these were not the only thoughts that occupied her mind.

If Charles Dashwood loved her, then why did he not declare himself? It had been days since she had seen him, although he had been in the house, visiting Marianne in his professional capacity. He could have taken that opportunity to let her know he was coming and requested an interview, but instead he had disappeared from society. Surely, he could not have been so upset by Caroline's refusal to withdraw from society altogether. If he could be so quelled by a refusal from a woman he had not wanted to marry in the first place, then she was extremely disappointed in him. He was not the man she thought he was if he allowed himself to be cowed so easily. It was all very puzzling, and he really was the most provoking man she had ever met. It was high time she dismissed him entirely from her thoughts and got on with her life. Longingly, she thought of Barton Cottage and the spring that would be fast approaching.

Hearing a knock at the front door and John Dashwood's voice in the hall, she hastened downstairs to pay her respects, finding him seated in the morning room with Marianne. "John," she said, taking his hand in greeting. "I hear that you are all returning to Norland tomorrow. How delightful! The park will be just showing the first signs of spring." He smiled joyfully at this thought.

"Yes, we thought it best for Fanny to live quietly at Norland in her delicate condition. Not that she suffers in any way. It is exceedingly lucky that she has a strong constitution and always enjoys the best of health. In addition, she will have Miss Parker's company, of course." He seemed resigned to that now, almost pleased that Caroline Parker would be with them to amuse Fanny.

"We called on Fanny this morning to take our leave, and I was very glad to see that she is in good health. She seems highly contented with the unexpected turn of events," Marianne informed him. "She is doubly blessed to be without the sickness that so troubled me."

"It was kind of you both to call," John said warmly. "Indeed, we are both overjoyed to be so blessed at this late stage in our lives. Fanny is more than well; in fact, she is positively blooming, and we must do our best to keep it that way. Norland is the ideal place to ensure that a happy state of affairs continues." John smiled at them both in happiness, giving no indication that anything was amiss. On the contrary, he was also full of the plans for the nursery and the improvements he intended to make to the park; it was unlikely he was hiding something. Later, after he had taken his leave, Margaret repeated this to Marianne.

"There was nothing in John's demeanour to justify our suspicions, and I begin to doubt our instincts. Can it be, Marianne, that we are completely wrong in this matter and John is the father, after all?" Margaret looked so very worried that Marianne sought to reassure her.

"Margaret, we are not naturally suspicious creatures, but consider the circumstances again. Firstly, Fanny has been nine years without conceiving. Secondly, before this event was announced, they were not a happy couple; anyone could see that. Thirdly, we have other circumstantial evidence. Do not forget the flowers and Fanny's blushes when I mentioned them to her. Not to mention Captain Dunning's unexpected appearance at the Norland Christmas party." It was clear to Margaret, Marianne had not changed her opinion and was still sure Captain Dunning was the culprit.

"I have further proof, although I thought nothing of it at the time," Marianne confessed. "I saw them walking together in the park at Norland on the day after the Christmas Ball."

"Why didn't you say?" Margaret gasped.

"It didn't seem unusual then," she explained. "Why shouldn't the hostess walk with one of her guests? With hindsight, now that other evidence has come to light, I find it highly suspicious."

"I agree, Marianne, the evidence all points to an affair with the captain, but one thing is certain: Fanny has managed to dupe John into thinking the child is his. He is simply incapable of carrying out an act in this way."

Meanwhile, at Grosvenor Street, Fanny and Caroline Parker were busy packing for their journey to Norland.

"I am sorry there will be no balls and parties for you to attend, Caroline." Fanny sighed, eyeing the ball gown that Caroline was carefully folding into the valise. "The best we can hope for at this time of year are a few local dinners. I do hope you will not regret your decision to accompany us to Norland, my dear. It would not do to blight your prospects of finding a match during the London season." Fanny did not beat about the bush as it was obvious to her that Caroline was in the marriage mart. "I hope you won't live to regret your refusal of Charles Dashwood's offer."

"Dear Mrs Dashwood, please do not upset yourself on my account. I am certain I will not regret Charles Dashwood, and it will be enough for me to be back at dear Norland and by your side," Caroline reassured her with a smile. "In any case, when you can spare me and the weather is fine, I intend to ask Mr Barrington to resume my riding lessons. I made a very good beginning on dear little Sally, and I would relish the opportunity for further improvement, that is if Mr Barrington does not object." Caroline looked conscious, and Fanny laughed at her embarrassment, seeing through her instantly.

"Why, yes, of course, you sly girl." Fanny looked at her with renewed admiration as the penny dropped. "I am certain that the gentleman will not object, Caroline, for what man could considering the inducement? But that reminds me, on the subject of the Barringtons, I have had some news. Miss Elizabeth Barrington has announced her engagement to Mr Harris. It is not a great match for her, but the families have been friends for many years. Although I have to acknowledge he is a gentleman, at least, and owns a very pretty farm." Caroline nodded in agreement, unsurprised by the news. She was constantly on the lookout for opportunities where she could press her advantage and rarely missed anything.

"I thought I detected some attraction between them at the Norland Christmas party. A love match then. How charming for them, Mrs Dashwood," she simpered, but Fanny was not so sure and gave her opinion in no uncertain terms.

"It is every girl's duty to marry as best she can; love does not come into it. Having said that, Miss Barrington is a good-humoured girl but no beauty, so perhaps she has done her best in accepting Mr Harris. Her fortune is not large, some ten thousand pounds, I believe. The Barrington Estate goes to Steven, of course. Still, it will be a very pretty wedding and something to relieve the boredom for you as it is to take place in the early spring whilst you are at Norland."

"I did not presume to think I would be invited, Mrs Dashwood." Caroline looked coy, but Fanny took her hand affectionately.

"Of course you will be invited, Caroline. I will insist upon it as you are my guest at Norland. Although it will not be necessary; the Barringtons know what is due to my guest." Fanny was quick to reassure her friend, and Caroline smiled at her adoringly.

"Now let me see, we must be practical if you are to succeed in your intentions. Let us not beat about the bush and pretend we don't understand each other. Do you have a suitable riding habit for these all-important riding lessons, my dear?" Fanny was warming to her new idea for Caroline's future, as if it had been her own plan. Caroline shook her head.

"No, Mrs Dashwood. I improvised as best I could before."

"Well, that was then, but it will not do this time. Such a situation must be rectified at once; we can't have you looking like the poor relation. Fetch me the dark green habit from the closet, and, look, here is the matching hat." Fanny produced a very stylish creation from a nearby bandbox, and Caroline was entranced. "I insist you accept these as a gift, Caroline, and I will not brook a refusal. After all, I will have little use for them in the ensuing months, and it's most important you should look your best." She smoothed her new silk gown over her increasing girth with a self-satisfied smile as Caroline pulled the elegant habit from the closet.

"My dear, Mrs Dashwood, how kind you are! It is the most stylish outfit I ever possessed." Caroline was quite overcome by Fanny's generosity and, at her insistence, tried on the outfit immediately. Caroline was amazed at the transformation expensive clothes achieved as Fanny examined the result with a critical eye, secretly very impressed. Caroline was, undoubtedly, a very pretty girl, but in that outfit, Fanny defied the Prince Regent himself to pass her by. She decided to supply the girl with new clothes over the coming months. It would be a very good investment, and who knows when Fanny might need the favour returned?

"My dear, how lucky we are similar in stature? It is almost a perfect fit. I will have Crane nip it in a little at the waist. Otherwise, it could have been made for you, my dear. How charming you look." Fanny smiled, very well pleased with the picture Caroline presented, imagining the reaction of someone else who, she envisaged, would be equally charmed.

Chapter 18
A Wedding Invitation

On the same day when the Grosvenor Street party departed for Norland, Margaret received a letter from Sussex.

My dear Margaret,
Allow me to say how much I have missed your company since you departed for London, and I hope that this letter finds you well and that your sister has recovered her health.
I have some wonderful news. Mr Harris and I are engaged, and we are to be married on ninth March. We, therefore, cordially invite you and the Brandons to join us for the ceremony and wedding breakfast. Dearest Margaret, I am so very happy. I know my parents were not overjoyed to hear our news, secretly hoping I would make a more prestigious match, but mercifully, they have come around. They know that we have been connected since infancy, so it's hardly surprising our attachment grew into something more. Nevertheless, we have been keeping it a secret, fearful my parents' disapproval would somehow separate us, but now the secret is out now and all is well. I cannot tell you what a relief that is to us. In fact, I believe my parents can actually see the advantage of me remaining in the neighbourhood. I am so grateful for this happy outcome, and I can only wish the same happiness for you, my dearest friend, when the time comes.
I understand that the Dashwoods and Miss Parker are arriving at Norland today. We received a note from Mrs Dashwood this morning informing us of this fact and a request for Miss Caroline to continue her riding lessons with Steven. I confess, I was rather surprised when Steven agreed readily, thinking he might be rather reluctant to school another beginner. It seems I was wrong, and he seemed quite glad to receive the request. Poor Steven. He must have been rather bored of late as I have been very much occupied with Frederick. At least it will keep him busy, while it is too early in the year for proper sport to begin.

I look forward to seeing you at our wedding in March. The time cannot go quickly enough for me.

Your affectionate friend,
Elizabeth Barrington

Margaret was overjoyed for her friend and went to find Marianne to give her the news. "Please say that we can attend, Marianne. Will you be well enough, do you think?"

"I do not see why not, Margaret, as the wedding is to take place three months before the birth. Perhaps Fanny and John can be persuaded to host us at Norland. I will ask the colonel what he thinks this evening. In truth, it would be a welcome break from London," she said with a heartfelt sigh. Margaret was not surprised that Marianne had changed her mind about being in town. To enjoy the capital's attractions, one needed to be in robust health and full of energy, and Marianne, though much better, was often fatigued. She wrote back to Elizabeth Barrington, sure of the colonel's approbation if Marianne wished to attend.

Dear Elizabeth,

Words cannot express my happiness for you, and I confirm that we shall be delighted to attend the wedding. We shall probably stay at Norland if that is suitable to Fanny and John.

I confess, I was surprised to learn of your secret attachment, but I did notice at the Norland Christmas Ball he admired you very much. I did not, however, suspect you of feeling anything more than friendship, but now I know the truth. I am so glad your parents approved the match. Nothing could bring more happiness than a love match between families who have been connected for years. It will be a constant source of comfort to you and your parents that you will always be near at hand. Most especially when there are grandchildren, if you will forgive my presumption.

My warmest congratulations to you and Mr Harris, and I depend upon being an early visitor at your future home.

Your affectionate friend,
Margaret Dashwood.

PS. Your brother is such a keen horseman that any excuse to keep him in the saddle will be welcome to him.

Margaret was right, and the colonel had no objection to attending the wedding, provided Marianne was well enough when the time came. He pronounced as much over dinner that evening.

"Although, ladies, I do have one stipulation. I am of the opinion we should not return to London following the wedding in Sussex. Events have rather overtaken us, and the circumstances are not the same as when we first arrived in London." The colonel's tone was unusually forceful, and it was clear he had made up his mind.

"You are referring to my pregnancy, I suppose," Marianne stated.

"Yes, my dear, I am, and I believe it would be prudent to return to Delaford after the wedding. I deem it unwise for you to travel in the later months of pregnancy, and I would prefer it if we could be comfortably settled at home by the middle of March. I have already consulted Charles Dashwood on this subject, and he is in complete agreement, although he cannot continue to attend on you in Devonshire himself." The colonel turned to Margaret apologetically, who had pricked up her ears at the mention of Charles.

"I know this is not what you expected, Margaret, but I hope you will understand that everything is different now. The Dashwoods are returned to Norland, and we must go home, for Marianne's sake." Margaret smiled at him reassuringly, secretly glad to be returning home, especially as Charles Dashwood appeared to have given their return to Devonshire his blessing. It was obvious his intentions to her could not be serious, and she must give up thinking of him.

"Please, Colonel, there is no need to explain; I quite understand. I have been thinking that it was unlikely we would remain in London for the entire season now, and it is but a few weeks early. I confess, I long to be back at Barton Cottage again."

"Do I have a say in this matter? Now that you have comfortably settled it between yourselves and Mr Dashwood?" Marianne interrupted, pretending to be put out, but Margaret could see she really approved the plan. In fact, she had virtually confessed as much to Margaret earlier that day, but the colonel looked abashed.

"My love, we were only thinking of your comfort, which is always my first consideration." He turned to her so apologetically that Marianne laughed out loud.

"I know that, of course, my dear. I was only teasing you, and I must confess, I would like to be home by spring. London is beginning to pall in my condition, and I long for the peace of Devonshire," Marianne admitted, and Margaret noted the colonel looked extremely gratified. He caught her eye and smiled.

"We must make the most of the last few weeks in London, though, for Margaret's sake." Marianne nodded in agreement, perfectly willing to chaperone Margaret about for the limited time left to them.

"On that note, I think I should be well enough to attend the assembly next week," Marianne added, and the colonel nodded in approval of the plan.

Marguerite Dashwood was the first person to greet them at the next assembly. As usual, it was a very crowded affair, but Margaret was disappointed not to see anyone of their acquaintance amongst the throng. Everyone we know has gone from London, she lamented to herself. Happily, at that moment, she looked up to see her friend making her way towards them through the crowd.

"Marguerite, how delighted I am to see you. I was feeling quite abandoned with not an acquaintance in sight," Margaret greeted her in relief, making room for her on the seat beside her. Marguerite nodded in sympathy, looking around her.

"It is true, many have left, but I have seen Miss Catherine Parker with her mama and also Captain Dunning and Lieutenant Carter, so we are not quite without friends here, but I must admit, London does seem a little thin of company with so many of our regular acquaintance absent," Marguerite concurred.

"Is your son escorting you tonight?" Margaret asked, unable to bear the suspense any longer, her heart beating fast as she waited for his mother to answer. Marguerite hesitated before replying, thinking of the difficult conversation she'd had with her son before she left the house.

"No, unfortunately not. He was called away to an emergency at the last moment. I'm afraid babies have as little respect for social engagements as they do for the festive season." She gave Margaret a wry smile, but her explanation didn't ring true to Margaret. It was as if he was purposely avoiding her, and some minutes passed before Margaret could speak, so great was her disappointment. It was fortunate that Marianne took over the conversation at that point. She explained to Marguerite their plans for quitting London soon, and Margaret was left to her own unhappy thoughts. He cannot possibly care for me if he is happy to see us return to Devon and steers clear of social engagements where he knows I will be present. Marguerite noticed with sadness her young friend's change of mood and resolved to have another word with her intransigent son, who was as obstinate as he was misguided. Fortunately, Lieutenant Carter joined them at this moment and led Margaret out to dance, leaving the other two ladies alone.

Marguerite decided to seize the opportunity of a private word with Marianne.

"Mrs Brandon, I can see for myself how much better you are, and Charles has confirmed you are over the most trying time."

"Yes, without doubt, and mostly due to your son's professional help. How is he? I do not see him anywhere here tonight, Mrs Dashwood. Has he entirely given up on society of late?" Marianne questioned her closely, and Marguerite was glad Mrs Brandon had begun with the subject she wished to raise.

"No, in truth, his spirits are a little depressed. Although when Margaret asked after him, I didn't tell her that. May I speak frankly with you, Mrs Brandon?" If Marianne was surprised, she didn't show it.

"Of course, Mrs Dashwood."

"No doubt, you know all the details of Charles' unfortunate entanglement with Miss Parker?" Marianne nodded sympathetically.

"Yes, a very difficult situation and not entirely of his own making. I believe my sister-in-law had a hand in that. Without her encouragement of Miss Caroline Parker's hopes, I'm sure she would never have dared to think of him seriously."

"Fanny is a strange person, I agree. She has three very amiable sisters-in-law, yet she prefers the company of Miss Parker." Marguerite was clearly astonished at this preference, and Marianne sought to clarify the situation.

"It has always been so, Mrs Dashwood, and it can only be explained by a fundamental difference between us. Fanny's values are very different from our own."

"I assure you, Mrs Brandon, I have seen that for myself, but it is a pity for your brother. I'm sure he would prefer the company of his own sisters rather than complete strangers."

"Yet John has also been distant to us all in the past, but Fanny has made him a happy man now," observed Marianne with irony. "But we were talking of your son. How does he feel after his narrow escape?" Marianne decided she must take this opportunity to find out more for Margaret's sake.

"I must be honest with you, Mrs Brandon. The affair has left him a little bruised and, uncharacteristically, lacking in confidence. He shuns society at present and has thrown himself wholeheartedly into his medical practice..." Marguerite paused, uncertain how to continue.

"What is it that has left him so uncertain? I did hear that he had no desire to marry Caroline Parker but felt honour bound to propose." Marguerite could see that Marianne was puzzled.

"My son is complicated, Mrs Brandon. Although he had no wish to marry Miss Parker, everyone wishes to be admired for themselves. He feels that the potential loss of the Norland inheritance has damaged his prospects in the eyes of the fairer sex and no one will want to connect themselves with a mere physician." Marianne's eyes widened in surprise.

"But that is utter nonsense, Mrs Dashwood. Charles has many personal attributes that a sensible young lady would find attractive." Marianne was clearly amazed that he could think otherwise. Marguerite shook her head with a sigh.

"You and I know that, but Charles can't see it, at least not at this moment. He is also ashamed of his impetuous behaviour that caused these difficulties. He prides himself on being wise, and indeed he is, at least professionally, but I fear we can all be fools in love. The trouble is, Mrs Brandon, I fear that by the time he comes to his senses, it may be too late." She looked significantly at Marianne, and Marianne took the opportunity to be frank.

"I won't pretend to misunderstand you, Mrs Dashwood, and I can tell you that you are right. Margaret is mortified that John tried to arrange a match between them, although I am not at liberty to tell you how she knows this. I also believe she is beginning to care for your son but is at a loss to understand his actions. She is a practical person and has no time for capriciousness. At heart, Margaret is a country girl and never sought to visit London. Thus, she has little patience with its fickle attractions, which are starting to pall. As I told you, we are to return to Devonshire after the wedding at Norland, and I believe Margaret is relieved to be departing. Her patience is wearing thin with such indecision. Unfortunately, propriety dictates the first move must come from your son, so Margaret can hardly write, summoning him to an audience with her." Marguerite was pleased that Marianne didn't beat about the bush, and she answered her with equal candour.

"I could not agree with you more, Mrs Brandon, and I quite understand how Margaret feels, as I, myself, have felt like shaking Charles in frustration. Matters have been left to themselves for far too long, and without some kind of interference, they may never progress satisfactorily. I know Margaret to be a sensible girl, but it is difficult to be in love for long without encouragement." Marguerite was totally in accord with Marianne.

"The difficulty is, by what method are we to bring them together, Mrs Dashwood, without raising their suspicions?"

"I have been desperately trying to think of a way, but he will not be prevailed on to go out in society at present, and I cannot force him," Marguerite answered with a sigh, and an idea started forming in Marianne's mind.

"Leave it with me, Mrs Dashwood; I have had a thought that might just do the trick. I will speak to the colonel about it, then send word to you in a few days." The two ladies smiled at each other conspiratorially.

Margaret was astonished to see Miss Catherine in the dance, noticing how different she looked – somehow more confident and prettier. She resolved to try and talk to her that evening, but Miss Catherine sought her out first.

"Miss Margaret, how fortunate. I was not sure if you were still in town as so many people have left." Catherine caught up with her at the refreshment buffet. She was flushed and animated, seeming much happier than Margaret had ever seen her before.

"We will remain in London for only two more weeks before we go to Norland for the wedding and then on to Devonshire," Margaret explained, pleased to see Miss Catherine looking so well. It was clear she was thriving away from the company of her dominating sister.

"How delightful! We shall meet again at the wedding then, Miss Margaret, for we are all invited. Caroline writes that she is vastly contented at Norland and has resumed her daily riding lessons with Mr Barrington." Catherine looked shyly at Margaret. "I am glad for you that Caroline rejected Charles Dashwood." Margaret sighed irritably.

"What makes you think that it could affect me in any way, Miss Catherine?" Margaret retorted with feigned indifference.

"I may be a fool, Miss Margaret, but not so great a fool that I cannot see when a man admires a woman. He does not stop looking at you when your back is turned. My sister also saw that but was determined to have him anyway – that is, until his circumstances changed. A lucky escape for him, I think, although she is my sister." She shook Margaret's hand meaningfully and took her leave as Lieutenant Carter joined them to claim Catherine for the next dance.

Margaret was still standing where Catherine left her, thinking over what she had heard when Captain Dunning greeted her.

"Miss Margaret, as lovely as ever." He bowed gallantly before her. "My congratulations on your excellent recovery. I do hope you have forgiven me now for our little adventure?"

"Of course, Captain, there is nothing to forgive. When do you return to Portsmouth?" Margaret asked, more for something to say than any real interest in his movements.

"I go first to Norland for the Harris wedding, then onwards to Portsmouth from there," he replied, to Margaret's astonishment as she had no idea that he was even acquainted with the Barringtons.

"You look surprised, Miss Margaret, and I confess, I do not know the Barringtons well, but as I am visiting Norland at the same time as the wedding, Fanny insisted I accompany them to the celebrations." The captain's explanation seemed rather weak to Margaret, and she regarded him dubiously, mindful of the crimes he was suspected of.

"You are very often with the Dashwoods of late, Captain. Do you and John share the same club?" Margaret was surprised by his familiar use of Fanny's Christian name and noted he looked exceedingly uncomfortable by her probing questions.

"John has invited me to the shooting party, but, I believe, it's just to make up the numbers," he answered, evading her question. Margaret was not convinced by his statement; sure the invitation to shoot would have been Fanny's suggestion. She knew well that John did not hold a social gathering of any sort without first consulting his wife on the guest list. Fanny was so well versed in matters of etiquette and fashion and could be extremely unforgiving if mistakes were made. She fixed the captain with a piercing stare.

"Is it not strange, Captain Dunning, that you, a seaman, have been chosen to make up the numbers for a shooting party when John has so many country neighbours that would better fit the bill," Margaret retorted, rather bored with playing games, observing another flash of concern in his eyes.

"Well, if you'll excuse me, Miss Margaret." He bowed to her with obvious relief, hurriedly departing. She returned to her seat in relief, where Marianne confessed to being rather tired and asked Margaret if she had any objection to accompanying them home. As it happened, she did not. The evening had been very disappointing, and Margaret was quite glad to bring it to a close. The information Catherine Parker had imparted troubled more than pleased her. If Charles loved her, then he should do something about it as nobody else could. Nothing would come of him shunning her company and society in general. He must know that she couldn't initiate a meeting between them. If the truth were known, she was beginning to lose patience with him. She was not particularly romantic, but in all the novels she'd ever read, faint heart never won fair maid. At this rate, she would be an old maid before he proposed, but if that was her destiny, then she must bear it with good grace.

Chapter 19
A Change of Scene

Margaret felt quite dispirited after the assembly, finding it impossible to settle into her usual pursuits. Listless and despondent, she was relieved when Marianne came to her suggesting a change of plan. Finding her sister in the little town garden, heedless of the chill February breeze, Marianne was concerned.

"May I interrupt, Margaret? I have been looking for you everywhere, but are you not cold?" Although the small walled garden was very sheltered, it was still winter, despite the luxury of some pale winter sunshine.

"Not at all, Marianne. It is such a solace to be outside after the long winter. There is a touch of spring in the air today. Can you not feel it?" Margaret enthused optimistically, her cheerfulness sounding a little brittle to Marianne's ears, especially as she couldn't detect any sign of an early spring. On the contrary, it was the kind of day that made Marianne think winter would go on forever. She sat down beside her sister, taking her hand.

"Margaret, the colonel and I have been talking. We are considering leaving London a little earlier than planned. The colonel wishes for us to have a little holiday before returning to our routine life in Devon. He is conscious that, aside from Norland, we have not been outside London, and he wishes to see a little more of the surrounding countryside. I confess, he is rather restless and dislikes to be so long confined in town, and I feel a little guilty for forcing his hand to come here for the season. It is true, I longed for a change of scene and the liveliness of town, but I must admit to being capricious, as I am now starting to pine for the peace of the countryside. I think I detect that your interest in London is also beginning to wane. Am I correct in that assumption?" Margaret laid down her book, surprised by this long speech.

"If anyone is allowed to be capricious, it is you, Marianne, but I own, you are correct. In fact, I found the last assembly quite irksome, so much so, I really have no heart to attend another. London has been an interesting experience, but like the colonel and yourself, I do now long for some peace and quiet and the green of the countryside. I shall be quite glad to go if that is what you and the colonel really wish." Margaret was pleased to be able to reassure her sister on this point. She knew Marianne would think she was denying her the opportunities the rest of the London season could bring, but, in truth, Margaret was heartily tired of the whole business and was resolved to return to Devonshire an old maid.

"Dearest Margaret, I am pleased to hear you say so, as the colonel is also in a fever to get me out of the city. In his concern for me and the child, he suspects disease and infection lurking in every corner. As you are in agreement with our little plan, we will make ready and leave this Saturday coming for Midhurst. The colonel informs me there is an inn there that has quite a history, so I think you will be fascinated, and I am really looking forward to seeing the place. It will be a fitting end to our adventure." The two sisters linked arms affectionately in complete accord as they returned to the house to begin packing but were interrupted by the arrival of a letter from John.

My dear Marianne and Margaret,

Of course, Fanny and I will be delighted to receive you at Norland for the wedding celebrations, and it is quite understandable that you all will return from here to Devon. If you care to arrive a few days earlier, I am hosting a small shooting party, which the colonel may enjoy after the constrictions of London. I am really sorry that you, Margaret, didn't experience a full London season, but I hope you have enjoyed the time you had. I think it unlikely we will return for much of the next season, so, unfortunately, it will not be in my power to invite you again soon. I am glad to report that Fanny is well, and she bids me tell you our news. Miss Parker has received a letter from her sister, Miss Catherine, who informs her that she is engaged to be married to Lieutenant Carter. You will meet them soon, as they are all invited to Norland to attend the wedding celebrations. It is a very suitable match for the younger Miss Parker, for whom Fanny did not hold very high hopes. She informs me that Captain Dunning will also join us as an extra gun, just to make up the numbers, you understand.

I very much look forward to welcoming you at Norland again.

Your affectionate brother,
John Dashwood.

"Goodness, what other surprises are in store for us? I did not think to see that mouse marry so soon!" Marianne exclaimed in astonishment, casting a surreptitious look at her sister to gauge her reaction to the news. Margaret felt she had to stand up for Miss Catherine.

"You do her an injustice, Marianne. Separated from the pernicious influence of her elder sister, she is quite a different girl. I talked to her at the last assembly and can see great improvement, both in looks and confidence. Personally, I am glad for her, especially as it appears to be a love match between her and the lieutenant." Margaret did not hesitate to defend the younger girl, who she'd increasingly felt was often tarred with the same brush as the elder, unjustifiably. Marianne looked surprised at her sister's outburst.

"I confess, I was completely in error then as I thought it was you he admired, Margaret." Marianne looked at her searchingly, and Margaret was able to meet her eye honestly.

"No, that could never be, Marianne. Lieutenant Carter is much more suited to Miss Catherine's compliant nature. Let's face the truth, Marianne, I am destined to be a crabby old maid," Margaret ended in jest, but there was something in the tone of her statement that made Marianne feel sad.

"I hope you don't really believe that, Margaret," Marianne admonished, but Margaret quickly changed the subject.

"What is your opinion of Captain Dunning being invited to join the shooting party at Norland?"

"I am all astonishment, but even John admits that it was at Fanny's suggestion. Although he makes the excuse that he is just an extra gun. I wonder if he can bear it." Marianne shook her head in disbelief.

"That is, if he suspects anything. I have to confess that Captain Dunning told me at the assembly he was invited to join the party. He implied it was John's idea, but we both know Fanny is the one who issues the invitations, and this letter is confirmation of that. Are we sure there is anything amiss, Marianne? John has suddenly become very proficient at subterfuge, if he is not the father, and would Fanny be so blatant as to invite the captain if there is really anything going on between them?" Margaret reiterated her earlier doubts, and Marianne considered this carefully.

"You are right, Margaret; John has not the character to be a consummate actor, which means that Fanny must have deceived him, as you surmised. We must be careful not to jump to the wrong conclusions, but my instincts tell me that we are right and the child is Captain Dunning's. Sometimes it is easier to hide things in plain sight. It is unlikely John would suspect something going on under his own nose. Take heart, Margaret, we will have ample opportunity of observing their behaviour together when we are at Norland." Margaret nodded thoughtfully before replying, carefully considering her sister's words of wisdom.

"I agree entirely, Marianne, that we must make the most of that opportunity. I am confident time will illuminate everything and show the proper course of action for us to take."

"I'm afraid this will cut short our stay in Midhurst to just a few days, but that may be for the best, as it will give us more time at Norland, which, as you say, Margaret, we will put to very good use."

"We are on to them now, so nothing shall escape our notice," Margaret concurred with determination.

The Brandons and Margaret arrived at Norland in good spirits on the afternoon of the sixth of March, having spent an enjoyable few days at the Spread Eagle Inn at Midhurst. Margaret was overjoyed to see Norland again and even more so because everywhere there were the hopeful signs of spring. After the mild winter, the park was bursting into life, and daffodils lined the sweeping drive, lifting her spirits and making Margaret more optimistic for the future. John's greeting was enthusiastic on their arrival, informing them that all the guests were due that day and a formal welcome dinner was to be held that evening. The ladies retired to their rooms to refresh themselves and supervise unpacking in readiness for the planned evening party. Margaret was just removing her outer garments when there came a knock at her door, and Lily entered with a broad smile on her face. The two girls embraced like long-lost friends.

"Oh, Miss Margaret, I'm that glad to see you again. It has not been the same since you left. Miss Parker is an exacting mistress and not above giving me a sharp slap if things are not to her liking." Margaret looked at her, horrified at this revelation.

"Can you not report this unseemly behaviour to Fanny?" she asked in disgust.

"The mistress wouldn't listen, and even if she did, she would take Miss Parker's part," Lily retorted. "Miss Parker can do no wrong in Mrs Dashwood's eyes, and they are as thick as thieves. No matter, it hasn't happened recently as Miss Parker is vastly contented over something, and it wouldn't take a very strong head to work out what." Margaret eyed her curiously.

"Go on, Lily, you now have me in absolute suspense."

"Mr Barrington, Miss Margaret. She has set her cap at him, and he is being drawn in," Lily enlightened Margaret with a sniff of distaste. "He doesn't deserve it, miss; he really doesn't." Margaret's astonishment was plain for Lily to see. Caroline and Steven Barrington? Surely not.

"I can't believe it, Lily. Are you certain? He is heir to the estate, surely his parents would never countenance such a match?" But even as she said the words, Margaret knew that Lily spoke the truth.

"Oh, yes, miss. I've seen them together down at the stables. She is all smiles and dimples, and he has the look of a man bewitched. The mistress has her decked out like a duchess, and to do Miss Parker justice, she does look the part. In this case, fine feathers have really made all the difference. No good will come of it, though, Miss Margaret. I can't see his mother and father agreeing to the match either. They will certainly look higher for the son and heir of the Barrington Estate." Lily shook her head in disapproval of such a mismatch. She was all for rags to riches, but this was too much. In any case, she wouldn't wish Caroline Parker on her worst enemy.

Frowning, Margaret pondered this new revelation. If Lily's report was accurate, then it was highly likely Miss Parker would be destined for another disappointment. Mr and Mrs Barrington may have been induced to allow their only daughter to marry a farmer, but she was not the heir to the Barrington Estate. Moreover, Frederick Harris was a gentleman and an old friend. It was most unlikely they would sanction a match between their son and heir and a Miss Parker of obscure birth and no fortune. Although Margaret had to hand it to Caroline Parker. She was very focussed on being the mistress of a great estate, and nothing seemed to stand in the way of her ambitions. Perhaps such determination might just pay off.

Margaret saw she had been right in assuming Miss Parker had another option in mind when she refused Charles Dashwood. It was clear that Steven Barrington had been on her mind since their first riding lesson together on the morning after the ball. Margaret remembered her surprise at the success of this first venture, recalling it took place unchaperoned as Elizabeth Barrington was not present. Caroline must have used her best arts that day, and Steven Barrington's change of manner towards her must have given her high hopes. All this, when a proposal from Charles Dashwood was uncertain. Now, deprived of his sister's company and bored stiff, Steven would have been ripe for the plucking. It all made sense to her now.

Chapter 20
Norland Revisited

That evening, Margaret was surprised when Marianne came into her chamber as she was dressing for dinner. Greeting Lily with a smile, she made herself comfortable whilst she waited for the girl to put the finishing touches to Margaret's attire. She wanted to see for herself the actual dress that Lily had picked for the occasion and was delighted with the maid's choice. Earlier in the day, Marianne had taken Lily into her confidence, and she was taking her role very seriously indeed. Marianne's instructions had been to make sure her young mistress was looking her very best for the evening, and as usual, Lily had obeyed this instruction to the letter. Margaret was looking extremely beautiful in soft rose silk, the rosy hue of the cloth reflecting the healthy glow in her cheeks, the result of an earlier walk in the park, and Marianne was delighted with the outcome.

"Goodness, Margaret, how you must have missed Lily in Bath Square," she said in admiration.

"I confess, I did, although I have never been used to the luxury of having a maid. Lily is so quick to know exactly what will suit me best, and her hairdressing skills are astonishing." Margaret did a twirl, admiring her reflection in the mirror and turning gratefully to the young maid.

"Thank you, Lily, but hadn't you had better go to Miss Parker quickly or there will be consequences, and there is still Miss Catherine to be seen to?"

"Then I will go to Miss Catherine first as she is now an engaged woman and must take priority over the elder sister. Miss Parker will have to wait her turn," said Lily with spirit as she left the room.

"I see Miss Parker has made an impact." Marianne laughed, offering her arm to her sister. "You look absolutely charming, Margaret. Shall we go down?" The two sisters linked arms affectionately.

The gentlemen were already assembled when they entered the drawing room as all eyes turned towards them. Marianne went to rescue her husband, who was being monopolised by Fanny, and Margaret was greeted by Lieutenant Carter, and she shook his hand in sincere congratulations.

"Lieutenant Carter, may I wish you joy in your union with Miss Catherine? I was so happy to hear your news." Margaret beamed at him, ignoring Captain Dunning, standing by his side for as long as she could.

"Thank you, Miss Margaret. I count myself very fortunate to have won such a prize. I am sure, ere long, you will receive an invitation to the wedding." Captain Dunning pointedly cleared his throat, and Margaret turned to him with reluctance.

"Good evening, Captain Dunning," she muttered, hardly able to bring herself to be polite, and he acknowledged her with a small bow.

"Miss Margaret, charming, quite charming," he mumbled, clearly distracted by the entrance of Fanny with the Miss Parkers in tow. Margaret was about to say something cutting when Marguerite Dashwood followed them, leaning on the arm of her son, stunning Margaret into silence and rooting her to the spot in astonishment. It was fortunate there was a chair behind her as her legs gave way, forcing her to sit down heavily, as she tried desperately to compose herself. She tried to catch Marianne's eye, but she was in deep conversation with Fanny and did not appear to notice. Only John, next to her, had witnessed her confusion and kindly came to the rescue immediately.

"Shall we go in, my dear?" said John, beckoning to his wife. "Mr Dashwood, if you would be kind enough to escort Miss Margaret?" he said as the young man approached, and Margaret dared not look up as she gave Charles her hand to help her up. The lieutenant followed with his betrothed, and the captain offered his arm to Marguerite Dashwood, leaving a disgruntled Caroline Parker to follow behind the procession unescorted.

It was some minutes before Margaret could speak, finding herself seated between Charles Dashwood and John Dashwood, so she was grateful to John for breaking the ice.

"How are you, Margaret? I trust not too disappointed to have your London visit curtailed?"

"No, indeed, John, and let me now thank you again for making it happen, but it would be unpardonable of me to resent the joyful circumstances that brought it to a close. I have greatly enjoyed my time there, and it has proved to be an experience I wouldn't have missed for the world. In fact, one I will remember all my life, but I am a country girl at heart, as you know. Besides, we now have two weddings to celebrate at present as well as new additions to the family. How does Fanny?" she remembered to ask.

"She is very well, Miss Margaret; very well, indeed. See for yourself." Margaret glanced over to where Fanny was seated between the captain and the colonel and had to agree.

Fanny was positively glowing. Pregnancy either suited her very well, or was it the man on her right who had something to do with it? She stared at them inquisitively but was distracted by Charles Dashwood.

"How does your sister, Miss Margaret?" he asked solicitously, and she steeled herself to reply with some semblance of normality.

"Much better, I thank you, Mr Dashwood. Still easily fatigued, but I think you advised that was to be expected. The colonel wishes us to return to Devonshire from here, as he wishes to be at home for the last months of Marianne's confinement. He distrusts that London can provide Marianne with all the comforts of home. Although, I know, he has been most grateful for your care of her during their sojourn in the city, he now has the family physician on high alert to expect Marianne shortly," she replied with tolerable control, keeping her eyes on her soup so she did not see his frown.

"The colonel did mention to me his wish to return to Devonshire in advance of the confinement, but I did not realise you would be going with them. When do you return to London?" Margaret was surprised by his urgency of manner.

"I do not expect to return to London, sir. The Brandons will remain at Delaford and have given up the London house, and my visit to Fanny and John has also ended. They also have no intention of returning to London this season and have also closed their London residence. They intend to remain here at Norland for the foreseeable future."

"I see, so you will continue your visit here at Norland, I presume?" he asked anxiously.

"No, sir, I am returning to Devonshire with the Brandons as I have not been invited to remain at Norland. Nor should I wish to be a burden at such a time. Indeed, Miss Parker is now Fanny's guest." She turned her attention back to her dinner, and they had no further conversation because Charles remained pensive and silent throughout the entire meal.

Later, in the drawing room, Marguerite sought the company of Marianne as soon as she could.

"Mrs Brandon, let me thank you for procuring the invitation for us to visit Norland again." Marguerite was grateful for her tactful interference and greatly relieved that Marianne's plan had succeeded.

"Do not thank me, Mrs Dashwood. In fact, it was not difficult to achieve as I think John was feeling that some special civility was due to your son after the announcement of Fanny's pregnancy, which may well disinherit him. Let us hope your visit to Norland achieves the outcome we hope for." Marianne looked at Marguerite meaningfully, and they both glanced across to where Margaret was seated with Miss Catherine.

"Could I ask you to do me a favour this evening, Mrs Dashwood? If music is required, then would you take my place at the pianoforte, and I will plead the excuse of fatigue? I need to be observant this evening, more I cannot explain, but I have a particular reason for asking this of you." Marianne was sure of her compliance and was not disappointed. Marguerite smiled at her, intrigued. She very much enjoyed plotting with Mrs Brandon.

"Consider it done, Mrs Brandon; one good turn deserves another, so I would be delighted to help you." They exchanged a look of complete understanding as Margaret came over to join them, catching their conspiratorial look.

"And what are you two plotting so secretly, may I ask, as if I didn't know?" she asked suspiciously, and they both laughed self-consciously, making Margaret even more suspicious. Just then, the gentlemen joined them, and Charles Dashwood immediately made his way to Margaret's side, where he stood in silence.

"Are you looking forward to the shoot tomorrow, Mr Dashwood?" Margaret asked, unable to bear his brooding silence any longer.

"As a physician, sworn to the Hippocratic Oath, I naturally abhor the taking of any life, even that of a game bird, so I will not be joining the other gentlemen. I have explained my point of view to John, and he quite understands." He hesitated, fiddling nervously with his pocket watch. "Miss Margaret, would you do me the honour?" He hesitated again, aware that Margaret was staring at him, wide-eyed. "That is, if you are not engaged with the shoot, would you do me the honour of walking with me in the park tomorrow?" he finished in a rush. Margaret could scarcely believe her ears that he had finally plucked up the courage to ask to see her alone. She looked him straight in the eye.

"I would enjoy that, Mr Dashwood, as I think we have much to say to each other." Her face broke into a delighted smile, which he couldn't help returning. Both were so absorbed in each other, they did not see the complicit smiles Marianne and Marguerite exchanged behind their backs. Margaret had great difficulty maintaining her normal composure for the rest of the evening and could only think of tomorrow and what it would bring. Thus, she retired as early as politeness would allow to find Lily waiting impatiently in her chamber.

"Do you have any news for me, miss?" Lily hovered about, helping her undress, clearly dying of curiosity, but Margaret eyed her sternly.

"I see you were in on the secret then, Lily. My sister, his mother and my friend plotting behind my back. Why didn't you tell me?"

"I was sworn to secrecy by Mrs Brandon," Lily explained apologetically. "I hope you are not really angry with me, miss?" She looked so worried that Margaret shook her head with a reassuring smile.

"No, Lily, not really; it's just that it would have been nice to have been forewarned. I could have prepared myself and not been so tongue-tied when I first saw him. I felt such a fool, but he has asked me to walk with him in the park tomorrow, so, at least, we can clear the air between us, if nothing else."

"Oh, miss," said Lily, rolling her eyes in ecstasy, indicating clearly to Margaret she expected Mr Dashwood to propose. Margaret wasn't sure what to make of his invitation but welcomed the chance for them to talk honestly together after all the misunderstandings.

The shooting party gathered noisily in front of the house before departing in search of the hapless birds, and Margaret and Charles stood by with some of the other ladies to wave them off. After they had disappeared into the distance, Charles offered Margaret his arm, and they walked in silence for some minutes, neither one knowing how to begin the conversation. At last, Charles took a deep breath and cleared his throat nervously.

"Miss Margaret, I think you and I have got off to a very bad beginning, and I owe you an apology and an explanation for my poor behaviour to you from the start." He paused to gauge her reaction to his apology.

"Please go on, Mr Dashwood," she encouraged, rather embarrassed by his candid statement. He cleared his throat again and continued.

"When it first came to my knowledge that I was to inherit Norland, I was not best pleased by the idea. I am a physician, first and foremost, and I wanted no more than that in life. The Norland inheritance seemed to be an inconvenience that would only get in the way of my true vocation, and I had no wish to play the country gentleman. When I was invited to visit Norland to make the acquaintance of John and Fanny, it wasn't long before John took me aside and suggested it would be right and proper for me to take you as a wife. Thus, righting the wrong that the entail had caused for you and your sisters." He paused again to judge her reaction, but she dared not look up, thinking it was not the right time to inform him how she knew this already. Her heart was beating furiously, and she dared not venture a reply. "Well, not to point too fine a point on it, I was incensed that John thought he had the right to dictate my choice of bride, simply because I was his heir. I confess, I was very angry, and that made me act rashly. You must have noticed, when I first met you, I was offhand to the point of rudeness."

Margaret nodded in silent agreement, remembering how puzzled she had been at the time. "As I said, I acted foolishly and thought to create a ruse to give the firm impression that I admired another. Miss Parker was the woman I chose for that role, and she played right into my hands, but unfortunately, I did not take her into my confidence, and she took me seriously. Although in truth, she didn't need much encouragement. In fact, it was her enthusiasm for me that gave me the idea in the first place. Not very gentlemanly of me, I know," he said, catching the look of disapproval on Margaret's face.

"Anyway, I was hoisted on my own petard. It was my mother who first warned me that my little charade was leading me into trouble, but I didn't take her seriously enough. It wasn't until Catherine Parker congratulated me on my forthcoming engagement to her sister that I realised I was in serious trouble. She blurted this out when I was seated next to her at dinner one evening. Needless to say, I was appalled and tried to extricate myself by leaving for London the next day. Out of sight, out of mind was the idea, but it was not successful. When I returned for the Christmas party, I could see Miss Parker was still wanting and expecting my addresses, aided and abetted by Fanny, who made sure her hopes were kept alive." He paused for breath.

"Yes, I could see that Fanny encouraged Miss Parker to think of you as a potential husband," Margaret agreed. "She is very zealous for her protégées, unless, of course, they want to marry one of her brothers," finished Margaret with feeling.

"Yes, I heard of that strange occurrence when Lucy Steele confessed to Fanny of her engagement to Edward Ferrars, and Fanny threw her out onto the street. Lucy Steele then transferred her affections from Edward to Robert, I understand, after Edward was disinherited. Yes, Miss Margaret, I see the comparison; there are similarities between the characters of Lucy Ferrars and Miss Parker." He was thoughtful for a moment before he continued. "Did you notice on the night of the concert that Fanny took me aside?"

"Yes, I confess I did notice that, Mr Dashwood, and was very curious to know what she had to say to you and why you were so serious afterwards."

"Fanny told me that I had been too particular in my addresses to Miss Parker, to be mistaken, and that, as a gentleman, I was obliged to make her an offer. Indeed, that everyone was expecting it of me. I was very unhappy, especially because, by that time, someone else was becoming very dear to me." He turned to look at her at this point, but she couldn't meet his eyes, suddenly very shy.

"You know the rest, Miss Margaret. I made the offer and was refused but only after Fanny discovered she was with child. Obviously, this impediment greatly diminished my worth in Miss Parker's eyes, and she wasn't about to take the risk of becoming the wife of a simple physician."

"It is true your chances are diminished by Fanny's expected child, but I do not think that is the reason Miss Parker refused you." Margaret felt it was time he knew the truth about Miss Parker's refusal.

"What other reason could there be?" He turned to her in confusion.

"I believe Miss Parker intends to be the mistress of a great estate, and Norland suited her very well until another opportunity presented itself. One that is more certain than Norland, especially as you were clearly exhibiting a great reluctance to get to the point, so to speak."

"You speak in riddles, Miss Margaret. I am not aware of any other opportunity for Miss Parker, or why would she have pursued me so relentlessly?"

"Do you remember her first riding lesson, Mr Dashwood?"

"Of course, I was relieved to be free from her attentions that day."

"Since that day, matters have progressed very well between teacher and pupil, and I believe Mr Barrington is in love with the lady. She chose to pursue this route after your inheritance became less certain. Now, she only has to win over his parents and she will become the next Mrs Barrington of Barrington House."

"Good God! Is there no end to the lady's ambition?" he exclaimed in disgust.

"No, Mr Dashwood, I don't believe there is," Margaret confirmed in sadness for Steven Barrington.

They walked on in silence for a few minutes before Margaret plucked up the courage to ask the question foremost in her mind.

"But Mr Dashwood, when you were refused, you were free to pursue the other lady. Why didn't you?" Margaret looked up at him, wide-eyed.

"Yes, that is true, Miss Margaret. I was set free by Miss Parker's refusal, but I thought that the other lady would also think my prospects diminished. Hurt pride prevented me from declaring myself, but I was also thoroughly ashamed of my behaviour and thought she would judge me harshly."

"Then tell me what has changed now, Mr Dashwood?"

"Time and my mother brought me to my senses. I realised that I had to, at least, try and win the lady despite the risk of rejection. It is better to try and fail than never to have tried at all. I still feel unworthy of her, but I am hoping she will understand and forgive me."

"I feel sure that she will, Mr Dashwood, especially as you have now explained yourself so clearly. That lady also knows you were, if not exactly an innocent party, the victim of two scheming women. What a pity John thought to interfere; it seems like he played right into their hands." Margaret shook her head, and he took her hand in gratitude for her understanding, looking seriously into her eyes.

"Margaret, tell me I have a chance of winning your affections." She had thought to dissemble and keep him guessing in payment for the many uncomfortable moments she had endured at his instigation. Now the time came, she had no thoughts of revenge. It had not been his fault, and they both were the unfortunate victims of circumstances beyond their control. She would not be the person to delay their happiness any longer.

"You already have won them, Mr Dashwood," Margaret replied simply, looking up at him with shining eyes and placing her other hand in his with complete trust. He stared at her as if unable to believe her words.

"You realise that you may be nothing more than the wife of a mere physician," he said, still unable to believe such good fortune had come to him so easily after such a period of anguish and uncertainty. Margaret laughed out loud.

"I can think of nothing that would please me more; in fact, I will only accept your proposal on one condition." Margaret looked up at him archly.

"Name it, my dearest Margaret."

"That you will let me help you in your work." Unable to resist any longer, he took her in his arms and kissed her, and they remained thus entwined for a long time, relishing the feeling of joy. Afterwards, wandering around aimlessly in the park, talking and laughing over past misunderstandings, they planned their future together. Margaret finally admitted to overhearing the conversation with his mother from the treehouse.

"What must you have thought of me?" Charles was horrified, but Margaret reassured him.

"I did not think any ill of you, but I was mortified by John's interference, and I began to understand your coldness towards me."

"Indeed, my mother thinks that John Dashwood has a lot to answer for, and without his interference, we may have come to an understanding much sooner," he declared, and Margaret nodded.

"Perhaps she is right; we shall never know now, Mr Dashwood, but can I ask a favour? Could we keep our engagement a secret whilst we remained at Norland? That is, we can tell Marianne and your mother, but no one else should know until we have left this place. Although, of course, I will write to inform my mother and Elinor. Oh, and I must include Lily in the secret."

"Of course, if that is what you wish, but why all the secrecy, my love? By the way, my name is Charles, you know." He lifted her chin to kiss her again, lingeringly.

"I don't want anything to mar our happiness, Charles, and insincere good wishes from Fanny and Miss Parker are more than I can bear," she confessed when he released her.

"I understand and honour your feelings. I have no wish for Miss Parker to lord it over you by implying she was my first choice. Consider it done, my love, but I hope you know I would never have proposed to Miss Parker if I hadn't felt honour bound to do so." He leaned forward to kiss her again, but she wriggled free, laughing.

"Of course, I know that, Charles; you surely don't expect me to take Miss Parker's leavings? Nevertheless, charming though this is, we must go in as you have a mother to inform and I, a sister, and both, no doubt, will be pacing the floor in an agony of anticipation, which is decidedly bad for Marianne in her condition, as well you know. I must also write two letters as I would not delay for a moment longer than I need to the news that will so delight my mother and Elinor. Not to mention Lily, who will also be waiting in my chamber, dying of curiosity, and I cannot keep her in suspense any longer. We have responsibilities,

Charles," she rebuked him playfully, and he caught her to him, holding her so tightly, she could scarcely breathe.

"You are right, of course," he agreed as he released her at last. "I am also very sure my mother has long been watching from her window for a sight of us." He kissed her again, reluctant to leave her side, still disbelieving that she was really his.

It was fortunate that Charles and Margaret arrived back at Norland at the same time as the shooting party. Amidst the furore of excited dogs, dead game and masculine laughter, their starry-eyed entrance went unnoticed. Margaret went straight to Marianne and Charles to his mother.

"Well?" was all Marianne uttered, eyes wide, holding her breath, and Margaret ran straight into her outstretched arms.

"He has asked me, Marianne, and we are engaged."

"I knew how it would be if we could only bring you to talk to each other. Marguerite and I think you are made for one another. My dearest, I am so happy for you. He is all that is charming and just what a young man ought to be." Margaret smiled to herself, remembering Marianne's previous comments about Charles being unromantic. At least she knew now he was capable of smiling as he had been doing it all morning.

"But Margaret, what about our suspicions of Fanny and Captain Dunning? Did you talk to Charles about it?"

"I confess, I did not, Marianne. We were much too taken up with the present moment, and I feel ready to forgive the world its sins, such is my current happiness. We cannot prove anything, and I have it from Charles' own lips that he did not want the Norland inheritance. We are so overjoyed with the way matters have turned out, and as I am more than happy to be a physician's wife, can we not let matters be?"

"Very well, Margaret; if you wish it, we will discontinue our detective work. Your happiness is my first concern, of course. But the truth will out. You mark my words," Marianne sagely replied as they went down to join the shooting party for a late luncheon.

Later that day, Charles and Margaret were able to snatch some precious moments together in the library. Sure of a little privacy, as it was always the most underused room at Norland.

"Charles," Margaret began shyly, "Marianne would have us married in Devon from the church at Delaford, with Edward performing the service. Does that meet with your approval?" He took her hands affectionately and raised one to his lips.

"I confess, I'd hoped for precisely that. A bride should always be married from home, and London is no place for a wedding," he agreed readily, to her delight.

"But Charles, how will it be possible to leave your patients for so long a period?"

"I've already thought of that, Margaret. My wise mother has long been advising me to employ an assistant as the practice has become so busy. What better time than now?" Margaret was still unconvinced.

"But how will you find such a person in time for the wedding? Won't your patients still want your personal attention?" Margaret voiced her doubts, mindful of his many absences from social events, but Charles was able to reassure her.

"Fortunately, I have somebody in mind, someone I've been watching for a while who comes very well recommended, and we have met several times to discuss how we might work together. Nevertheless, you are right, Margaret, my patients will still want me personally for a time, certainly until they get used to a new face. As soon as I return to London, we will begin our partnership, and if I'm not much mistaken, the patients will soon come around. In any case, they can hardly begrudge me time off to get married." Margaret laughed.

"I hope we can always agree on everything so easily," she replied with an arch smile, and he laughed outright. A rare occurrence in her experience.

"I think you will find a way to make it so, Miss Margaret Dashwood," he said with a smile, but Margaret was suddenly serious.

"Marianne and the colonel want to set out early on the day after Elizabeth's wedding, so we must be separated for a while, Charles." She sighed, and he took her in his arms, looking at her searchingly.

"My dearest, considering how long it has taken for us to come to an understanding, this short separation will be nothing compared to the agony of uncertainty. We must bear it as best we can and take heart from the knowledge that our hearts belong to each other, even if we are parted. Besides, we will have many tasks to keep us occupied. You, to organise our wedding and me, to train an assistant so as to give me leisure time with my wife. In any case, I think we should marry at the end of April. They say May is unlucky, and I can't wait until June. Can you be ready in time, my dearest?" She smiled up at him a little tearfully.

"In half that time, Charles, if you say the word. I have such beautiful gowns from my London season that I don't even need to wait for a wedding gown to be made up. My sisters and mother will need new finery, however, so it would be prudent to wait until the end of April if we must, but no longer," pleaded Margaret, tilting her face upwards to receive another kiss.

Chapter 21
Home Again

Margaret Dashwood was, therefore, restored to her mother at Barton Cottage by the middle of March, more than a month earlier than either of them had expected. Her much-neglected garden was waking up, and all of nature was in bud to welcome her home. Moreover, the London visit had produced the desired result, and she returned home an engaged woman, much to everyone's delight, but most of all, her own. Mrs Dashwood's and her sisters' only concern was that she must make her home far away in London, but a winter visit to London would always be a great attraction, just as a summer one would be in Devonshire. This must be their consolation. Some days after her arrival, Margaret received a letter of congratulations from John and Fanny after her mother had written to apprise them of her engagement.

My dearest Margaret,

I write to offer Fanny's and my congratulations on your forthcoming wedding to Charles Dashwood. I confess, it is what I always wanted, especially when he was the heir to Norland. It would have redressed the imbalance of the entail. Now, of course, that this is less certain, however, I am no less pleased. We are very glad that our invitation to London has culminated in this desirable result. It would have been such a pity if you had returned to Devonshire unengaged, and Fanny is particularly pleased that the gowns she purchased for you have not been wasted. Unfortunately, we will not be able to join you for the wedding celebrations because of Fanny's delicate condition. She will be in the sixth month by then and cannot travel safely. Although she continues in excellent health, the doctor's advice is to take every care. By arrangement with your fiancée, we send you this wedding gift with our very good wishes for your future happiness.

I have other surprising news to impart to you, however. You will be astonished to learn that Miss Parker and Steven Barrington are engaged. I confess, I was never so surprised in my life, the lady being completely without fortune, but it seems Fanny was expecting the announcement. She is vastly pleased to have Miss Parker always nearby. I am even more astounded that his parents have agreed to the match, but they have always been an indulgent pair, and this is the result. Both children marrying without adding to the family fortunes is always a sorry state of affairs. In my opinion, it is the duty of the offspring to add to an estate where they can.

We wish you well, my dear, and I hope we will often meet in London when you return with your new husband.

Your affectionate brother and sister,
John and Fanny Dashwood.

Margaret smiled at their method of congratulations. How typical of Fanny to think of the gowns first. So, Miss Caroline Parker had succeeded in gaining her desire; whether it was her heart's desire was another matter. This confirmed, beyond any doubt, why she had refused Charles Dashwood when his prospects were diminished by Fanny's pregnancy. Caroline had secretly nurtured high hopes of catching Steven Barrington so would not take the risk of becoming a mere doctor's wife. A great deal must have happened between them on the afternoon of that first riding lesson for Caroline Parker to take such a risk. Margaret took comfort from the fact that Steven Barrington was a sensible man, and she doubted if he would easily be taken in by flattery. Perhaps there was true affection between them that sparked on their first afternoon alone together. Margaret hoped so. It was also unlikely Mr Barrington would stand any nonsense from his future wife. In fact, the more Margaret thought about it, the more she was convinced they would probably do very well together. Their characters were much better suited than Miss Parker and Charles Dashwood. Then she remembered the wedding gift John and Fanny had sent her.

"Mama, was anything else delivered with this letter?" she called to her mother in the drawing room.

"Yes, my dear, I will bring it through to you now," her mother concurred, and Margaret looked up to see her mother and Lily standing in the doorway, laughing at her open-mouthed astonishment.

"Lily?" For a moment, Margaret was speechless. "How?" Lily handed Margaret a note in Charles' writing.

"I'm sure this will explain everything, miss."

My dearest Margaret,

I send Lily to you, my love, with this note. I know you will find her help invaluable, not least with the wedding preparations. I have managed to extricate her from Fanny's employment, which she is very glad to leave. In truth, Fanny has no further use for her now that Miss Parker is leaving Norland to be married, and she could hardly reduce her salary back to that of a kitchen maid. She will be accompanying us back to Harley Street, where she will be your personal maid, of course, but also take over the housekeeping duties from my mother. You will understand, my dearest, that a mere physician cannot afford both. Lily is completely happy with this and desires nothing more than to be in your service. I know you will approve of these arrangements, my love, and I am glad to make you happy.

My mother has decided to take a long-desired trip to France after our wedding now that she will be released from the onerous care of her bachelor son. She wishes to visit her mother's relations, many of whom are elderly, so this may be her last chance to see them in this lifetime.

You will be glad to hear I have successfully employed an assistant and am in the process of training him into my ways. Although, in truth, he hasn't needed much training and seems to know exactly what to do instinctively. I think you will approve of him as he is a bright young man with an infectious sense of humour, something that is sorely needed in our profession, as you have lately pointed out to me. His name is Andrew McCauley, and he is a Scott by birth. His qualifications are exemplary, so it's likely that he will be able to teach me more than I can teach him. It is a fine thing to have acquired such a partner for my practice and a great relief to be able to leave it when the time arises in such capable hands. You will be reassured to hear that the patients have taken to him enormously, so much so that I feel quite superfluous already.

As to our honeymoon, my dearest, what do you think of Bath? I have a yearning to take the waters, and I hear it is charming in spring.

Take care of yourself, my love, and I will be with you in just four weeks from now. I am busy counting down the hours.

Your loving fiancé,
Charles Dashwood.

"Of all the gifts that I could have received as a wedding present, this is by far the most delightful." Margaret turned to Lily with an affectionate smile. "I had absolutely no idea that this was planned."

"Mr Dashwood approached me before you left Norland, miss. I think he could see how unhappy I was, and I had no hesitation in accepting his terms, as you see, miss. I am so looking forward to helping you prepare for the wedding. Oh, and before I forget, miss, I have another letter for you from Mrs Harris."

Dearest Margaret,

I was so excited to hear the news of your engagement to Mr Charles from John, and thank you for the invitation to attend the celebrations, which we are delighted to accept. I thought you looked rather coy when I confessed to thinking him handsome. How useful, though, for you to be married to a physician! It will be delightful to have you nearby in London, and I will make Freddy bring me for a visit whenever the countryside becomes intolerable.

Likewise, I hope you will not wait for an invitation to visit us at the farm whenever you need a breath of fresh country air.

By now, you will have heard the news that Caroline Parker and my brother Steven are engaged. At first, Mama and Papa were dead set against it, but it came as no surprise to me when they finally relented. Steven could always get his way with them, and Caroline presents such a picture of duty and respect that I can even bring myself to think her affection for my brother is genuine. They are to be married quietly from Barrington House and thence to Paris, which is somewhere Steven has set his heart on visiting, and I do not see any objection on the lady's part. I confess, I am a little envious myself. Perhaps I did not care for her much at first, but now I really believe she is so sincerely attached to Steven that she has quite changed in personality.

Thank you for coming to our wedding. It was a blessing for me to have so many well-wishers and friends there. I am only sorry not to have had the chance to spend time with you all, but the day passed in such a whirl.

I look forward to meeting you again next month on your own happy day.

Your affectionate friend,
Elizabeth Harris

Lily soon became such an indispensable part of the Dashwood household that mother and daughter wondered how they had ever managed without her. She slotted in with the chores as though she had lived there all her life and threw herself into the wedding plans with every enthusiasm. When the day of the wedding finally dawned, she found herself helping all the ladies to dress, in addition to her most important duty of attending to the bride. Margaret and Lily had chosen a white satin ball gown for the bridal ensemble. This was the finest of the gowns purchased, intended for the grand ball, the finale of the season, which, in the end, Margaret had not been able to attend. It was the creme de la creme of her gowns, perfect for a wedding and fashioned by one of the top sempstresses in London, at the insistence of Fanny and at John's expense. Little did Margaret think, when being fitted for this exquisite creation, it was destined to be her wedding gown.

Mrs Dashwood and her other daughters joined Margaret to watch Lily add the final touches to her attire, and all were overcome with emotion when the bridal veil was finally in set in place. She was to be given away by the colonel in the absence of John, and the little church was full to the brim, as they began the slow walk to the altar. Edward was waiting in his ecclesiastical ceremonial robes, and Charles Dashwood had enlisted Lieutenant Carter as groomsman, resplendent in full naval uniform. Everyone who attended agreed wholeheartedly that it was a very pretty wedding as they waved the happy couple off for a week in Bath.

Chapter 22
Loose Ends

Two months later, back on Harley Street, Mr and Mrs Charles Dashwood were seated at dinner in their newly decorated dining room. It was still a luxury to have dinner without interruption, made possible because of the services of Andrew McCauley. It was a pleasant time of day and one that Margaret looked forward to most of all. Charles raised a glass of wine to toast his wife in appreciation before beginning the conversation.

"My dear, I had a letter today from John Dashwood containing some astonishing news." He passed it over the table for her to read, and she looked at him in concern.

"Not bad news, I hope, Charles?" She frowned, hating the thought that their newfound happiness could be marred in any way.

"No, my dear, not bad news. Read the letter, and all will be revealed," he said mysteriously, and Margaret opened the letter with some trepidation. It was from John, very brief and to the point, most uncharacteristic of him.

My dear Charles,

I write to inform you, as my heir, that Fanny has given birth to a little girl who is to be named Anne. You will be pleased to learn that mother and daughter are in very good health, and, needless to say, we are overjoyed.

Please give my kindest regards to your wife.

John Dashwood.

Margaret laid down the letter and looked questioningly at her husband.

"Charles, is this not a month too early? I thought that Fanny and Marianne were due to give birth at about the same time." She was puzzled.

"Yes, you are correct, my dear; it appears it is a little early," he corroborated. "Perhaps the dates were wrong, which is not unusual in an older mother when things become a little irregular," he replied lightly, occupied with a slice of roast beef, not quite meeting her eye.

"But I don't understand, Charles. Surely, if a baby comes that early, there is some doubt as to its survival, yet John reports that mother and child are healthy." Margaret still looked puzzled, not believing for a moment that muddled dates alone could be the reason for such an early birth. All her old suspicions were flooding back immediately.

"That is not always the case, but you are right, Margaret, if a child is born that early, it's usually undersized and often more vulnerable."

"So what is your real opinion then, Charles?" She looked at him quizzically.

"Let us say, my dear, that Fanny has been fortunate and leave it at that. I am not her doctor and was not in attendance, so it's not for me to venture an opinion." She nodded, seeing the good sense of his advice and glad to return to her dinner, but another thought struck her.

"Charles, John wrote to you as his heir. Does this mean you are, once again, heir to Norland, then?" Margaret was looking at him intensely now.

"Yes, my dear, it appears it does. In the absence of a male child, rightly or wrongly, the entail to the male line cannot be broken, so little Anne may not inherit her father's estate." His expression remained inscrutable as he picked up his wine.

"To the Norland inheritance, my dear." He grinned, seeing her delighted smile.

The next news arrived a month later from Mrs Dashwood.

Dearest Margaret and Charles,

Forgive my short note.

I am delighted to inform you that a baby girl has been born to Mr and Mrs Brandon. She is to be named Elizabeth (Eliza), in memory of the colonel's cousin. I am pleased to be able to confirm that mother and child are both in good health despite a protracted birth, which left Marianne quite exhausted. Although, I am also delighted to be able to reassure you, she recovers her strength daily.

You will appreciate I am much occupied at present but will write again shortly to keep you updated on the progress of your new little niece and, of course, her mother.

Your loving mama.

Two months after that, Charles received another letter sent from Norland, this time from John's lawyer.

My dear Mr Dashwood,
　I am sorry to be the bearer of sad tidings. John Dashwood has suffered a stroke, which has left him partially paralysed, hence the need to write to you in his stead. I believe that it was brought on by the shock of his wife's departure for the protection of Captain Dunning, taking with her the child, Anne. As you are probably already aware, Mrs Dashwood has her own independent fortune, over which she has complete control; thus, she is not beholden to Mr Dashwood financially. In addition, I believe, there was also an unexpected legacy left to her recently by her mother. Fanny Dashwood has become quite an heiress in her own right and has no need of her husband's protection. This is borne out by the note she left for her husband on her departure. It is, of course, a terrible scandal and one that John Dashwood will find hard to weather at his age. In his current state of health, John Dashwood will require a great deal of assistance in the running of the estate, and you, as the heir, are the natural person on whom that responsibility should fall. Doubly so, because your wife is Mr Dashwood's sister. I entreat you to come to Norland as soon as you can to set your affairs in order.
Your obedient servant,
Edward Delamere.

PS: I enclose the note that Fanny Dashwood left for her husband as verification.

Dear John,
　We have long been unhappy together, and the death of Harry simply brought that to a head. When I found out I was pregnant, however, I was prepared to try again for the sake of the Norland inheritance. Now that Anne is born and Norland is lost to us forever, I cannot see the point of sacrificing my future to a

loveless marriage. I am sure you will be very shocked to learn that Anne is not your child but Captain Dunning's daughter, and I am leaving you for his protection. By the time you receive this note, we will be on our way to Portsmouth. I make no apology for the scandal because, I believe, we were both equally to blame for this sorry state of affairs. Our marriage has long been a marriage of convenience, devoid of any affection, and now that we have lost the second chance of the Norland inheritance, I see no reason to continue with it.

Yours sincerely,
Fanny Dashwood.

    Charles handed Margaret the letters in stunned silence, and she read them through with increasing anguish. It was true then. Everything she and Marianne suspected had been confirmed, and Margaret was very sorry indeed. She was shocked to the core by Fanny's callous leave-taking of John. Whatever her current feelings, he was her husband of many years standing and deserved greater respect.

    Fanny had only waited at Norland long enough for her little daughter to gain the strength to make the journey. She had been toying with the idea of leaving the marriage since she first learned of the additional legacy. Her final decision was made on the day she gave birth to a daughter, which meant that Norland was lost to her forever. She had no hesitation in casting aside convention and throwing herself under the protection of her recently acknowledged lover, Captain Dunning, the father of her child.

    With a light heart, Fanny had Crane pack her belongings and those of her child. They met the captain at Petersfield and from there went on to Portsmouth, where the captain had procured lodgings for his new family in the best part of the town. Portsmouth society, he assured her, would not be so particular as fashionable London and she would be received there by almost everyone as his mistress. The fact that she was a wealthy woman would also help considerably to ensure that no doors were closed against her. Thus, on their arrival in the naval town, Fanny made sure she and the captain entertained lavishly, and very few could resist an invitation to their home. The gallant captain was very pleased with this new arrangement. His pecuniary embarrassment was at an end, for Fanny was generous with him, as she had not been with her husband. He was also really quite taken with Fanny, who knew how to make herself agreeable when necessary, and he genuinely loved his daughter. Little Anne, a spirited little thing with her father's good looks, had completely captured his heart. Fanny was not so besotted with her lover as to let him rule her completely. She took care not to let her fortune slip through her lover's fingers, only allowing them to live on the interest, but as this amounted to three thousand pounds a year, it proved to be quite sufficient for their wants, especially in Portsmouth, where money stretched a lot further than in London. She was also safe in the knowledge their fall from grace in London was likely to be only a temporary setback. She had already received Mrs Barrington's absolute assurances that she and her husband would receive them as soon as they were ready. She congratulated herself on her investment in Caroline Parker. It had been well worth the expense of providing her with an entire wardrobe, especially for the entrapment of Steven Barrington. It might be that she and the captain would have to wait to be married until they could be received, but Fanny had it on good authority from Mrs Barrington that John Dashwood was very unwell. She tried hard to feel some remorse at this turn of events but couldn't help thinking John had brought it on himself.

Chapter 23
Postscript

Nearly a year later, on a fine August day, Charles and Margaret were hosting a picnic at Norland Park. The site chosen was beneath the ancient oak containing Margaret's treehouse, it being near enough to the kitchen for servants to ferry back and forth. The treehouse was almost hidden by the abundant leaves of summer, and the heady scent of damask roses, buzzing with bees, had induced a post-prandial contentment. John Dashwood sat in his bath chair, in the shade of the tree, every now and again checking the precious contents of the perambulator placed purposefully by his side. Baby John, his namesake, was born to Margaret and Charles three months ago. He was a robust little thing, with his mother's hair and eyes and his father's determined chin. Just at the moment, his chubby fist clasped a silver rattle, presented to him at birth by his uncle, who rarely let him out of his sight.

These days, baby John was the only person who could bring a lopsided smile to his uncle's stricken face.

John Dashwood had recovered a little from the stroke, but he was not the man he was and never would be again. He had aged considerably, and his face had the transparent appearance of a much older man. He looked up as Margaret handed him some lemonade and checked that the wool blanket was safely tucked in around him. Despite the heat, he always felt the cold these days. Margaret saw how he weakened daily and reflected sadly it couldn't be much longer before Captain Dunning would be able to make an honest woman of Fanny.

News of the pair reached them often from Mrs Carter, who was in correspondence with Margaret and mentioned them frequently in her letters. Fanny and Caroline Barrington were also regular correspondents, and Margaret was aware the Barringtons had visited her and the captain in Portsmouth on several occasions. They had set up house together in Broad Street, a fashionable part of Portsmouth, where, as the captain had predicted, there were few society doors closed to them. It was said they were a devoted couple, although Margaret found it difficult to believe that Fanny could be devoted to anyone but herself. How difficult life can become when one marries for the wrong motives, she pondered. It was clear Fanny and John had never been suited, and once the Norland inheritance was lost, Fanny had no reason to remain by his side. Obviously, their marriage had been based upon the shaky foundations of money and status without the mutual respect needed to ensure a lasting union. The unexpected inheritance left to Fanny by her mother had been the final nail in the coffin. Perhaps Fanny really did care for the captain, as she had never cared for anyone before, and their liaison had made a new woman of her. Love conquered all, apparently. Margaret hoped so, for both their sakes. For her part, she would be forever grateful for the fate that had led her to Charles. She was glad, that when she'd accepted his proposal, there had been considerable doubt as to whether he would ever inherit Norland. It meant he would always know that she'd chosen the man and not his prospects. It made their current good fortune all the sweeter.

Caroline Barrington was an open champion of Fanny, making no secret of their visits to Portsmouth, and Margaret was sure that Fanny and her captain would be received at Barrington Court just as soon as they were married. Although it was unlikely that the couple would be welcomed back into the first circles in London, at least at first, Margaret put nothing past Fanny's ingenuity. Aside from Fanny's absolute focus on getting her way, she was a rich woman with many influential connections, and these brought all kinds of benefits. Not to mention Captain Dunning's own reputation as a handsome rogue and the darling of the ton. Of course, Margaret made absolutely sure that John knew nothing of this state of affairs. Fanny's name was never mentioned before him. It was as if she had died.

The ladies of the party were charmingly grouped around John and could have been the subject of a Gainsborough painting; he reflected admiringly as they were a handsome bunch. Mrs Dashwood sat with Marguerite Dashwood under her parasol, keeping one eye on a chubby toddler going by the name of Eliza, daughter of Colonel and Mrs Brandon. Eliza was the prettiest little thing, but a headstrong child who reminded Mrs Dashwood strongly of Marianne at that age. Privately, the colonel had also observed she was uncannily like her namesake and resolved to keep a very close eye on her in the future.

Mrs Edward Ferrars held a fine baby boy on her lap whilst helping to make Kitty a daisy chain. Edward was playing boules with the gentlemen, and Elinor was keeping one eye on the game. She and Edward had invested the unexpected inheritance wisely, and the extra interest made all the difference to their small income. Margaret was pleased to note her sister was wearing a fashionable new gown.

Elizabeth Barrington was big with child, which had not stopped her from riding over from the Harris Farm that morning with her husband to join them. She and Margaret remained the greatest of friends, and the two couples were very often at each other's houses.

Steven and Caroline had also been present at the picnic but wandered off to explore the park, as Steven could never sit still for very long. Despite all odds, they seemed happy, especially now, as Caroline was expecting their first child, and Steven Barrington was considerately careful of his wife. Margaret had received every arrear of civility from her now that they were no longer rivals for the same man. You would never know that Charles Dashwood had once been the object of her desire. Margaret felt she'd done her an injustice by comparing her character to that of Lucy Ferrars. It was clear now that Caroline had achieved her object of marrying for position and money, she could relax, and Margaret thought she really loved and respected her husband. It was a happy outcome for both of them, especially as Caroline was now a marvellous horsewoman. Only Marguerite Dashwood succeeded in outshining her these days.

Marguerite returned from France a few months ago, having visited all her family and friends, and Charles and Margaret had begged her to make her home at Norland with them. Similarly, Margaret's mother had also been persuaded to give up Barton Cottage and move from Devonshire to Norland, and she and Marguerite were the best of friends. It delighted Margaret to see them together, and between them, they ran the house. This was the perfect solution as this left Margaret free to help her husband in the herbal apothecary.

Lily set off for the kitchen in search of more lemonade, and Margaret watched her go with admiration. The young maid had always been quick and smart, but now she really shone with happiness in her new station. Margaret knew she was not the only one to have noticed, having seen the looks the butler sent her when he thought the mistress wasn't looking. Luckily, when the time came, there was a cottage on the estate that they would be most welcome to.

Marianne was favouring the company with some country ballads, most befitting to the occasion, whilst the colonel looked on adoringly. Their sojourn in London appeared to have done the trick, settling Marianne down to motherhood and a country life at Delaford. The rest of the gentlemen were occupying themselves with boules and laughing at Charles Dashwood, who had said something amusing. Margaret looked up from tending her child at the sound of his laughter and smiled in happiness. How fortunate he had been able to leave his London practice in the capable hands of his assistant and move to Norland with his wife, Margaret, and baby son, John Dashwood junior, the future heir to Norland.

THE END